QUEEN OF MOONS

THE BLOOD MOON PROPHECY

BOOK THREE

SUSAN PERSON

PERSON
PUBLISHING

For my parents who believed in me and told me I could do anything

QUEEN OF MOONS

CHAPTER
ONE

Darkness stole more of my soul with each day even though I tucked it into a corner inside me. Anger built in me. I wanted to burn down the world and inflict unspeakable pain on others. The only thing that kept me in my right mind was my pink aura and Nick's love, and the pink aura weakened with every second. I knew the battle I'd avoided since I learned of The Blood Moon Prophecy was inevitable.

The two weeks allotted for mine and Nick's honeymoon were at their end. We had to return for the final two moons of the tetrad. They counted down to the prophecy's end like it was doomsday. *Maybe it is.* I had promised myself to try to put it out of my mind for the honeymoon, so I could enjoy a brief blissful period with Nick fairly sure it would be all we would ever have. And I did try. I tried and I failed. Darkness and the prophecy crept into my thoughts every day.

The car came to a stop in front of the Great House. An elegant archway covered the oversized door at the top of the stairs. The mansion looked the same as when we left. Before Cecily had chosen me, I preferred to use the back entrances versus this one. The way it was inside an arch embedded in stone at the top of the steps was a statement, but it was also beautiful. I'd thought of the Great House as my home long before I was required to reside there. Since assuming the role of the Queen, it felt more and more like a prison.

The car door opened, and a guard's hand extended to help me out. I ignored it. Queen or not, I could still get out of a car on my own.

Nick stood beside me and wrapped his arm around my waist. "They honored your request for no pomp and circumstance upon our return, but you are the Queen, my wife."

"And I'm still me. I believe I showed you, Vampire King, who that is," I whispered to him.

His cheeks tinted pink in a vampire blush. "Multiple times a day the past couple of weeks."

I smiled and leaned against him. "Reality awaits. Is it too late to run?"

"I'm afraid so. Your schedule is already in their hands by now." He squeezed me to his side.

"You have super vampire speed though. You could carry me and run far far away." The prophecy would find us even if we did. The last two moons were on our heels and Alastair would know it. He would eventually find us. This was the end, and I needed to throw everything I had at the damn prophecy to stop it and Alastair.

"I could, and I would if you so desired," my husband whispered in my hair.

Nick at my side brought me comfort, but tension

spread through my body at what reality would bring being home. We walked up the steps. I glimpsed my Coven's bronze insignia before the guard opened the massive door for us. Nick's stride matched mine down the long marble hallway.

The familiar scents of the mansion drifted around me. I inhaled deeply, taking in the aroma of burning sage. "You are sure giving into my every whim. What's up with that?"

I glanced up at him and love glowed in his eyes. It warmed me and awakened my desire. His love seemed to be a barrier against my darkness, and I clung to it.

"You are the Queen, and you are my wife."

"I'm not your queen though. You have your own brood to rule. Nasty as some of them might be." And there were some terrible vampires.

"Careful now. Alastair is among your subjects, and he's not a shining example of good." I couldn't argue with that. His very name raged the darkness in me, and my pink aura let a sliver of it slip through. Alastair had told us some enlightening news hidden from witch and vampire history, and he made us forget. For some reason, the memories flooded back the first day of our honeymoon. Alastair was unaccounted for, and not even his son and my friend, Cal, knew where he was. The answer as to why Nick and I suddenly remembered eluded us. Nick and I decided to stay on the honeymoon knowing Alastair wanted us and hoping he would seek us out there versus where our loved ones were. He'd made no move on us though.

"True. He is the worst of the coven," I said. Nick was hiding something. He held back. I didn't need magic to sense it. His secrets weren't always bad news, but I'd had enough surprises to last a lifetime, vampire or witch. "Spill it, Nick."

"I don't know what you're talking about." His fingers wrapped around my elbow. He tugged gently to get my attention. He'd stopped us in front of the large ornate doors to an area he couldn't walk alone.

My heart filled with love and chased away the darkness nibbling at the edges. Happiness could be ours if we could stay here in this moment.

"Ahhh. You want something from me, Mr. Domenico." I leaned up and kissed his cheek.

"I do. I'd like my wife to take me into the chapel." He said, his voice low against my ear. His breath slid along my skin like a warm caress.

"When you say it like that there is no way I can deny you." I held out my hand palm up.

He cocked his head to the side. His hand covered mine as his fingers laced through. "Like what?"

"Your wife." I sent my pink aura out around him. "Open the door." I smiled up at him. His love reinforced my pink aura, but the use of it would be a wash against the space darkness occupied. Nothing lost and the peace he experienced inside the chapel radiated like a crown jewel each time he stepped inside. It was more magical to me than anything I could do on my own.

His eyes widened a little. He smiled as he grasped the knob and turned, pushing the door wide. My heart swelled with the joy visits here brought him.

We crossed the threshold together. I'd made it my mission to do everything alone. Until I met Nick. He changed me for the better. I believed in love, and moreover, I wanted it from him and my family.

Nick let out a breath. His shoulders relaxed. "I feel different in here. At peace. Safe."

"I can see it in the way the tension leaves your body." I studied him. His thick dark hair faded on the sides with a little more length on top suited his features. Those emerald-green eyes were the first thing I noticed about him, and they glowed a little when he was in here. "It's the only time I see your walls go down."

His voice was low and full of remorse. "I don't have walls with you, Brie."

"We all have defenses, Nick. Products of the emotional baggage we carry." I'd stuffed Darkness so deep inside me, but it waited for the time to rise up in me. I knew it. Nick knew it.

"I've had two hundred and fifty years to deal with mine. It's long since been directed and discarded from my old life."

His human life was so short compared to his vampire life, and he'd struggled with some of the duties he performed under Stefan. *Maybe the peace here could help him through those.* "What about your vampire life? You've been carrying around a lot of strong feelings about it. Not to mention you lost Stefan."

He shuddered. Nick rarely bared a crack in his armor, but we'd seen into each other's past twice, once with a new lovers spell I cast and the other when we became Blood Bound.

"I do wish I'd been able to talk to him before he died, but not for the reasons you think. I would never forgive him for his part in the plan to use you to raise this army Alastair is Hell-bent on building. He was evil."

I cringed when he said Hell. Hell would be where I'd go after this life because I chose Darkness to save my family and coven out of love. My actions unknowingly brought my father back from Hell when he sacrificed himself for us. He'd chosen Darkness too. My fate sealed in those choices. I'd never see Summerland.

"Are you afraid you'll be like him?" I asked. It had been my fear once for myself, and it came to fruition.

Nick looked away.

Guilt ate at my insides for asking him, but his action told me the answer. I placed my free hand on his cheek and nudged his face back to me. "You could never be like him. He'd forgotten all humanity. His own and the preciousness of it. Greed took him over. It was a power trip. You are not like that."

"I almost was, Brie. That scares me." His eyes reddened and his face paled, pale even for a vampire.

I softened my voice. "You were under a spell cast by Alastair. That is not the same."

"Are you sure it was all the spell? A part of that could be in me," he said, regret laced his words.

"It's not. I know." I locked eyes with him. His confusion cast a dullness over his usually bright eyes, but our special connection navigated him back. Electricity coursed through my body. One look and I was undone.

His forehead rested against mine. "I wish I was as confident as you."

"The fact you are soul searching and have doubt shows

your humanity is still alive. That should give you confidence."

He turned his face into the palm of my hand and kissed it. His head tilted so his cheek rested in my palm. "You save me every day with your love."

"I don't mean to brag, but I did go against a prophecy for you." I smiled at him.

"Yes, you did, and married me even though I'm a blood-sucker." He leaned forward and pressed his lips to mine.

"I'll confess I called you that a few times." I giggled.

He threw his head back and laughed. "I know, Brie. My hearing works pretty well."

The door opened and footsteps echoed behind us. I turned my attention to the shadow at the corner, annoyed we were already discovered. Even having refused a grand arrival for my return, the council and staff would have been informed.

"Right on time. I trust you had a good trip," Cal greeted both of us and waited at the front. His olive complexion a little pale and dark circles marred his usually clear tone. Cal's dark hair was perfectly in place and his amber-colored eyes were bright. The stress, either from being my second in command or his father or both, started to affect him. I knew the signs, and it took a lot of missed sleep for a witch to have dark circles in the afternoon.

I hugged his neck with one arm and kept the other hand firmly in Nick's. "Good to see you. The island was," I paused. "Wonderful."

Cal smiled, and his cheeks reddened. "I'm glad you were pleased."

Nick winked at me. "Cal." He extended his free hand for a quick shake.

"I scheduled a private dinner tomorrow for your family since you're booked so heavy today, and there is a dinner to greet the new European Coven representative tonight." Cal gestured between us.

For the first time in my life that I could remember, I was on good terms with my entire family, and I looked forward to time spent with them. "Thank you. That was thoughtful. Will you and my brother be joining us?"

Brandon and Cal went public at mine and Nick's wedding, and it was the happiest I'd ever seen my brother.

"My." He stumbled over his words. "I..." He shoved his hands in his pockets. Cal was a polished member of society, and this was out of character for him.

"You don't usually get so nervous about dinner with us. What's up?"

His forehead wrinkled as he met my gaze. "My girlfriend, Clara, is here from London. I was going to have dinner with her."

"Your..." My voice trailed off, and I paused to regain my composure. My brother hadn't been in a serious relationship until Cal. He had to be hurting. *Why didn't I feel it with our twin sense? Darkness.* "Has the rest of the family met her yet?"

"Just Brandon," Cal said, his voice full of defeat. He walked with Nick and me to just outside the chapel.

"I'll see you later." Nick kissed my cheek and headed toward our suite of rooms.

I had so many questions I wanted to ask as a friend and queen if it wasn't so awkward. "Why don't you bring her to dinner with you tonight?" *Why did I just say that? Is Brandon ok with this? I'm an idiot.*

A tight expression formed on Cal's face. "If that is what you wish."

"You decide. I don't want to make it uncomfortable for either of you, but I would love to have you both there." *Goddess, can you shut my mouth? I keep making it worse.* Heat crept across my cheeks. "Any news on your father?"

Cal's shoulders softened. If he was relaxed more talking about his father, then things were bad with Brandon. "According to the latest activity of his known supporters, we believe he is in London."

"You think he is hiding under the guise of protection in London?"

"It would seem so, even though we haven't been able to confirm it," he paused. "It's the reason I brought Clara here."

"You..." He brought her here. His decision. *Fuck. Stop meddling, Brie.* "I don't blame you." I plastered a fake smile on my face and stepped forward down the hall. My chin stretched over my shoulder. "Can you ask Brandon to join me with the Elders?"

He grimaced with a nod and headed in the opposite direction. It was rare for me to walk the corridors without a guard, and the space gave me a moment to clear my head before my meetings.

The echo of my heels down the hall made a very different sound from the leather boots I wore for hunting. I missed the hunt, not the killing, but when Darkness crept in, it made me question myself. *Had it always been there waiting for me to realize it? Is that why I enjoyed hunting vampires so much? Nick changed everything for me. He's not like other vampires... but maybe there are others like him.* Voices stopped me before I turned the corner by the Elders' office.

"Michael is never wrong. His visions may change, but they are true until someone in them has a change in path," Fergus, the head Elder, said.

I leaned further around to see who was with him. *Orion. Michael trusted him. I need to find Michael and ask him about this vision. I haven't had one since before the wedding.*

"We must tell her. She may have already seen it in a vision of her own," Orion said.

Fergus narrowed his eyes. "We should not be the ones to tell her this."

Why wouldn't he tell me? Fergus would never have my trust. *And what is it with this vision? It was like Michael saw me die or something. Maybe he did. Maybe he saw me burning in the flames of Hell.* I shifted and my heel squeaked on the floor. *Fuck.*

Both the Elders looked toward the corner I peered around. *No sense in hiding like a child stealing cookies from the cookie jar.* I stepped forward.

"My Queen," Orion said in a bow. Elder seemed a strange role for him considering his age. He wasn't much older than me. He'd risen to the role quickly with his photographic memory and loyalty to Cecily. Michael trusted him, but I was still on the fence.

The head elder, Fergus, took a wordless bow.

"Bowing is not necessary."

"It is our custom," Fergus said.

"And we know witches are nothing if not traditional." I

bit my lip at my sarcasm. Darkness made it harder to control comments better left unsaid. I'd promised myself to try to honor some of the traditions important to them, and the Darkness coursing through me made my lips loose.

"Yes, we are very proud of our traditions." Fergus folded his hands in front of him and straightened his shoulders.

I nodded to fight rolling my eyes. *How the fuck does anyone think bowing to a leader is needed in the twenty-first century?* Darkness liked those thoughts and knocked on the door of the internal compartment I'd placed it in. "What was the vision Michael had?"

Orion opened his mouth only to be interrupted.

"I'm sure you will see your own, my Queen," Fergus said.

"I am asking you," I paused, reigning in my anger. "Of course, I can go speak to Michael directly." I pivoted to continue down the hall.

"Let us go to the Elder's Council chamber to discuss. This is not a subject for all the ears of the halls." Fergus gestured toward the chamber. His words were polite, but his features tightened.

I nodded. He'd do anything to keep me away from Michael. It started before the wedding, and I hadn't expected it to change when I returned. We walked in silence the rest of the way to the room. My heels clicked along the floor, unlike the silent moves of the elders.

"Wait here. Make sure no one disturbs us," Fergus said to Orion.

Orion was the youngest of the elders in appearance, and he looked more like a warrior to me. *Of course, I look like a huntress rather than a queen, so who am I to judge?* I looked down at my heels and dress. *Not so much like a huntress today.* My attire became more queen-like every day.

Michael sat at the end of the table. "My Queen. You look happy and well. Forgive me for not standing to greet you. My legs are not cooperating today." His gifts often took a toll on his physical body. He either refused to use magic to heal or something prevented it. Michael deflected the question when I asked.

I made my way around the table to squeeze Michael's hand. "No need for forgiveness. Formality isn't required with us, my friend." Michael and I had become close the last few weeks before my wedding. He had taken up the void Grandmother would have filled in my reign. Sorin, my father, had left on a sabbatical and Mother went with him. They promised to return if anything changed with Alastair, but it nagged at me not having their presence here. I understood Sorin's need for space, and the further we were spread out, I figured the likelihood Alastair would attack was reduced.

I ignored the chair Fergus had pulled out for me at the other end and took the seat beside Michael. My hand rested on his. "What ha...." The room grew fuzzy around me. My voice trailed off as the vision took over. The putrid smell of burnt flesh assaulted my nostrils.

Vampires standing against Nick.
Witches standing against me.
Against us.
So much hate.
Revolt.

The room returned to focus around me. I gagged and gasped for air. The taste of death clung to my lips.

Michael and Fergus exchanged looks.

"I need to know what you saw," I said to Michael, my voice shaking.

He focused on me with a guarded expression. "It would seem I saw the same as you."

"Did I project the vision?"

Michael glanced at Fergus. I followed his gaze. Fergus shook his head that he didn't see it.

"Yes, I could see it," Michael said. He squeezed my hand.

The few times I projected before had been under stress and to everyone in the room. *Why and how was Michael the only one that saw it?* The vision made me nauseous.

"We finally have peace. Why would they turn on us?" No matter how much oxygen I sucked in, all I could smell was charred skin and smoke.

"I know only what you know, my Queen. You will need to find out why and change the course of the vision."

I looked at Fergus. His presence stopped me from asking Michael the question that burned into my brain.

Michael's hand covered mine, and he squeezed it hard.

My attention returned to him. His lips were pressed tightly together.

He looked me in the eyes. A slight movement towards Fergus and a slow blink. He didn't want me to say it in front of Fergus either.

"I need to meditate on the vision for clarification. If you two will excuse me." I pushed my chair back. My body recovered from the vision, but my mind was chaotic with the scene I'd witnessed. *I have to stop it.*

"Of course." Fergus bowed.

I nodded to them both and escaped the room. A guard waited on the other side of the door, but it wasn't Alan, my trusted head guard that had traveled with Nick and me on our honeymoon. I waved him away. "I don't need an escort inside the mansion."

"Elder Fergus asked me to see you safely to your destination."

Of course, he did. My stomach twinged. Michael tried to convey something to me about Fergus. *What happened while I was on my honeymoon that Michael didn't trust the head elder?*

"As your queen, I'm telling you I do not require your services at the moment."

He bowed in front of me. "Yes, Your Majesty." He backed away.

Relief at his obedience dissipated. I turned and hoofed it to the library. There had to be something in the prophecy I'd missed about it and how to prevent this. *Maybe the only answer is to stop the prophecy...*

My body slammed into something as I rounded the last corner. It knocked me to the ground. "Hmph."

"Sis, I didn't think I'd see you before dinner. Welcome back." Brandon extended his hand and helped me to my feet. He hugged me. "I just saw Nick, and he told me you were in meetings."

I'd been worried about him after Cal's confession. My twin and I didn't have the strong twin sense we once did, but there was a connection that remained. It helped to center me, and my mind calmed some.

"I did." I studied him for a second. "Wait. Nick told you? Not Cal?"

Brandon deflated. I wished I hadn't asked. "He has a girlfriend."

"But you two looked so good together." I looped my arm through his and tugged him toward the library. My urgency was hastened by the dejection rolling off my twin.

"I thought so too," he said, his voice dripping with sadness.

Our twin sense may have waned with the darkness in me, but his heartache came through like a megaphone. Darkness prodded me to poke the pain, but my pink aura engulfed it. I urged my pink aura to soothe him, but there wasn't enough of it to go around. I quickened the pace, and he stayed in step with me.

He inclined his head toward me. His eyes were full of hurt. "Let's talk about it later. Where are you dragging me to in such a hurry?"

I glanced around and leaned in to whisper as low as I could. "Something's going on, Brandon. Fergus and Michael were both acting off. I don't think Michael trusts our Head Elder."

He looked around, eyes darting up and down the hall. My office was in sight. "Let's step inside." Everything looked just as I had left it. The teapot sat in the middle of the coffee table in the sitting area, the couch on one side and two wingback chairs on the other. Earl Grey scented the air, despite my two weeks away, and the familiar smell was like home.

He made sure the door closed before he said anything else. "Michael has been in isolation since shortly after you left."

"Why didn't anyone tell me?" If the only Elder I truly

trusted was in seclusion, that should have been enough for them to break the no-contact order on the island. Michael wouldn't lie to the council, but he would isolate himself.

"You were on a private island celebrating your honeymoon. Do you think anyone was going to disturb you?"

I nodded. If they didn't want to contact me, then the next person would be Sorin. He was the closest person to an Elder outside of the council. "What about Dad? Did anyone tell him?"

"I promised we wouldn't contact him unless it was news on Alastair." Brandon had done as we asked, but I didn't agree with it. When our ally was in self-imposed lockdown, shit either had happened or would happen. I was back, so we could let Dad stay put.

"Then it's us. I don't trust Fergus. I never have." He'd tried to control me more than once. I hadn't seen anything that resembled collaboration from him. If kicking him off the Council had been an option, I'd have done it before I left.

"Me either. He gives me the creeps."

"It's more than that. Michael had a vision. When I met with him, I had my own vision, and I projected it to him. Fergus acted like he didn't see it. I don't even know if that's possible." Visions changed. Each turn we took could prevent them or could lead us right into them. Whether Fergus saw it or not mattered, because it could be his actions that lead us here. I didn't see him, but maybe Michael did.

"Same vision?" Brandon's eyes furrowed.

"I'm not sure. Michael made it clear not to ask in front of Fergus."

"He doesn't trust him either."

"Nope," I said.

Brandon swiped his hand down over his face. "Fergus was one of Cecily's most trusted advisors."

"And he hasn't been thrilled about me as queen." My aunt set her own death in motion to put me on the throne and stop this prophecy. Guilt spread like a poison across my chest, but darkness sucked it up. *How had she trusted Fergus? Had she known what a conniving bastard he was?*

Brandon chuckled. "Only because you don't follow the rules."

"Exactly. He wants a puppet on the throne that will do as he says without question. And I don't get it, because that definitely wasn't Cecily." She took the role when my father, the first warlock in centuries to be allowed to sit the throne, abdicated from his battle with darkness. Cecily was a strong queen that maintained peace. Our people loved and respected her.

"But she did believe in upholding the traditions, and the entire coven knows how important that is to Fergus," Brandon said. "So, what was in this vision you had?"

If my vision wasn't stopped, it was war. It was the apocalypse. How do I even begin to explain the death I saw? *The odor.* I had to try to make him understand, but I couldn't wrap my own thoughts around it. "I don't know exactly, but it was filled with hate. Everyone turned on Nick and me, but I don't know why."

"That seems unlikely, Sis. Everyone is enjoying the peace we have. That is only possible because of you and Nick."

"Except Alastair isn't a fan. He may have left with his tail tucked between his legs, but he'll be back." *And he'd left me with the darkest of Darkness inside me, and I don't know how much longer I can keep it boxed up. How am I going to tell my brother that?* Brandon knew I was battling Darkness, but he had no idea what happened with Alastair at the church. *Fuck.*

"With a plan."

"Which is what worries me," I said.

"I hate to ask this given our relationship status, but Cal..." He paused. "Are you sure he's the right person to watch for his father?"

"I'm not debating Cal again with anyone." *Harsh Brie.* I softened my tone. "Yes, he is. His loyalty is with me."

"Sorry. I hated to ask because I don't want to think of it either. He's the only reason I can think of the people would turn on you," Brandon said, his voice sad.

Cal proved his loyalty over and over, and I trusted him. "Unless something has happened in the last two weeks, most people don't even think about his relationship to Alastair."

"They don't forget though. Sis. You must know they don't."

"I know." I chewed on my fingernail and looked out the window facing the courtyard. The witches and vampires practiced drills side-by-side as they had since we implemented the Conservatorship bringing our people together.

My hand went to my neck and slid over the ancestral necklace until my fingers found the hidden vial of Vampire Death. I'd kept it in the safe while Nick and I honeymooned, but it was back in its place of pride. It weighed heavier around my neck. The tiny vial could end any vampire in close enough proximity, including my husband. The necklace symbolized my heritage and had been given to me by my grandmother and her mother to her and so on down our line for at least two hundred years. Maybe longer. My mind was all over the place, and I needed something singular to shift my focus.

The training masters held classes for hunters. All hunters were required to train for so many hours a week. I missed the training sessions. The practice created an outlet for all my nervous and frustrated energy, and the real answers I needed were locked inside me instead of the library.

"Let's go spar. You are one of the few left who won't take it easy on me." I tapped his shoulder.

Brandon narrowed his eyes and cocked his head. "Don't you want to find out what your vision means?"

I smiled. "You know I do some of my best thinking when I'm kicking your ass."

"Kick my ass?" He laughed. "Meet you there in ten minutes."

I took a deep breath when he left. My gaze fell back to the courtyard. Everything looked strong on the outside, but I feared I was on the outside looking into a cracked snow globe.

Nick jumped from the couch and met me at the door. "Your nose is bleeding."

"Meh. Brandon got a lucky hit in." I wiped it away with my thumb.

"Brandon?" His eyebrows shot up.

"My twin brother. My sparring partner. Yes, Brandon. I responded with a foot sweep." I smiled. Pain shot through my nose and made me cringe. "Shit." My hands covered it.

"That's my badass wife." He smiled. "Have a seat on the couch. I'll get you some ice."

"I can—"

"No arguments. Yes, you can do it yourself and you'll heal fast enough, but I want to do it."

I plopped down on the couch. *How do I tell him we are leading a crumbling kingdom? Hey honey. Guess what? Everyone is going to hate us in the near future. Or my darling husband, our world is about to go to shit. Again.*

"Head back." Nick emerged from the bar area with a towel full of ice. His love language. He needed to show how he cared. I wasn't big on talking, much less about my feelings before I met him.

"It's not that bad." I rested my head against the back of the couch as instructed.

"Trust your husband." He pressed his lips against my forehead.

"Always," I said in a nasally voice. The ice-filled towel rested over my nose. Perfect excuse to run through how I would break the news. A dozen ways passed through my mind, and I lifted the ice pack off my nose. Straightforward was best with us. I'd learned that. *So why is it so damn hard to tell him?*

"Maybe I should try to heal myself. I haven't tried since we," I paused. "Remembered." The last word came out with almost no sound and hung in the air between us.

Nick leaned back against the couch with only his fuzzy silhouette visible in my peripheral vision. "You're a witch and your gifts are part of who you are. I worry about what Sorin told you when we learned of the prophecy. If the only way he can keep the Darkness dormant is to not use his powers, then it would stand to reason, it would work the same way for you."

I tilted my head in his direction. Worry etched his face, and I didn't want him to stress over me. He'd checked in with Malachi, his second in command, on our honeymoon, but he hadn't been to the vampire mansion yet. He wouldn't leave my side if he had concerns.

"I do still heal fast," I said. "And using magic isn't necessary for this injury." I wouldn't use magic for something so minor as a bloody nose, but he understood how Darkness waited to capture another piece of me each time I did use it.

His face relaxed. "Not as fast as vampires." He slid down on the couch next to me and pressed his lips to my forehead again. "The swelling is already going down."

"I feel a lot stronger after our honeymoon too. It did me good to get away from the stress here."

"It did me good too." He wagged his eyebrows at me.

"What has gotten into you?" I laughed.

"You, Brie. That's what's gotten into me. You." He slipped his hand under my neck. His other hand held the ice pack on my face with the softest touch. I leaned back against his chest. His arms slid around me.

"You certainly know how to make me feel special," I said, relishing the safety of his arms. I sighed. He needed to know what the vision was, and I would tell him tonight.

He leaned his chin on top of my head. "We need to decide what name we are going to take."

Since we formed The Blood Moon Conservatorship, the Coven Elders and the vampire leadership had struggled with how to style us. I'd planned to take Nick's name, but he wasn't sure if he wanted to keep Domenico.

"Oh, were you buttering me up for that question?" I teased him.

"You've been avoiding it, and we have to file it in the next two weeks."

"Only for the traditional marriage. Witches do not need that affirmation."

"I do though." As much as he supported my plight to

break from many of the witch traditions, his heart wanted some of the human ones upheld. He didn't care what our last names were as long as they were unified, like the future we wanted for our people. *A future we might not see if I can't figure out how to stop the vision.*

I leaned my head back and looked up into his eyes. He tilted his down and met my gaze. Our special connection was as powerful as ever, electricity sizzled through my body. A different jolt hit at the end. *Darkness.* I tamped it down. *How long would I be able to?* "We'll decide soon. I promise." *I had to tell him now. Tell him our last name could be mute if the vision came true.*

He pulled me closer to him. "Something's on your mind. Are you going to let me in on it?"

I leaned my head against his shoulder. "Life sucks."

His head rested over on mine. "Looks pretty good from here."

"We don't get any time to be us."

"You're the Queen of the Witches. I'm the King of the Vampires. We have responsibility. That doesn't mean we don't get to be us or make time for us," he said, his voice confident. Nick had so much hope for us... for the future.

"You didn't have to run off to the castle though." Darkness fed me resentment. I'd accepted my duties, but Darkness could find the little openings and pry them wide.

"I video chatted with my team," he said.

"That's not good enough for Fergus," I snarled, but I would have still wanted to see Michael in person. Emotions were harder to read over screens.

"Fergus is an odd character."

"He's not a fan of ours," I said.

"I gathered."

"There's more." I pulled the ice pack away and sat up to face him. The peace and collaboration The Conservatorship offered meant so much to him. I had a hard time imploding his dream.

He tucked some loose hair behind my ear. "Out with it, wife."

"I get a feeling from him, but I can't focus on it. He's well protected," I said, trying to think of some gentle way to say it, but there wasn't an easy way to do it.

"That's to be expected."

"Michael had a vision. I had my own when I sat down next to him. Fergus was in the room, and Michael indicated to keep quiet. He didn't want me speaking about it in front of Fergus." The odor of fried flesh came back with the memory and made me nauseous.

Nick's forehead wrinkled. "I thought they were close."

"Fergus was close to Cecily, but he didn't agree with me for her successor. Michael did. I guess that drove a wedge between them." Michael was the Seeing Elder. He'd known before anyone I was the one the prophecy wanted. He'd told Cecily. He'd probably even known of her fate before she did. Fergus liked control and he would never have that over Michael.

"More so when you and Michael grew closer after your grandmother's death." He nodded. "Maybe Fergus is afraid you'll replace him with Michael."

"No, it's more than that. I'm sure of it." Fergus's actions were calculated, and my suspicion heightened around him.

"What about the vision? Was it related?"

"Not sure." I hesitated. Nick needed to know It was about him as much as me, and vampires would turn on him because he chose me. Because he loved me.

His voice softened. "We are leading our joint followers. The Conservatorship is about transparency. You need to be able to share information with me. This is us, Brie. We have to be honest with each other."

I bit down on my lip. "That's not why I'm hesitant."

"Then what is it?"

I grabbed the bridge of my nose and winced from the pain. "It's like a shit storm follows us around."

His hand rested on my shoulder and squeezed. "Unfortunately, I think that is normal for us."

"You're right." I sighed. *He needs to hear it. Just say it, Brie. The truth is the truth even when we don't like it, and he deserves to know.* "I saw a revolt."

"Revolt?"

"Your people turning against you. My people turning against me. Everyone hating us." The memory of everything we knew in flames was hard to relive, but it was even harder to share.

"What else?" His features tightened.

"That was about it. It was short, but I could smell burning flesh and smoke. I projected it to Michael but not Fergus or so he said. Michael saw details but I don't think what he saw as the same snippet by the way he reacted."

"We need to talk to him," he said, his tone insistent.

"I'm not sure how to get to him without Fergus know-ing." The guards loyal to Fergus would tell him I was at Michael's door before I ever crossed the threshold.

"Teleport," Nick said. The risk against Darkness would be worth it if we didn't have a living and breathing alarm system.

"It's a mansion full of witches. Some trained to sense those subtle movements in the energy around us. They'd think it was an intruder." There were so many incantations in place, even before I took the throne, but they were increased tenfold after Stefan's alliance with Alastair was discovered.

"And find their queen. No real harm there."

"Find their queen sneaking around her own home? That won't raise suspicion at all."

"Then just go see him. You are the Queen. The leader. This is your home. You have the right to speak to who you want." He was right, and if the relationships weren't already strained with the Elders, I would. The peace we had was fragile, and I couldn't risk anything that might cause them to withdraw their support from The Conservatorship.

"If I summon Michael here, Fergus will know." *He'd know before Michael even got through my door.*

"And?"

"Fergus suspects we have secrets. I don't have to sense it to see it in all his actions." Michael's safety concerned me. He'd already put himself in seclusion, and Fergus knew he'd had a vision.

"If he already suspects it, then you have nothing to lose," Nick said matter-of-factly.

"Michael seemed to think differently."

"Don't overthink it. You already know the answer."

The answer formed in my gut, heart, and mind. An answer that scared the hell out of me. If I pursued it, the dynamic of the world witch coven would be forever changed. *Am I ready for it to change on that scale?* It was one thing to make subtle changes here in Dallas to bring us into modern times, but a forced reset worldwide would have ramifications. The visions made it clear change was here. I'd summon Michael in the morning on the chance it would seem less obvious.

"I do have to make a trip to the vampire mansion. Dinner here tonight?" He sounded regretful.

"We have the new European Coven representative dinner tonight. The other one was an Alastair follower and disappeared right after he went into protection."

"Have they chosen a leader for their coven yet?"

"No, as long as a queen," I paused, hands out. "Is in place there's not as much of a rush. It does leave things in flux though."

"And we're sure this representative isn't an Alastair follower too?"

"Yes, she's been through a circle bound by truth, and one of the elders oversaw the ceremony."

"Not Fergus I presume."

"No." I patted his arm.

"How are you so calm about everything? You know our lives are going to change... again, right?" I searched his eyes. "A lot."

He slipped his arms around me and pulled me close.

"Brie, I've come to the realization there isn't anything we can't do together. I'm more concerned why my wife hasn't figured that out as well."

Because she's a realist who doesn't know if we'll survive a revolt.

CHAPTER
THREE

I entered the dining room to pomp and circumstance. An emotionless expression plastered on my face, but in my mind, I rolled my eyes so hard they should have stuck. I don't know if it was my dislike for setting someone apart in such a way or Darkness, but this traditional sign of respect seemed more like a way to enforce power and control.

"All stand for Her Royal Highness. Queen Brielle, leader of and mother to all Covens," the guard at the door announced.

The room went silent, and all eyes were on me. The spotlight was not a place I liked to be in. I wished my husband was by my side to offer some of his wise encouragement, but his meetings at the mansion had run long. My first official engagement since our honeymoon, and I did it alone. That wouldn't have bothered me before him.

I tilted my head back. *Light, my friend, bring me strength to calm my nerves.* She answered like the Goddess she was, and her power coursed through me. *I will make it through the night.*

Chairs scraped back as the attendees took a knee in a formal bow.

"Please rise." My voice boomed out over the room. *Maybe a little too much Light.*

I made my way to my seat, relieved to see Brandon to my right and Cal to my left. A beautiful raven-haired woman with pale skin sat next to Cal. *The girlfriend...* I looked at my twin. His eyes focused on me, no emotion on his face. *Definitely the girlfriend.*

Why didn't I keep my mouth shut? I just had to suggest Cal bring her. Now my brother is uncomfortable, and it's my fault. And it's going to make the dinner with the new representative awkward.

Brandon pulled my chair out for me, and I took the offered seat. Everyone remained standing. *Oh yeah. Stupid formalities.* I spread my upturned hands out and smiled. The dinner crew took their seats. Alan stood just over my shoulder, ready to deter any unwanted visits.

I leaned over to my brother and whispered. "Are you ok being here?"

"Of course." He smiled, but it was forced and didn't reach the rest of his face.

Cal cleared his throat. "My Queen."

I turned in his direction. "May I introduce Clara Carmichael?"

"The girlfriend," I said. "Hello, Clara."

She placed her hand over her heart and dipped her head. "Your Majesty."

Despite not wanting to like her, there was something warm about her. "Brie, please."

Clara smiled. "Thank you," she paused. "Brie."

"Of course," I said. "Cal is a dear friend of mine, and his girlfriend is welcome at my table." *Did any past queen have to deal with this situation? I feel like I'm betraying my brother by being nice to her.*

I glanced around looking for the European Coven representative, but I didn't see any unfamiliar faces... except for. I looked back at Clara.

"I'm honored to serve you as the representative from the European Coven."

Fuck me. Insert my fucking foot right in my mouth. So, fucking awkward. If I weren't the queen, I crawl right under this table for the remainder of the dinner.

"Apologies, Clara, I didn't realize."

"The fault is mine, My Queen," Clara said.

"No, it is mine," Cal said. "I should have mentioned it this morning."

"We'll not worry about it any longer," I said, smiling at them both through the annoyance Darkness wanted to twist into anger. "I'm pleased you are here, Clara. How does the Coven fair during the transition from Alastair's leadership?"

Cal flinched. It was a small movement, but I wondered if they had found something on Alastair's whereabouts. I'd had that same thought every day since he disappeared.

"The European Coven is strong and is thrilled to have a strong queen to lead us into a new era," she said, her voice full of enthusiasm. *Too much enthusiasm.*

"And what of my husband? What does the coven think of

my husband?" Most covens still didn't recognize my marriage. My own coven barely did, and I wanted to know where she stood on it. If the European Coven were to show support, others would follow.

She exchanged a worried look with Cal.

He nodded.

"The European Coven has not taken any steps to officially recognize marriages between our kind and vampires, but they are not opposed to it."

Not opposed to it. Like two people's love should be subject to approval. It made my blood boil, but I appreciated her honesty. Most people wouldn't be so forthright in the same situation.

"Thank you for your candor, Clara. It is only through honest discussions that we will see true change in the world," I said.

"I couldn't agree more," she said. *Right answer.* With someone like her in place, the European Coven would remain a strong part of the worldwide coven leadership and the kind of ally I needed for the upcoming events.

☽ ☽ ● ☾ ☾

BRANDON WALKED me back to my room after the seven-course dinner. *Why are seven courses necessary?* We'd attended these state-type dinners before, but it was different at the head of the table.

"Have you and Cal talked?" I looped my arm through his. I'd hoped to hate Clara for being the wedge between my twin and Cal, but she was intelligent and strong. She was an asset to the Coven.

"What's to talk about? He has a girlfriend."

"But his eyes were on you most of the dinner," I said. "Not that you would know since you didn't look his way at all." Other than occasional comments to me, Brandon had made conversation with the representative on the opposite side the entire dinner.

"Oh, I looked. He should have told me," Brandon said. "It hurts he kept it from me."

"Coming from someone who is an expert at hiding everything from her feelings to an impending apocalypse, I hid things because I didn't want to burden anyone. It was out of love that I didn't want them to suffer because of me." When we were kids, Cal was the one who thought of others, and he seemed the same as an adult. I believed he didn't want to hurt anybody, and that's why he hadn't told Brandon, not unlike what I did with my visions.

"It sounds like you are siding with him, Sis," he said.

"No, I'm advocating for communication as someone who has to live daily with her mistakes of not communicating," I said.

"You sound like a wise queen these days." He leaned into me.

"I've always been wise. I just didn't talk much." I laughed.

He chuckled. "I'll talk to him tomorrow."

Me giving Brandon relationship advice. No one would have believed it. It gave me hope for them that he was going to talk to Cal though.

We reached my door. "Good choice," I said. "Can you stay for a few minutes? Because speaking of not hiding things, I need to tell you something about my honeymoon." With Nick gone to the vampire castle, I didn't want to be alone, and Alastair's spell on our memories was something Brandon should know.

Brandon held up his hand. "I don't need any details from the last two weeks."

I leveled my gaze on him. "This you do."

His hands lowered in slow motion and his expression sobered. He opened the door and held out a hand to motion me to enter.

The room was dark, and I flipped the light switch instead of using magic. The history... the real history would change what we all knew as witches. We'd grown up in the safety that witches were the guardians, but a part of our history was dark and ugly. It wouldn't be easy for Brandon to hear, any more than it was for me. When the knowledge got out to the masses, it could change the dynamic between witches and vampires yet again.

He closed the door and locked it. "What happened?"

"The first day on the island. I sat out on the lounge chair while Nick walked the security team out."

"And a giant magic crab crawled out of the sand? What Brie?"

"I wish." I shook my head. "We both had memories returned to us. Memories deliberately taken from us by Alastair."

"How would he have done that? What memories?" Brandon asked concern rippling off of him.

"Turns out we did find him at the old chapel by the battlefield Ella sent us to," I said.

His mouth fell open. "What the fuck?"

"My thoughts exactly," I said. "He elaborated on the history of how witches made vampires."

Brandon stiffened. "Witches what? I don't understand."

"Vampires are born of a very old and dark incantation only performed by dark witches."

"And you believe him?"

I nodded. "Unfortunately, I do." The truth of Alastair's words still pierced my pink aura and prompted Darkness. It was the truth.

"Why would he tell you that and then take the memories?"

"I don't know, but the spell he cast on us was very old. Old enough and dark enough to suppress the Darkness in me. It's the only way I've been able to keep it compartmentalized, but I can feel it growing in strength." Self-doubt in my ability to control expanded. Darkness rejoiced as if my verbal acknowledgment opened the door for it.

"And why do you think the spell wore off? Do you think he's dead?"

"Death wouldn't have been enough to break that spell. When he cast it, he said until he asked us to remember. He broke it for some reason," I said.

"And you two kept this to yourselves for two weeks why?" The hurt in his eyes pierced me.

"We were hoping he would come out of hiding or try to contact us. But he hasn't. We figured it would be better if he thought the spell was still intact."

"That's a good bet." Brandon scratched the back of his neck.

My hand went to my necklace and rubbed the vial of Vampire Death. *Why did Alastair want us to remember at that moment? It didn't make sense.*

"Don't tell anyone else," Brandon continued. "We should keep this among us until we know more about the spell. Write down the exact words he said, and I'll start researching in the library."

I found a piece of paper and scribbled down what I recalled Alastair had said. Folding the piece of paper in half, I handed it to Brandon. "Thank you," I said. "Thank you for understanding."

"You don't have to thank me for being your brother or your Protector." He hugged me. His acceptance of me had never wavered, even when he didn't agree with my decisions or called me out on my bullshit. I was thankful for my twin.

The door handle jostled, and I could sense my vampire on the other side. Butterflies flitted in my stomach. I waved my hand at the door to unlock it. A stab in my gut hit me. Darkness tried to punch its way through the temporary box, and I knew it wouldn't hold forever.

Nick stepped through the open door with massive dark circles under his eyes. Vampires didn't look that tired unless they were hungry. *Had he not fed?* He'd been gone long enough to. *Why wouldn't he have?*

"I'll leave you two for ..." Brandon's voice trailed off with a smile.

I waved to him and laughed. "Get out!"

Nick kicked the door shut behind Brandon and enveloped me in his arms. "I missed you, my wife."

I melted into him. The safety of his arms was everything I needed. It washed away my fear and replaced it with strength.

"I missed you, husband." I reached up and slid my fingers into his dark hair. My awareness of his body grew.

He leaned in and brought our lips together. His passion devoured my lips, and I returned it. He pulled away, leaving me breathless. His hand slid into mine. He led me to the couch and pulled me into his lap.

I tucked my head into the crook of his neck and inhaled the vanilla whiskey aroma. All Nick and wonderful, the scent aroused need inside of me.

"How were your meetings?" I asked, intoxicated by his scent.

"Rough," he said. "There is so much dissension in my house, I'm not sure it can be saved, and the whole time I was thinking about your vision." Vampire inner activities were vicious but stable under Stefan, and Nick was used to those cutthroat tactics in their daily business. It was worse if he bothered to mention it, and that meant something more built. And I knew what that was thanks to one of my gifts.

The visions are a blessing and a curse. Something I've known since they started.

CHAPTER

FOUR

M y chair rolled back from the desk, louder than usual in the quiet office. I'd sat down and stood up a half dozen times while I waited for Michael. I'd tried to make the visit request sound as benign as possible around guidance for better meditation. My hope was the guise would be enough to convince Fergus. He was the leader of the Elders and with that came a certain power and respect among the royal families. A lot of influence held in the balance between us and the support of the masses would be crucial if this vision were to come to fruition. I pushed back again and stood up to light the blood orange candle on the table in the sitting area, inhaling the calming scent.

There was a *rap tap tap* at the door. I jumped and forced myself to calm down before responding. "Yes."

Alan opened the door. "Elder Michael is here for you, Ma'am."

"Thank you, Alan. Michael is always welcome here."

He nodded and held the door for Michael to enter.

Michael moved slower than he had before I left. He was one of the older elders, but his health had been fine before my honeymoon trip. The decline was rapid. Fear spiked in my neck. *What happened in the two weeks I was away? Why hadn't Brandon or Cal mentioned Michael's struggle?* I met him at the edge of the sitting area and took his hands in mine. His skin was cold.

"My Queen." He kissed each of my cheeks. "I was pleased to receive your invitation."

Alan closed the door behind us.

"Please sit." I took a seat on the sofa, leaving the space closest to him open.

"Are you well?" I asked.

He eased down on the plush cushions. "There is no need for you to worry," he said. "I assume you didn't request my presence to discuss meditation techniques."

Nope. I chewed the inside of my jaw. "Not exactly."

"You want to know about the visions." He settled into the seat. His gaze was distant.

"Yes," I wiped my damp hands on my slacks. "Were our visions the same?"

"They were indeed," he said.

My stomach knotted and my hand found the vial of vampire death in my necklace.

"Yet, they were different," he said. "In your vision, Nick was still a vampire."

"Still?"

"In my vision, he was a witch." Michael turned his head

and met my eyes. There was no fear or worry there. It was empathy that looked back at me.

My heart raced, and my thoughts fuzzed over. I couldn't have heard him correctly.

"That's not possible though. What does it mean?" *Vampires can't become witches any more than they can become human again.*

"I believe that is what you must research, My Queen," he said. "Although not possible from what we know today, magic has a way of twisting power to make the impossible happen."

That's the truth. Vampires were born from such acts. "Where should I start?"

He rose from the couch. "If it were me, I'd start with the old dark magic texts used to make the dark witches."

I sucked in a breath and exhaled slowly. The best source was the Fire Book, and I hadn't touched it in weeks. *I'm not even sure it will let me now. Will Darkness unsheathe itself if I do? I'm not sure I have the strength in me to come back if it takes me again.* Darkness scraped across my pink aura as if to answer me with pain. The Fire Book was the worst idea, but it, also, seemed like the only logical choice.

Michael made his way to the door in slow steps. I followed him. He stopped and turned around, holding out his hands. I placed mine in his.

"Trust in yourself, Brie. Trust your decisions. The ancestors gifted you for a reason, and they are rarely wrong," He sounded so much like Grandmother in the moment. Tears sprung to my eyes. He gave my hand one last pat and left.

The little ball of light I was convinced was Grandmother

hadn't appeared since before Nick and I got married, but I looked for her everywhere in the Great House.

"Grandmother, if you are here, I'll do my best to figure this vision out, but I miss you and your wisdom."

No ball of light came in response, but I did have an overwhelming sense of warmth like a hug. *Love.* I smiled nowhere in particular.

The door cracked open, and Brandon poked his head in. "Sis?"

I waved my brother into the space, relieved to see him and not Fergus. "Come on in. I'm alone." I didn't feel alone though.

He closed the door and dropped into one of the chairs in the sitting area. His brow furrowed. "I was waiting outside and saw Michael leave."

"Yes, he came as soon as I requested." I sat in the chair opposite him.

"Were we right about Fergus?"

"We didn't talk about Fergus," I paused. I'd been too engrossed in my thoughts of understanding the vision to even ask him about Fergus. *Facepalm.* "We talked about the vision we both had."

"So, they were the same?"

"They were except for one tiny difference," I said. "Nick was a witch in Michael's version." *Could Nick really become a witch? Was there a spell in the Fire Book capable of changing a vampire to a witch?* I couldn't let myself muster hope. Even if there was a spell, Nick might not want it.

Brandon barked out a laugh. When I didn't laugh too, his face turned stoic. "You're serious."

"Yes, but he wasn't in mine," I said. "I'm not sure what to think."

"It's not possible. None of these ancient texts we've read have mentioned a vampire being turned into a witch. They are sacrifices," he said, his tone indignant.

He was right. Everything we read said it hadn't ever happened. *But that didn't mean a new spell couldn't be written.*

"Did he say anything else?" Brandon leaned forward on the chair.

"Just to do research," I said, frustrated. "Always research."

"I've got that covered," Brandon said, his voice turning compassionate. "I'm pretty good at digging through the old books. You can carry on with your duties, so Fergus doesn't suspect anything."

I nodded, staring out the window. The last thing I needed was Fergus scrutinizing me more than he already was. "The one source I think will be the most helpful is one that I don't want to touch."

"The Fire Book," Brandon whispered. "Stay away from it. Nothing good comes from that book."

I nodded again, but I knew it was where the answer resided Michael wanted me to find. I knew it as sure as I knew I was the queen of my people. My hands would have to touch that book again, and the cost would likely be my soul.

"And Brie?" The concern in his voice drew me back to him. "Are you going to tell Nick?"

"No, not until we know more," I said. There wasn't anything to tell yet. He knew my vision and telling him Michael's wouldn't change anything. Nick's focus had to be on his people, and this would be a distraction. "And you shouldn't either."

He gave me a tight smile. "I wouldn't. He's your husband. It should come from you."

"I know…" My voice trailed off. "He just has so much to deal with right now, and we're trying to establish the conservatory."

"But." Brandon waited.

"But he deserves to know," I said. "I think Grandmother possessed you instead of gifting you. You act more and more like her every day.

He laughed. "I wouldn't put it past her. That would be one way to make sure we listened to her."

I laughed too. As absurd as it was, the thought was comforting. "I miss her so much."

"Me too." Brandon grabbed me into a bear hug. "She's always with us, Sis. Even if we don't see her."

I blinked back tears and cleared my throat. "Ok. Enough of the mushy crap. Go see what you can find. Let's keep it between us for now," I said. "At least until I get the chance to tell Nick."

"Deal," he said.

A rapid knock echoed through the door. "Yes?" I called.

Brandon opened the door and Alan stood there.

"Ma'am, Mr. Kingston is here."

I could see Cal's tuff of black hair behind Alan. I hated that every time he introduced him as Mr. Kingston, I thought of Alastair first. If I thought it, then others did too, and it hurt my heart for Cal to have that kind of burden.

"I'm on my way out," Brandon said, his tone flat.

Alan moved aside to make room. "We're still sparring later, right?"

Brandon met his gaze. "Of course."

He'd shut down as soon as he saw Cal. I recognized it because I'd done my share of it when the pain was intense. I wanted him to be happy, but this was his relationship to figure out.

"Come in, Cal," I said.

He didn't seem to hear me though. His eyes locked on Brandon like a lost and feral animal. *Don't interfere, Brie. Don't interfere. Keep your damn mouth shut.*

"Cal?" I called.

He blinked and looked at me. "Sorry, Your Majesty."

I enjoyed not being noticed. Since being queen, every move I made was under scrutiny. "No harm. Come on in."

Cal cleared his throat.

I took my seat behind the desk.

"I don't mean to take up much of your time, but I wanted to apologize for the mix-up at dinner," he said.

"There are no apologies needed, my friend," I said. Cal's had better manners than me, and he cared what others thought of him. It wasn't his fault I didn't read the room. "I should have put it together myself."

"It's my job to keep you informed though," he said. "As your subject, your friend, and your successor." The anguish in his voice reverberated in me. His eyes were ringed with dark circles. He must have thought about this all night.

"If only life were that easy, Cal, but you are always my friend first." I smiled. "Above all else."

"Thank you," he said.

"And we're in private. You can call me, Brie"

"I want to explain," he said. "About me..." He fidgeted and swallowed a couple of times. "And Clara."

I held up a hand. Brandon and Cal needed to figure out their relationship stuff, and Brandon was my brother. A line needed to be drawn. "I don't think I'm the one you should be having that conversation with today. The person you should be having that discussion with is in the library doing some research for me. You could go there if you want to have that talk now."

"I've tried to have it with him." Cal's hands covered his face.

I love both of these idiots. How am I supposed to support my friend and protect my brother in this situation? Why can't they just talk?

"Why didn't you tell him?" I asked. *Brie, this is crossing a line. Don't get into it.*

"Clara knows," he said.

"Knows what?" *Why am I asking questions? Fuck me.*

"She knows I'm bi-sexual," he said, his tone apprehensive.

"You know the coven doesn't like to use those human labels," I said. "But Brandon and most witches for that fact are too, so I don't understand what the issue is."

"She assumed I would want them both," he said.

A silent oh formed on my lips. "Well, polyamorous relationships have been going on in the coven forever," I said. He stared down at his hands, and it clicked. He didn't want both of them. "But that's not what you are saying."

"No," he said. "I only want to be with Brandon."

"And Brandon?"

"He only wants to be with me." He looked up with tears in his eyes.

My heart cracked at the sight. It hit me what his concern was. "You don't want to hurt Clara."

Tears threatened to spill over. He mashed his lips together.

"But you are hurting all three of you by letting it go on like this," I said.

"If I do tell her the relationship could be strained between the covens because of this," he said, his voice shaking.

Duty. It was different in our roles. The expectations it placed on us were a heavy burden. It crushed me that two people I cared about were challenged by a political situation not all that different from what Nick and I faced.

"I don't know Clara like you do, but she doesn't seem like the type that would make a mistake like that. Has she ever done anything to make you think that?"

"No, she's always been kind and fair."

"Then, I think you should trust she will handle this the same way and be honest with her," I said. The irony was not lost on me that I'm advocating for honesty while I debated on telling my husband about Michael's vision. *Hypocrite much, Brie? I should not have gotten involved, but they love each other. They just need to fucking talk.*

He nodded, regaining his composure. "What if Brandon won't take me back?"

I didn't have any answers. My brother hadn't been in any serious relationships until Cal. I was pretty certain Cal was

Brandon's first love, but that would definitely cross the line to say.

"I don't know what my brother will or won't do, but I do know he respects honesty," I said. "And I'm sure Clara would too."

"I'll talk to him," Cal said. His face creased with stress. "And Clara, but Brandon first."

"It will work out, however, it is supposed to, Cal." *Even if it isn't what we want or what makes us happy.* I didn't add the last part, but it hammered against my soul.

"I'll leave you to your day, Ma'am," he said, his tone formal.

"Brie," I said. "I'm just Brie to you."

He turned and left. A twinge caught in my stomach. I worried my brother would be angry at me for meddling. And I was angry at myself for debating about telling my husband the truth about the visions.

I read through the reports from the last two weeks and hoped something would stick out about Alastair. If I'd thought it would really be that easy, I'd have been disappointed. The dossier on Clara sat in front of me. As the queen, my job included reading it. Our personal entanglements caused me to hesitate. *If there is information on Clara and Cal, their names even fit together, would I be able to separate the personal from my duty?* I picked up the folder and turned my chair toward the window. *Duty first, Brie... And curiosity.*

I broke the seal on the file and opened to the first page. Her basic information listed on the paper like she was livestock made me cringe. *I know that is part of the dossier prep, but it's so ugly. It reduces witches to a number instead of people.* Clara's lineage was on the next few pages. She had numerous royal families intertwined. Her skills were the most impressive part. She was top in the European coven in her youth for most of the activities, and the top of her class in secondary school and university. She was good at everything she did it would seem. She held the top marksman award for the European coven and chose to train the current group of youths. What I noticed absent from the file was her relationship with Alastair. Her relationship with Cal was reduced to a few lines with an expectation of marriage, but there wasn't anything about her interactions with Alastair. But they had to of crossed paths given her achievements. My anxiety spiked. Something had been left out of the folder, and that bothered me more than anything I read. *Redacting a dossier for the Queen borders on treason. Who would risk that?*

My cellphone buzzed in my pocket. A text from Brandon.

Found something.

Come to the library.

Answers. I teleported into the library, and Darkness latched on to my magic. Instead of my usual surefooted landing, I stumbled across the room. Brandon jumped up and caught me. The force drove us against the bookshelf. Books scattered around and on us.

"Hmph," Brandon grunted. He steadied me. "Are you okay?"

"Darkness gripped onto me as soon as I used my gift," I said. My hold was almost non-existent, and Sorin was right. It was harder to control. No one else would understand except Dad, and he wasn't here. He had his own battle. "What about you? A bookshelf to the spine with books raining down couldn't have felt good either."

"Not particularly, but I'm fine. Maybe you should save your magic for now until we need it."

"It's so much a part of me and my instincts. I have to consciously think about not using it. If I relax a fraction or get stressed it happens. Maybe I should bind my powers?"

"After all the shit you gave Mom for trying to do that when we were young?" Brandon shook his head. "Nope. I'm not supporting that."

He was right. I'd been horrible to Mother, and I regretted most of it.

"Besides, your gifts are the best defense we have against Alastair if he shows up. You're the only one powerful enough to fight him," Brandon said.

Darkness would be freed in me if I let go to fight Alastair. My family was worth it. One last sacrifice, I'd give if required.

"Not the only one," I said. Dad being the name unspoken between us. As little control as I thought I had on Darkness, Sorin's was far less. I'm haunted by it. I'd brought him back from death. *What is his future? And what is mine?*

"The only one here," Brandon said.

This wasn't the time to tackle that heavy subject. I scanned the room for Cal, but he wasn't there, and I sighed. I hoped I would find him here with Brandon.

"What did you want to show me?"

He directed me to the table where he had several books laid open. "This book." He pointed to one, and I picked it up. The book was heavy, and the leather was worn with age not use. "It's old, and it has some text about a vampire revolt."

"We know they were used to make dark witches, so that shouldn't be a surprise," I said.

"But look at this passage." His finger traced along the first line of a paragraph.

"For he was the only one capable, his fangs sunk deep into her neck. The queen no longer reigned the witches. She now, too, was vampire." I reread it several times. My translation had to be wrong. It was impossible, especially for a queen with ancestral power.

"It says what it says." Brandon took the book from my hands and flipped a few more pages and handed it back to me. His finger pointed to another passage.

"Though she no longer wielded the might of Light. She could no longer wield pure Darkness either. She was now a ruler of vampires and all her ancestral gifts taken in the change. Yet, she had the power to make people forget." Nick had made me forget the time I was his brother's victim. He'd made me forget the time at the castle when I was a dumb nineteen-year-old, but he'd never been a witch. Alastair cast a spell on Nick and me to forget the history of how vampires were made until he wanted us to remember. But these were specific witch and vampire actions. What I had experienced weren't the results of transformations like this text, but it was interesting. "So, a vampire lived a long time ago that was powerful enough to turn a witch into one of them?"

"Yes," Brandon said. "And he died a very gruesome death. They hacked him up into tiny pieces and tossed them into a fire. He was still alive... well undead when they started the process."

"That's inhumane and disgusting," I said. The irony was not lost on me that I was in fact a vampire killer. The best one until I met Nick. My desire to hunt disappeared when I met Nick, and with the knowledge we'd uncovered, it turned my stomach what my kind had done. "I'd want revenge for that."

"So did the queen he turned into a vampire. Evidently, they had quite the love story. They fell in love before he became vampire, but her coven wouldn't sanction her marriage to a human. They eloped, and her father gave him to the vampires. He tried to erase the marriage, but enough people knew that he couldn't totally expunge it. Her husband, now a vampire, killed her father. Or so he thought until her father came back as a vampire. They ended him together. She thought the coven would make her pay, but they made her queen instead."

She killed her own father. I can't even think that, but Sorin hadn't, nor did I think I would do what her father did. The covens tolerated my marriage to Nick at best, which was why The Conservatorship was so important. We needed to solidify our unity. "Why didn't she just try to build a treaty with the vampires?"

"I don't know, but I suspect it has to do with she didn't want anything between her and her husband."

"I can understand that." I didn't want anything between Nick and me. "So why did she let him make her vampire?"

"She wanted to be with him forever and be like him," Brandon said. "They didn't know if it would work or not, but she insisted he try."

The desperation to be with the one you love does crazy things to you. I'd been willing to sacrifice myself for Nick, and I'd do it again if required. Darkness stabbed at me. It wanted a vessel, and if I died, it would have to find someone else. No one deserved the curse.

"The coven revolted against them and dethroned her, obviously not wanting a vampire to lead them. The vampires dethroned him because he'd betrayed them by making a witch a vampire. Both sides feared them. He was ended first. Then her. They made her watch. There are so many parallels to their story and yours," he said, his tone foreboding.

And many I'd rather not see happen in my life.

"There are," I said, suddenly exhausted. Too many for my comfort. I'd bring down the entire coven before they could force me to watch Nick's murder. After centuries, we stood in almost the exact situation, and that scared the Hell's Fire out of me. "Did they try anything to bring her back from vampirism?"

"Not that I've read." Brandon rested a hand on my arm. My twin offered comfort, but it was short-lived. "We both know there isn't a way to bring anyone that has been turned back."

"Yet." I forced optimism on myself. "Maybe we can figure that out with some meditation and incantations."

Brandon sat in silence like he waited for me to make a decision. As much as I wanted to be hopeful, I had to be a realist. A realist who knew enough to be dangerous, but didn't have enough information to make a sound decision.

I leaned back. There had to be more information, and we needed to find it. "I know you think this would help Nick, but I have to consider what it might do to the delicate balance we are walking with the current peace agreement. I can't act until we know more."

Brandon nodded. "Understood. One reference isn't enough, but this is pretty detailed, Sis. I'll keep digging."

"Not to change the subject." I chewed on the inside of my jaw. "Ok. Totally changing the subject. Have you spoken to Cal?"

He avoided my eyes. "No, and there isn't anything to say."

"Are you sure you don't want to listen to his side?"

Brandon leveled a gaze on me, and it almost made me think he might have consumed some of the Darkness. I held eye contact with him, not showing weakness.

"Are you seriously taking his side?" Brandon asked.

"No, I'll only ever take my brother's side," I said. "But you gave me perspective with Nick, and I wanted to do the same for you."

"Brie, stay out of it," he said, his voice stern. He was the laid-back one, and it caught me off guard to hear the harshness in his words.

"Fine," I said. "Just don't be a stubborn ass about it. That's all I'm saying."

Brandon chuckled. "I believe you have earned that title over and over again."

"I suppose you're right. I won't ask anymore, but I'm here if you need me."

"I know you are." He patted the top of my hand. "Now go do your queen stuff and leave me to do my job and research."

I smiled at him and teleported to the office since no one knew I left except Brandon. The rush in close proximity should have caused a little breeze, and I could see him shaking his head. The image made me giggle. Darkness twinged. I landed on my feet without issue. It was harder not using my gifts than I could have anticipated.

The door opened and Alan stood with a concerned look. "My Queen, there has been a sighting of Alastair. The intelligence team was unsure since his hair has turned back dark."

My chest tightened, and cold covered me.

His hair isn't white anymore? The red was still mixed in mine. Never mind hair color, Brie. Focus. "Where was he cited? What part of London?"

"It wasn't in London, Ma'am." Worry lines creased Alan's face.

"Then where?"

"He was getting off a plane in New York," Alan said.

"Why would he leave the safety and sanctuary in London to come stateside? That doesn't make any sense. How long ago?"

"The report just came in through the face recognition software, so it's been less than an hour. The intelligence team sent it over for confirmation. I reviewed it myself, and it is him."

"Let Brandon know right away." Nick and I can get him. We can end this.

"Yes, Ma'am. I've requested the security go on the highest alert and secure the coven perimeter."

"Very good," I said. "I need to make a few calls. Can you ask Clara to come to my office too?" Alan left me alone. I inhaled a deep breath and focused on what I needed to do. If this wasn't handled right, Alastair would slip through our fingers again. He'd gone under the radar for so long. It was suspicious he appeared now. He might want me to come after him, and if that was the case, he would get his wish.

I tried to call Nick, but it went straight to voicemail I texted him a brief alert.

Alastair has been spotted at an airport in New York.

I dialed Ella. We weren't friends, but I trusted her despite her history with Nick. "Brie, you shouldn't be— "

"Alastair has been spotted in New York," I said.

"What?"

"Yes, we don't know anything except he landed in the last hour."

"Why are you telling me?"

"I texted Nick first." I paused. "You know why, Ella. What I still need you to do if it comes to it." I closed my eyes. Death was not what I wanted, but I needed to know someone could do it if I had to use Darkness to defeat Alastair again. "I don't know what Alastair's plans are, but I will give every part of me to stop him."

Ella said, her tone anxious. "If Nick finds out about our pact..."

"If it comes to that, tell him I cast a spell on you to control you. The decision and blame for this should all rest on me." Nick knew my power and my mind well enough to believe it.

"Every time I wonder why he loves you, some stupid sacrificial statement comes out of your mouth, and I get it."

Ella and I didn't necessarily like each other, but there was mutual respect between us.

"That's me the sacrificial idiot queen," I said.

Ella laughed. "Don't make me like you. It will be harder."

"Never. The ex-fiancée and the wife are not allowed to be friends."

Ella laughed harder, and I joined her. "Let me know the plan when it's set, and I'll be there for you," she paused. "However, you need me to be, Brie."

"Thank you," I said. "I know, with the vampire bonds and loyalty, it is hard to give me your word."

She ended the call. I checked messages even though my phone hadn't buzzed. Nick hadn't texted or called me back yet. I tried to call him again, but his voicemail came on right away.

A swift knock made me jump. I jammed my finger into the red button. The door cracked open. "Clara is here, My Queen," Alan said.

"Please send her right in."

She entered at a brisk pace and stopped in front of me to fist a hand over her heart. "My Queen."

I motioned to the chair in front of me.

"Is this about Alastair?" She started before her butt hit the chair.

I interlaced my fingers and set them on the desk. "It is. What can you tell me?"

"Not much. Just that I got an alert of a possible sighting." She fidgeted in the chair.

Something was off. She shouldn't have had access to the intelligent report, but we were on high alert for Alastair. All covens were on notice. *Or does she have a direct line to his whereabouts that was redacted from her dossier?* "Has something happened, Clara? Something you want to talk about?"

"No," she said, but she looked out the window.

Where was the strong woman I met earlier? The woman in the dossier?

"Alastair is our biggest enemy. The biggest threat to peace. Keeping secrets about his plans or whereabouts is considered treason."

She flinched at my last word, and I was glad to see her react to it. Clara wasn't a traitor. At least by choice.

"I don't know anything else," she said.

Her lie twisted in the air and stabbed my skin like a handful of needles. Darkness inhaled it and offered up anger in return. I closed my eyes and recentered. When I opened them, I kept my voice neutral. "If he's threatened you, we can protect you."

Tears welled in her eyes. "It's not me..." Her voice was quiet, almost inaudible. She met my eyes, and hers were full of fear. "He has my sister." She sobbed. "My little sister."

I moved around the desk and hugged her to me. *Why hadn't she told us this sooner?* I handed her a tissue from my desk. "Tell me what you know."

She blotted at her eyes. "She was at university. He took her as soon as I was chosen to lead the coven."

"We'll have the team review the video to determine if she is with him. Then, we can figure out a course of action. I'll not endanger her life." That promise I made freely.

"Thank you, but this is my problem to deal with. I couldn't ask a queen to interfere." Her sobs were less frequent.

"You're not. I'm insisting, especially since it involves our most wanted enemy."

She swallowed hard. I could see her throat move in a painful motion. Her lips closed in on each other, and she nodded. "Thank you." Her voice was strained and quiet.

Alastair had kidnapped and imprisoned people before, and it was strategic and with reason. He took my father to get to me. *So what is his reason for taking Clara's sister?*

"Have you contacted your coven?"

She shook her head.

"Why don't you go call them and see what information they have? I've already got the team here working on it." I doubted her coven would have more information than we had. If they did, it was an advantage we could use.

I walked her to the door and gave her another hug. She looked like she needed it and held on for a long time. I put my arm around her shoulders and walked her into the waiting area.

Cal stood up. I hadn't expected him this early. His eyes darted between the two of us. He took Clara's hand in his. "Are you ok? What happened?"

"He took Ivy," Clara choked out the words.

"Who took her?" Cal asked. His gaze landed on me.

I tilted my head not wanting to say his name out loud.

He nodded, understanding my unspoken message.

Clara brought a shaky hand to her forehead and swayed.

"We'll find her," Cal said. He pulled Clara into his arms and held her close. "She'll be fine I promise."

My heart constricted in my chest for her and her sister. I'd been here with Brandon and my father and Nick while he was under Alastair's spell, and as powerful as I was, I'd felt helpless at moments. Clara had to be overwhelmed.

Brandon rounded the corner book in hand and froze. He pivoted to head back the way he came.

"Brandon," I ran after him.

He stopped but didn't turn around. *Damn it.* My twin's timing sucked, and his pain plastered the air around us. Cal consoled Clara. It was nothing more, but Brandon didn't know that.

"He has her sister," I said. "You know how it feels. Come back, and I can give you details."

"I got the message," he said. "Still not turning around. Let me know when they are gone, and I'll come back."

"Of course." I didn't try to stop him as he walked away.

His hurt rolled from him into to me, and when his met mine, it ached enough I wanted to call Darkness to make me numb. It didn't need my call though. It was ready to pounce on any opening I gave it, and I could feel my hold slipping further away. The part of me that wanted to let go sided with Darkness, but the other part of me that wanted to stay with Light was still in control. *For now.*

◗ · ◗ · ● · ◖ · ◖

Brandon didn't want to be found as evidenced by my not being able to locate him. I wound down the hall toward my private residents in the coven's mansion. If I used teleportation, Darkness would gain another small piece of me, so I walked instead. Nick never responded to my text. I suspected he might try to take Alastair down without me, and the more time that passed the surer and the more pissed I grew. Darkness lurched in me. It agreed with me.

Thankful we didn't have a formal one on the itinerary, I'd asked the chef to prepare something for dinner to send to my room. My phone sat on the coffee table and taunted me with silence. I couldn't sit still. I stretched out on the couch and curled up on my side. Alastair was at the forefront of my mind. I stood up and paced the room debating on whether to go after Alastair on my own.

A knock at the door startled me. My dinner had arrived, but Nick hadn't. *Where was he? Why hadn't he answered my calls?* The answer was in my head before I even finished my thoughts. *Alastair. Nick better be okay, because I'm going to singe his ass with Hell's Fire.*

"My Queen, I hope you like what I prepared." The chef lifted the lids off each item. "Tonight, as requested, we have blackened pork chops with steamed vegetables and fingerling potatoes."

"It looks delicious." I smiled, but I had no appetite.

"And I know you didn't request it, but I remembered how you liked it, so ..." He lifted a small lid. "Chocolate cake."

My smile grew enough my cheeks hurt. "You are an angel," I said.

"I'm glad you approve, Ma'am. We found that recipe for the chocolatinis as well. We can prepare them anytime you wish."

I could use a giant chocolatini right now. "I'd love to serve them the next time we host a cocktail hour."

"Very good." He bowed and left the room.

I glanced at my phone. Still no word from Nick. *Where the fuck is he? Teleporting would be great ... if I knew where they were.* I grabbed the fork and took a bite of the chocolate layer cake. It tasted like pure heaven. "Mmhmm."

I hit the call icon next to Nick's name. It went straight to voicemail. *Was he declining me? Was his phone off? Maybe his phone battery died. There could be a legit reason for not answering, Brie.* We both added the feature to our phones where we could locate each other. It seemed unnecessary with his inhuman speed and my ability to teleport, but my finger hovered over the option. I didn't spy on him. His boundaries were so few, and this wasn't one of them. Tracking him over the phone felt so intrusive, and I debated on whether to do it.

My finger pressed the screen, and the tracking function searched for a ping on his phone.

The fork slid from my hand and clanked against the plate. "What the actual fuck."

His phone showed to be in New York. The last place our surveillance spotted Alastair. I fought the urge to chunk the phone across the room. Nick went after our enemy without me. My anger spiked and Darkness chewed on it.

I called Nick again. Straight to voicemail again. *Mother fucker.* "So, I just used that new feature you added to our phones, and I'm surprised to see you are in New York. I'm extremely pissed and disappointed you would do this without talking to me."

I stabbed my finger against the end button. Dissatisfied with the result, I chucked it all the way to the bed.

I paced the length of the room. If he thought I'd sit still, especially after his communication talk, he'd be shocked. The only places I knew well enough to teleport to in the city were public or residences. *The Coven house in New York City could work. The queen showing up unannounced might cause a stir though.*

My phone buzzed from the bed. I walked in there and picked it up. *Nick.* The fury in me rose like the sun on a hot Texas morning.

"Speak of the vampire," I answered, keeping my tone cool.

"Don't be angry, my love," he said, in his melodic tone.

"Don't use your vampire voice on me," I said, my voice menacing.

"We had a lead that needed to be acted on right away," he said. "I tried to call you, but it didn't go through."

Without me. I ruminated on his words, and my irritation ballooned.

"My phone never rang," I said, letting the anger enunciate every syllable.

"It said it was on do not disturb."

Shit. I pulled up the menu. *He was right.* I disabled the function and a voicemail showed up.

"Okay, I'll cut you slack this time if you tell me whether the lead you had was before or after the text, I sent you."

"It's shared intel. I knew as soon as the team notified us."

I chewed on side of my jaw.

"Talk to me, Brie," Nick said.

"Where are you now?" I could teleport there with a little more info and help capture Alastair.

"We're getting on the plane now to come home. The lead was a dead end." Nick's voice was quiet.

"Dead end as in you killed him?" Vexation rose in me. Alastair's assassination was mine to claim. Darkness drove home the thought with a bite in my gut.

"No, we didn't find him," he said, his tone a mix of anger and discouragement.

"Probably because he is on his way here," I said. Even without confirmation, I knew his target. *Me.*

"We don't know for sure what his plans are," Nick said.

"But you and I both know it includes me. His whole setup when we tried to pull Darkness from him was to supercharge me." I paused. Fear spiked up my spine. Darkness nibbled on it like a dessert. "Nick, come home. I need you here."

"I'll be there as fast as I can." His voice was rough as if he was in pain.

"I love you," I said to him.

"I love you too," he said, his tone apologetic.

My irritation with Nick subsided. Fear of what Alastair planned for me, and my loved ones took the spotlight. I tossed the phone on the nightstand and heaved myself onto the bed.

I didn't know Alastair's exact intention for me. The memories weren't a smoking gun. If he'd wanted dark witches, he didn't need me for that. The only option that entered my mind was that he planned to make vampires.

Vampires could make other vampires, but they were loyal to the bloodline of their creator. Nick hadn't turned many in his long life, so he had very few naturally loyal. However, the King's Loyalty passed to him when Stefan died. There were thousands of vampires across the world now that would do his bidding.

Alastair couldn't create that bond unless he created a line of his own. *A vampire army he could control.*

He needed a powerful witch to cast that spell and no one that walked with Light would do it. *That's why he chose me. My darkness. My love of it. The ease with which it consumes me and controls me. The way I welcomed it in.* He'd waited for someone like me. *For me.*

I'm such an idiot. Everything in motion led us here. Alastair arrived right after the assassination attempt on me using natural gas when I first became queen. He visited as my gifts became known and my link to the prophecy was in the limelight for the Coven. His own son didn't know. He'd wanted to drive the wedge deeper between the vampires, so he could seize control. *He sacrificed his relationship with his son to achieve what? What would this army gain him? What did he want to do with them?* If it was the Coven he wanted, he would have only needed to out me for the way I invited Darkness into my soul. There was more here, and we were at a disadvantage.

And Clara's sister. My stomach twisted and rolled. *What part is she play in his plan? Is she just to lure us into yet another one of his traps?* He hadn't been two steps ahead of us like the saying, he'd been at least a dozen the whole time. My ego took a hit from that, but I had to keep going as long as there was one innocent life at risk. If he harmed Ivy, I would make him pay with every single ounce of Darkness in me and send him straight into the abyss of Hell.

·)·)·●·(·(·

The door shut, and I sat up in bed. "Nick?"

"It's me, my love." He slid onto the bed next to me. His lips brushed mine. "I missed you."

"Then you should have taken me with you," I said, happy to see him safe but agitated as fuck.

"Still mad?" His hand rubbed up and down my arm. My skin heated in his wake.

"Very." I pressed my lips to his and bit down on his bottom one.

"Mmmm," he hummed against my lips. "I like you mad like this."

"As much as I would like to show you just how mad I am, we need to talk," I said.

He leaned back. "Why don't you get some rest, and we can talk tomorrow?"

Is he seriously trying to manage me right now? I can't believe him. Urgh. "No, I want to talk now. I'm not the one that made a cross-country trip today."

He flipped the table lamp on and held up his hands. My eyes trailed down his bare chest, and I forced my eyes back up to his mouth. "You're right."

"Why did you go without me, Nick? You could have come here first," I said.

"I wanted to make sure he didn't get to you, Brie." He took my hand and squeezed it in his. He'd tried to protect me from the time we met, even when his brother captured the naïve teenage witch a decade ago. I wasn't that same witch, but I understood his fear. Mine for him was the same.

"That's a sweet gesture, Nick, but I am the leader of my coven," I said. "And in case you forgot, there is a very powerful witch sitting in front of you."

"Who consumed Darkness not once but twice to save me." He looked me in the eyes, and I saw fear. Not the fear one powers through but the kind that cripples one's judgment. "I don't know Alastair's plan, but I know it involves you. I assumed he couldn't fulfill his plan if we forced distance between you."

Any anger that lingered in me withered away. He wanted to protect me, and he was prepared to take whatever punishment from me to do so. *And hadn't I done the same more than once?* But Alastair was a warlock, and his fate should be in the Coven's hands. *My hands.*

"While that is admirable and I love you for the gesture, I don't need you to fight my battles for me, Nick. I need you to stand with me and face them head-on together."

"Of course, my love," he said. "I know you are strong in both powers and will. It was my mistake, and I promise to be better by my wife's side." He kissed my cheek.

"Thank you," I said, hoping he meant his promise. "There is more information. Did you know he has Clara's, our new European Coven Representative, sister Ivy?"

His eyebrows squished together. "And this Clara is also Cal's girlfriend?"

"The very one," I said.

"And Alastair took her sister?"

"Yes, her younger sister. It makes me sick. We have to rescue her as soon as possible." I reached for my necklace, but I'd taken it off for the night. The empty space on my neck left me vulnerable. "If he does anything to her..." I couldn't finish the sentence out loud.

"You won't use Darkness. We'll find a way to rescue her that doesn't involve magic," he reassured me. "Interesting the intelligence reports didn't have the kidnapping in them."

"I don't think Clara has told anyone else."

"But the others traveling with him were known conspirators, both vampire and witch. There wasn't anyone that went unidentified."

"So, where in the Hell's Fire is she?"

"Careful saying that," he said, his tone cautious. And rightly so. Hell's Fire answered my call any time like a best friend ready to deliver vengeance.

"Hold on," I said and swooshed us into my office to avoid the watchful eyes Fergus had placed up and down the halls. We landed on the floor together instead of on the couch. *Ooops.*

"A little warning next time you plan to teleport us." Nick stood up and pulled me with him.

"I said hold on."

"Why are we in your office?"

"Because I wanted to look through some files." I moved to my desk and flipped on the lamp. The files on my desk were still in the order I'd left them. I found the one with the intelligence report and opened the magic seal. "Were all these people with him?"

"We never caught up to him, Brie," he said, exasperated.

"Were they all in your version of the intelligence report?" I pushed the file closer to him.

He scanned the document. "Yes, those are all the same ones in the file I saw too."

"Why wouldn't there be a picture of Ivy in here?"

"Because he left her in London?" Nick said.

"Or someone is deliberately removing her from the files," I said. A traitor sat among us, and I suspected that person worked for Fergus. He had the most to gain. If we didn't catch Alastair and The conservatorship broke down, he'd be able to remove me easily and replace me with someone more traditional.

"Why would they remove her?"

"I don't know, but she's his leverage on Clara," I said. "Which gets him to me. I can't see him leaving someone that important in London."

"You're on to something. How do we prove it and find out who he is working with that has the right access?"

That was the question, but the only answer I had included some folks from my past. It had to be them though.

"What about Clara?"

Clara didn't have the direct access, but she could have someone on the inside like I'm about to reach out to. It seemed more logical someone wanted us to think it was her. "No, I don't think it was Clara."

"I don't want to tip our hand, but I do know two people on the team that deciphers the intelligence information. They were in my class." I hadn't spoken to them in years despite how much time we had spent together back then. They had gotten me out of trouble a number of times during training with their skills.

"And you trust them? They are friends?"

"I wouldn't call them friends today, but we ran in a lot of the same circles until our roles were chosen," I said. *I'm not sure they still consider me a friend after the way I cut them off when I became a huntress.*

"Well, let's go talk to them," he said.

I glanced at the clock on the wall. "I don't think we should show up there at three in the morning." They weren't early risers when I knew them, but their roles were like mine with no set hours. "I think I should give them about five hours."

"Good point," he said, his voice warm and soft. "And my beautiful wife needs her witchy sleep."

I rolled my eyes. "Witchy sleep? Is that part of witchiness?"

He chuckled and pulled me into his arms. "It is because I declare it so as king. And since we can't do anything else tonight..." He pressed his lips against mine. I laughed against them.

His kiss deepened, and I parted my lips to let him claim my mouth. Our connection coursed to life. Sparks danced out from my spine and down my arms and legs. His hands slid into my hair and held my head in a gentle caress. I undid the buttons on his shirt and peeled it off, desperate to touch his skin.

He leaned me against the desk and pulled back enough to speak. "Here?"

"Yes," I whispered my lips brushing his.

His hands slid down my sides and lifted the hem of my nightgown. He yanked on the thin strap of my panties and ripped them away.

"I like it when you use your vampire strength to destroy my lingerie." I kissed my way down his neck and along his collarbone.

A deep throaty sound rumbled from him. "I promise to do it more often then."

"I'll hold you to it," I said, my voice raspy.

He squeezed my thigh and lifted me onto the edge of the desk. His fingers skimmed over my belly.

Electricity hit every place he touched.

His hand moved down my abdomen and a finger slipped between my folds. Pleasure sparked like a current. He worked his kind of magic.

I moaned burying my head into his neck. The pleasure intensified with the speed he applied. His belt pulled free with ease, and I tossed it aside. My hands worked on the button to his pants.

He fisted the hair at the back of my neck and that magic finger drove inside me. "Yes," I moaned. My head fell back, thankful his other hand was there to catch me.

"Pants," I gasped and struggled to pull his down.

The absence of his hands and pleasure left me panting.

He yanked his pants off and exposed his hard length. I was ready for him and dug my fingers into his hips pulling him toward me.

He hesitated. His hips lined up with mine. He looked me in the eyes, and our special connection lit up like fireworks between us. A shimmer of light enveloped us. Nick drove into me hard.

His forehead rested against mine. "Brie." My name came out in a deep raspy whisper.

He stroked harder and faster deep inside me. "Yes, Nick."

We met together at the summit, and warmth spread around me. Nick held me close to him. His cheek against the top of my head.

"I love you, my wife." He said in a husky tone.

"I love you too, husband."

"Hold on," I whispered.

He picked me up and cradled me to him. I teleported us back to our room. He placed me gently on the bed.

I'd have to get to the office early to retrieve Nick's clothes and my shredded panties. *Can't have anyone else finding the Queen's mangled underwear when they drop off the latest intelligence files or my tea.*

Nick's lips brushed my forehead, and he crawled into the bed next to me.

"I don't think I'll ever have enough of you," he said. His lips pressed against my cheek.

"Ditto, husband. Ditto." I turned on my side to face him and captured his lips with mine.

Nick's laptop was open in front of him, so he must have been up for a while.

"Morning, my love," he said.

I ran my hand over his arm. "Morning." I stretched and grabbed my phone to look up my former classmates. I texted Crew and Dahlia as much detail as I could without giving too substantial away. It was more of a risk for them than for me, so disclosing less to them kept them safer.

"Sent," I said.

"Your friends? What should we do until they respond?" Nick wagged his eyebrows at me and leaned in close.

"You must already have an idea of how we can be productive." I wrapped my arms around his neck and rested my temple on his. My phone dinged on the table. I leaned over and picked it up. My anticipation justified by the response on the screen. "They'll meet us at the lake house in an hour."

"And they know how to avoid being followed?" Nick's forehead wrinkled.

"They are intelligence officers. If they are followed, it's because they want to be."

He nodded, disappointment in his eyes. "I guess we'll have to finish this later."

"Why?" I smirked. "I'm teleporting us there, which means we have about 45 minutes to do other things." I'd arranged for a distraction for those monitoring the magical vibrations, so we could travel without being seen. It would cost me with Darkness, but it was worth the risk to avoid Fergus learning we'd left.

"This is why I married you," Nick said, his voice deep.

"And if you want to stay married to me, you better fuck me like you did last night." I pulled my sleep top over my head.

"Keep talking like that, and I won't stop." He scooped me up in his arms.

❩ ❩ ● ❨ ❨

NICK PEERED out the window of the lake house. "It's been an hour," he said. "Shouldn't they be here?"

He was nervous about the timing, but I was more nervous they might tell stories from an awkward phase of my life. *Focus, Brie. You are here to see if they can help you identify the traitor.*

"They weren't punctual when I knew them before either," I said. "I guess being in intelligence hasn't fostered better habits." I'd expected them to be on their timetable, but I thought they might be on time since I was the queen now. *Wrong.*

"We got here early, and we had time to fu- "

I pressed a finger to his lips. "Ssh. Let's keep that detail to ourselves."

Nick chuckled and licked my finger. "Whatever you say, my love." He cocked his head to the side. "A car pulled up out front."

"That must be them." I smoothed out my clothes and walked to the front door.

The thud of footsteps stopped just on the other side. I could see the silhouette of Dahlia's spiked green hair through the frosted glass. A memory flashed through my mind of the three of us sitting in one of the training rooms passing a bottle of vodka back and forth and laughing. I smiled and reopened the door.

"Dahlia," I said, my voice warm with recollection. She hadn't changed much. A similar build to me, she wore all black that matched her black lipstick and eyeshadow.

"Brielle." She held out her arms.

I hugged her. She pulled away and waved to the person in the car. Crew's tall frame unfolded from the two-door sports car. His tatted arms were on full display.

"I guess I should address you as My Queen now," Dahlia said.

"Don't you dare," I said. "This is my husband, Nick."

Dahlia threw her arms around him. "For the record, I've never had a problem with sexy vamps." *Still the same.*

Nick patted her back in an awkward hug and screwed his

face up when he looked at me over her shoulder. He pulled her arms away. "That's good to know."

Crew swaggered his way up the steps. Nick stiffened beside me. Crew had that effect on people, especially other men. His chiseled face and tall athletic build garnered attention. Model scouts had stopped him on the streets and in clubs when we were out in Dallas. He exuded testosterone and confidence.

I slid my arm around Nick's waist. He relaxed into my touch.

"I always knew you were a princess, but look at you now, My Queen." Crew drawled in his thick accent. He took a knee and fisted over his heart.

"Don't you dare bow before me. I'm still just Brie to you."

Crew dragged his eyes up my legs and over my body until he reached my eyes. Nick's fingers twisted in my shirt. "You are anything but just Brie, My Queen."

I held my arms out to him trying to manage contact, but Nick dropped his arms, giving Crew the access he needed to show out.

He pulled me into an embrace. "I missed you, princess." He lifted me off the ground.

"Crew, put me down." I'd missed him and Dahlia too. He set me on my feet and spun me around in a circle. I stopped him at one spin. "Won't you meet my husband, Nick?" I gestured to the side Nick was on. "Nick, this is my old friend, Crew."

"Princess, you know how much I hate to be called old."

I laughed. "You know what I meant."

"No offense taken." He held his hand out to Nick. "You

are quite the handsome vamp. I can see why Brie would be interested in you."

"I assure you it is more than interest and deeper than my looks," Nick shook Crew's hand. My husband appeared cordial, but his coolness didn't get past me. There might be a little jealousy and possessiveness in his actions. *And I might like it a little.*

"I have no doubt." Crew turned his gaze on me. His lips twisted into a crooked smile. "I heard you got yourself one of these." He ran his hands over his tattooed arms.

My mark hadn't been much of a secret, unlike how we'd been able to keep Nick's more to ourselves. Most of the coven knew about the prophecy and my role, so I wasn't surprised Dahlia and Crew would have found out.

"Yes, but mine came a little less conventionally than yours." I pushed up the sleeve on my shirt so he could get a better look at the sword with the scrollwork and four moons, two filled in and two open for the two left in the tetrad.

Dahlia reached out to touch it. "Beautiful," she whispered.

"That is some piece of art, Princess." Crew slid a finger over it. "I got a new one too." He tilted his head up to expose his neck. I'd spied it already. It looked like an old altar with the words of an ancient spell entwined in it. I swallowed hard.

"Nice," I said. "Didn't that hurt on your neck."

"Nah, Princess, you know I have a high threshold for pain." Crew winked.

Dahlia's eyes widened and she cleared her throat.

Damn, Crew. I'll be answering that question later. I shifted closer to my husband and glanced at Nick. His expression was neutral, but his body was stiff. It convinced me he wanted to rip Crew's head off.

"Shall we go inside?" I opened the door and held it for everyone.

Crew reached around behind me. "We should be holding the door for our queen, princess."

His personality had always been big. I should have anticipated this and prepared my husband for it. It wasn't like Crew and I had ever been a thing though. There were a few random hookups and ended up being friends. He was the reason I met Dahlia. They had a friends-with-benefits relationship. *I wonder if they still do.*

I took Nick's hand and led the way to the table. He deserved an apology later. I should have told him the history. *Maybe this wasn't a good idea. No, Brie, they are the right people for this job, and you know it.*

The table had room for all of us and then some. Nick pulled out a chair for me and took the one next to me. Dahlia and Crew sat across from us. The faces in front of me turned serious, and the awkwardness dissolved.

"So, I know Alastair is the reason you wanted to meet with us, and I'm assuming you wanted to meet here because you don't trust the intelligence you are receiving," Dahlia said.

I glanced at Nick for confirmation I could include vampire business, and he nodded. "Nick and I both feel we are receiving cleansed intelligence files. Yes, that is accurate."

Dahlia looked at Crew. Crew drummed his fingers on the table. "They are coming for you, Brie," he said.

My stomach tightened. *Fuck. Is it worse than I thought?* "They who?"

"The elders, or at least part of them," Dahlia answered, her tone irritated. "The part that wants a traditional queen and traditional leadership."

Crew leaned forward. "There are some that support you. Our age group, of course. They are more progressive."

That's why Fergus isolated Michael. He planned to challenge my right to rule. That didn't explain why there was no mention of Ivy in the file. I didn't doubt their loyalty to me. They'd risked a lot, maybe their lives, to come here.

"I need to ask you something extremely sensitive and confidential."

"It was Fergus," Crew said, in his signature candid bluntness. "We don't like him, so take him down, princess."

Why did it sting getting confirmation for what I already knew? Fuck. I'll make him pay with or without Darkness.

"I can handle Fergus. My question is about someone Alastair kidnapped," I said.

"Who has he abducted besides you and your father?" Dahlia asked. Her eyes flicked toward Nick. They must have heard how Alastair marked him.

I narrowed my eyes in a warning not to ask the question she wanted. It wasn't necessarily a secret, but those events still haunted Nick, even though he couldn't have done anything against the ancient spell. I waited for her to lean back in the chair before I continued.

"Clara Carmichael, the new representative from the European coven, has a younger sister. Her name is Ivy, and we don't see anything about it in the files."

"No, and you won't," Dahlia said, her tone matter-of-fact. If she was surprised I knew, she hid it well. "There's a directive written into the program that erases any mention of her before the file is created and saved on the servers."

"What?" I asked. Nick squeezed my knee under the table like it confirmed his suspicions. "Why?"

"We don't know," Dahlia said, frustrated. "We weren't told when the code was put in place."

"I stumbled across it running some checks on data. I didn't tell anyone except Dahlia," Crew said, his tone somber. I wasn't surprised Crew found it. He could read code better than most people could spell their names.

"That's when we started surveying outside the network using untraceable paths," Dahlia said.

"So, you know where she is?" I reached for my necklace. *This was good news, so why do I feel so nervous about it?*

"Yes, princess, we do," Crew smiled, but it didn't reach his eyes. "She's here in Dallas. She arrived last night."

I gaped at him. *She's here? In Dallas? Does that mean Alastair is here too?* "Are you sure?" I didn't wait for his answer and faced Nick. "We have to rescue her." I looked up into his green eyes.

"We will," he wrapped his arm around my shoulders.

"I'm not sure she wants to be saved," Dahlia said.

"What do you mean?" I leaned forward. *Who wouldn't want to be saved from the tyrannous bastard?*

"That young woman seems pretty free to come and go as she pleases. I'd say she is part of Alastair's supporters," Crew said.

No one would stay with Alastair willingly. *Well, except for his followers. Was she one of his followers? Clara said she was kidnapped. Ivy must be under a spell if he is giving her that much freedom.*

"She can't be," I said. Clara would be devastated if that were the case. She was convinced Ivy wasn't there of her own choice. "Is Alastair with her?"

"We haven't had eyes on him yet, but I suspect he is. Every single one of his known cohorts is there. A report went out on their arrival as we left to meet you."

I hadn't been told about it, but the report might be in my inbox... unless Fergus had found a way to keep that from me too.

"And where is there?" Nick asked, his tone cold.

"At the old church— "

"On the battlefield," I said. *Alastair had a thing about that damn church.* He'd stolen my and Nick's memories from our time with him there. *Was it his base of operations now?*

"Yes, there is a secret passage to an underground bunker," Dahlia said. "It's heavily guarded." She turned to Nick. "You should know some of your vampire leadership visits there frequently."

Traitors on both sides of the treaty.

Nick stayed stoic. "I'm not in the least bit surprised. My father had many enemies, and they would love to end the reign of the Domenico family."

"I'd change that name if I were you, dude," Dahlia said.

"The thought has crossed my mind." Nick gave her a tight smile.

"We can continue to provide you with information," Crew said. "But we need to keep our distance and limit our in-person contact." He paused. "As much as like seeing you, Princess."

Nick's leg twitched against mine. He'd been patient, but I needed to wrap this up before he killed Crew.

"I understand," I said. "Let me know directly if Alastair is spotted or if Ivy leaves the old church alone."

"Or if anything is revealed about their plan," Nick added.

"But protect yourselves." I continued. "If you get caught, I don't trust Fergus to bring you in front of the council for trial." They were risking their lives to help me. Fergus could bind their magic or sentence them to death for crimes against the coven if he removed me and they were discovered.

"Brie, you are the queen. Fergus doesn't have our loyalty. You do," Dahlia said. Her pledge reassured me.

"Always, Princess," Crew said. "And when this is all over, we'll smoke a little something together."

I laughed. "I haven't done that since our training days." My tone echoed nostalgia for those times. Life seemed hard then, but it prepared me with the perseverance for my role. "I do appreciate what you are doing, and I will gladly smoke one with you when we rid the world of this threat."

Crew's eyes shot to Nick and then landed on Dahlia. "We better get going." He extended a hand to her. They bowed their heads and fisted a hand over their hearts.

"Long live our Queen," they said in unison.

"Long live our peace," I said, my voice quiet as I contemplated how unharmonious our future would be.

I walked them to the door. Once goodbyes were said and the door closed, I leaned back against it and let out a breath.

"They are..." Nick paused. "Interesting."

"That they are." I slipped my arms around his waist and looked up into his green eyes.

"And you — "

"It was a long time ago, and I was particularly rebellious then."

Nick's brows shot up. "As opposed to now?"

"I guess I've never liked being told what to do or how to act." *Not then. Not now. Not by anyone.* That's why I'd been such a loner before I met Nick.

"That sounds like you." He kissed the tip of my nose. "Ready to go back?"

I glanced around the lake house. This place should be our sanctuary, but it reminded me of hiding out. "After we get Alastair, let's spend a few days here. Just you and I."

"You want to get me alone, wife?"

"Every second of every minute, husband," I said. "And we need to make some more good memories here."

"Another reason I love you," he said. "Whoosh us back to reality."

"As you wish." With my arms wrapped around his waist, I teleported us back to the suite in the Great House.

CHAPTER
NINE

⟩ · ⟩ · ● · ❨ · ❩

The royal apartments were quiet as we left them. I scanned the area for hidden cameras. I didn't think the council would stoop so far as to monitor me in my private suites, but I hadn't expected to confirm Fergus's plan to move against me either.

"I need to go to the mansion." Nick kissed my temple. "I'll see you this evening." He was gone out the door before I could respond.

"Bye..." I whispered. Strange he didn't even want to discuss what we learned in our meeting with Dahlia and Crew.

Nick had my trust, but I hated how we kept things from each other. When he concealed his identity at the beginning, it nearly devastated me. I wasn't sure I could trust him then, but those days were past us. *Aren't they?*

A knock at the door jarred me from my thoughts. I opened it. Cal stood with Brandon at his side. *Something happened.* I glanced between them, and my eyes settled on my brother. His contentment rolled onto me. They must have talked. *Good.*

"What's up?" I smiled and moved aside for them to enter.

"Michael has asked to see you right away," Brandon said. "He says it's urgent, but he didn't want anyone to know."

"We'll stand outside and make sure everyone thinks you are still here while you teleport to his chambers," Cal added.

"They will sense the energy fluctuation," Brandon continued. "Fergus had them cast incantations about an hour ago."

What the Hell's Fire? They are monitoring for teleporting now. Fucking fuck. They must have sensed me come back. I hadn't told Brandon I was going to see Dahlia and Crew. *Shit. Shit. Shit. I'll deal with that later.*

"How do I teleport to Michael's chamber under their radar?"

"We're going to create another disturbance here to cause several fluctuations," Cal said. "They will think something is off with the spell."

"Tell me this doesn't put you at risk of exposure."

"The monitors will never know it was us," Brandon said. His contentment changed to concern. "Go."

My concern mixed with his, but I nodded.

"On my way." The whoosh enveloped me. I landed on my feet inside the door of Michael's chambers. Teleporting into someone's personal space equaled eavesdropping in my book, but I was invited.

"Brie." Michael sat on the couch. He'd become frailer. *Why is he not healing?* "Come sit by me. I need to show you something."

I took the seat next to him. "How can I help you? Can I heal you?"

"Ready?" He asked, ignoring my questions.

"Yes, of course."

He took my hand in his like I would when teleporting someone. Light flashed in front of me, and a vision took hold. Nick wielded magical gifts. Blue light danced at his fingertips and formed into a ball. He cast it toward something or someone, but I couldn't make out the intended target. My gut twisted at the thought it might be me. I shivered. My sight cleared back to the room. *A vision is subjective.* Fear swirled in me like a whirlpool in the ocean and threatened to drag me down.

Michael held my hand tight in his. I met his gaze and knew he saw what I saw.

"What does it mean?" I asked.

"My sweet child." Michael patted my hand. "Our past is dark and twisted from what our destiny was meant to be. Darkness, as you know, corrupts, and it will eat the weak. Our predecessors did horrible things, and as we moved forward, those things were concealed. I believe you know what I'm referring to."

I nodded, acknowledging I understood. Alastair had made sure of it.

"There are those like Alastair who seek to return to those dark times, and his followers are growing. Many want to purify the witches and return the vampires to our control. They don't believe in our stewardship of the human race. Power can corrupt and none is better at stoking those flames than Darkness itself."

"Darkness is embedded in me, Michael. Deep and dark and wound into me like my veins. I haven't told anyone else, but it burns in me like it is burning down my defenses one by one with Hell's Fire. It sears me inside like poison." Tears pooled in my eyes.

Michael squeezed my hand. "Your life was never destined to be easy, Brie. Nor do any of us choose the time we are called. You must decide every day what you will fight for, and you will have to decide your entire life whether you have Darkness in you or not."

His words settled over me like a weighted blanket. This would never end. There would always be another battle or moment in time to save the world. *This is my life. Until the end.*

"What role does Nick play in this?"

"I can only confirm what you saw can come to fruition if you stay on your current path."

My destiny was written from the day I was born. My ancestors chose me. This is my path. "But how? How can a human-turned-vampire have the gifts of a witch?"

"They can't." He took my hand and pressed it over my heart. "You already know the answer if you would only allow yourself to feel it." He paused.

A human can't turn into a vampire with gifts like a witch. So how... "He was a witch turned into a vampire." I blinked trying to erase the words from my mind, but there was no taking them back. *Like the story Brandon found.*

"He is," Michael said. "And as such, with enough magic from a strong enough witch, he could be returned to his witch form."

The implication was clear. I was the witch who could do it. The coven would be more accepting of Nick and our marriage if he was a witch. Life should be easier, but the vision didn't make it seem easier.

"How does he not know? Was it erased from his mind?"

"I don't think he ever knew. He came from a time when our ancestors were scattered and in deep hiding. Not too long after the time he was turned was the time we formed the international coven. And now you have the conservatorship."

"It's going to fail though," I said. A conservatorship couldn't survive with this dissension, and not only would the truce between vampires and witches break but the coven would fracture. *Unless I can stop Alastair. And Fergus.*

"No, it will do what it is meant to do," Michael said. "Have faith in it and yourself."

"Do I tell Nick about his heritage? I hate to get his hopes up about something I don't know how to fulfill and risk raising the already high tension he is dealing with among the vampires."

"I cannot answer that for you," he said.

Knocks wrapped on his door. I jerked like we were caught breaking an ultimate coven rule. It had to stop. *I'm the queen. I shouldn't have to sneak around to see my advisors.*

"That will be Fergus," Michael said. "You should go."

"Thank you, my friend." Fergus better not touch him. I hesitated a moment and teleported back to the corridor of my suites.

Brandon and Cal stood side by side outside my door.

"You were gone a while," Brandon whispered. "We need to get you to your meetings."

He didn't ask what we discussed. Maybe he already knew. Maybe Michael had told him. No, he wouldn't have told anyone besides me since it was about Nick. *Should I tell Nick? He's keeping something from me too. Would he even want to be a witch?*

"Brie?" Brandon drew me from my thoughts.

"Yes," I said.

"Did you hear Cal?"

"No," I said. "What was it, Cal?"

"Fergus is first on your list today," he said.

"Of course, he is," I said, my tone flat. "But he was at Michael's door when I left."

"He was probably checking to see if you were there. I'm sure he will be waiting for you by the time we get to your office."

We walked in silence the rest of the way to my workspace. I willed my nerves and anxiety to calm down because my outer image needed to be calm and in control. *Goddess knows that's not my strong suit. I'd rather shoot the traitorous bastard with a big enough ball of energy to obliterate him.* Killing him in cold blood wouldn't earn me any points with the Coven or the Elders, whether there was proof or not.

"Fergus," I greeted him in the waiting area with a false calmness. His expression was neutral. If he knew I'd talked to Michael he didn't show it, and he hadn't bothered to hide his disdain for me any other time. "Shall we?"

Brandon took up his Protector position on the opposite side of the door from Alan. Cal swung open the door for us, his eyes cast down. Despite his high rank and respected position, he struggled to fit in here. I identified with that imposter syndrome.

"My Queen." Fergus bowed in front of me. I didn't interrupt him or ask him to call me by my name. He could bow down to me every day as long as he lived, or I reigned. His despicable behavior earned him that. Darkness liked those thoughts and jabbed at me from the inside.

I stepped through the door. "Cal, please join us today."

Fergus rose with a grimace on his face. He recoiled back like I was a snake that would strike him. *And maybe I would the way Darkness bit at my aura.* "My Queen, I hardly think that is necessary. He has not taken the oath yet."

Cal froze in the doorway. I smiled at Fergus and narrowed my eyes. "But we both know that can only come when my death is near, and my successor should be familiar with the inner workings just in case fate decides my destiny should change." I motioned for Cal to enter.

He gave me a hesitant nod but entered my office.

"You are wise, Your Majesty." Fergus lowered his gaze as if he was being submissive. It only lasted seconds before he met me eye to eye. His hatred for me burned there almost as hot as Hell's Fire.

I wanted to vomit, but I gestured to the sitting area and took one of the wingback chairs. Cal took the other, leaving the sofa for Fergus. The coffee table had the tea service on it with my morning hot tea.

"What is on your mind today?" I asked, expecting his usual bullshit about traditions and how evil the vampires were.

Cal leaned forward and poured a cup of tea for each of us. He handed me a cup and sat another one in front of Fergus. Fergus didn't touch his, but Cal leaned back in the chair and sipped his. I picked my cup up and thought of how wonderful it would be if Fergus's tea was poisoned.

"I know your husband is one of them," Fergus paused.

My heart sank. *Does he know? He couldn't know Nick was once a witch. Nick doesn't even know. Just Michael and I. Unless he saw my vision... or Michael's. Could he know? I'll have to kill him.*

"But the vampires are conspiring," he continued. "They are not cooperating with our joint intelligence teams under the conservatorship."

Oh. He meant a vampire. Of course, he did.

I lowered my voice. Not that there weren't very obvious issues we were dealing with, but he'd looked for every possible reason to dismantle the conservatorship. "What do you mean?"

"We've asked them for information, but they refuse to give it to us."

"They've refused?" I raised an eyebrow to reinforce my false concern.

"Yes," he said.

"What information did you ask them for?"

"I wouldn't trouble you with that, My Queen," he said with fake abashment.

"But you are here to seek my help." I forced a smile. "Or rather my husband's. I'm unable to ask for his help if I don't know what I am asking."

He inclined his head toward me. "Your assessment is

accurate, Ma'am. We believe the vampires are concealing Alastair's whereabouts."

"I see," I said. Nick wouldn't conceal that from me. *From Alastair likely but not me. Not after our talk.* My confidence in him didn't stop the dread pitted in my stomach. "That would be an important piece of information requiring shared intelligence reporting. Let me text my husband now while you are here."

I pulled my phone out of my pocket.

> Fergus is in my office right now. He believes the vampires know where Alastair is. Can you confirm and let me know?

I hit the send button. *Please answer fast. Please answer 'no.'*

"He had a full calendar today, so it might take a few minutes for him to respond." I sipped my tea. My phone buzzed on my lap. *Thank the Goddess.*

I clicked on the alert to read his text.

> Since you can't tell him what we both want to. The vampires do not know where Alastair is.

Sweet Goddess, thank you. I locked the phone and returned it to my pocket. "The vampires do not know Alastair's location any more than I presume we do."

His gaze flicked up to mine at the glove I tossed down.

"I see." Fergus's eyes shifted to my jacket pocket where I placed my phone like he could read the text through it.

"Was there anything else today?"

He stood up. "No, My Queen. That was all I needed to cover with you today."

"Very good then," I said and walked him to the door. *Goddess, give me the strength not to shove him out the door, magically or physically.* "Will you be presiding over the ceremony for Clara's confirmation?"

"Yes, Your Majesty. It is my honor and my duty." He bowed in front of me.

"Wonderful," I said.

I stood like a statue in the doorway until Fergus disappeared. I jerked my head towards Brandon to join Cal and me in my office.

Brandon shut the door and walked to the sitting area with me.

"He is up to something, isn't he?" He asked. "We all know it."

A unified front was our best defense against the vision, and the time to share what I'd done with Brandon and Cal had arrived. "I can confirm that. He's been limiting the information in the intelligence dossiers by having them scrubbed of certain data."

Cal set his teacup on the table and focused on me.

"What data?" Brandon asked.

"Data about Ivy," I said. "The worst part is that Ivy appears to be working with Alastair's team, and I'm not sure how we break that news to Clara." I met Cal's gaze. Disbelief in his eyes. He shook his head.

"She wouldn't," Cal said.

"Brie, you didn't reach out to certain old friends, did you?" Brandon asked.

Of course, he knew I'd contact Crew and Dahlia. "I did."

Brandon heaved a big sigh. "They will want favors in return. Just keep them away from Nick. I don't want to be the one charged with cleaning that up." *Too late, bro, too late.*

"Who are they?" Cal asked.

"They are Dahlia and Crew," Brandon said.

"And they already met Nick and are still walking," I smiled. "Crew and Dahlia are intelligence officers now with the highest clearance, and I trained with them several years ago."

"I see," Cal said. "And you trust them?"

"I do." I nodded in a slow motion. Darkness twinged in my gut like it questioned my words. I trusted them. *Should I?* "But as Brandon said, they will want favors in payment. I knew there would be a price when I reached out to them."

"And Crew has been in love with you for years, Princess." Brandon snickered.

I rolled my eyes. "There was definitely some tension with Nick," I said, my tone as flat as I could make it. "But everyone survived."

"What did Michael have to say?" Brandon dropped a foot on the coffee table and crossed his legs.

"I have to sort through it first," I said. Nick wouldn't forgive me if I told them first, and I didn't know if or when I should tell him.

"Was it about Ivy?" Cal asked.

"No, nothing to do with her." I turned to my desk and shuffled some papers. The secret bubbled inside me like Old Faithful before it erupts. I wanted to shout it out. *My husband was a witch, and he can be again.*

Brandon's feet thudded to the ground as he stood. "I can feel your nervousness, Brie. Just tell us."

"There's nothing to tell," I said. "At least not yet. It doesn't make sense." It was the only truth I could say. It didn't make sense. My husband had once been a warlock, and he didn't even know it.

Brandon leaned up against the desk next to me. "It's not like you to keep things from me, but I'm sure you have your reasons." He took a step back. "Cal and I need to take care of some things, but Alan will be here for you."

I glanced between them both and smiled. "I bet you do. Bye." I waved to them. Those simple times when you first fall in love are so rare. *Except Nick and I didn't really have those. Our relationship had been complicated from the very start.* My smile broadened across my face until it hurt because I wouldn't trade those memories. My husband meant everything to me. *He caught me at my most vulnerable. He fought for me when I didn't want to fight for myself. He made me feel loved when I didn't think I deserved it.* Brandon and Cal deserved that kind of love too without the struggles Nick and I had faced.

That stupid vision clouded my thoughts. *What in Hell's Fire am I going to do about my husband?*

CHAPTER

TEN

I smoothed out my ceremonial queen's dress. Nick wasn't allowed to attend Clara's confirmation, and I'd only seen him over video chat for a moment. The vampire disorder worsened by the minute, and I suspected Fergus seeded similar discourse for the witches. Brandon and Cal accompanied me for Clara's ceremony. My Protector and my successor flanked me on either side. Sexual tension rolled off them both. It made it awkward to stand between them.

"You two should just do it and get it over with," I whispered while facing forward down the hall.

"Don't be vulgar, Brie," Brandon scolded. "It's unqueenly."

I didn't try to hide my smirk. All the times he'd embarrassed me deserved some payback.

"Besides, we are waiting," Cal said.

Heat radiated from Brandon, and I didn't have to look to know his cheeks were crimson.

"Hmm hmm." I cleared my throat. "Waiting for what? And if you say marriage, I'll hit you both with an energy ball."

Brandon squeezed my arm. "No, not marriage. Just until we get to know each other better."

"That's really sweet," I said. "So much so I might gag, but I'm proud of you two."

"Don't say another word or I'll trip you when we walk into the room," Brandon said. "In front of everyone."

"You wouldn't," I said. "Not to your queen."

"You know I would," Brandon said, his tone lethal.

I looked at him. His face set in a wicked smile.

"Asshole," I whispered.

"Stubborn ass," he whispered back.

I composed myself, and our trio entered the meeting hall together. The room had been prepped for the ceremony. The aroma of sage hung in the air. I inhaled deeply and let it fill my lungs with its sweet scent. Candles were lit around the room. The overhead lights dimmed. Brandon and Cal released my arms, and I walked up the stairs to the center of the platform with the confidence of a queen backed by her ancestors.

The royal families of the coven filled the space from wall to wall. Brandon and Cal positioned themselves on either side of the stage. Fergus met me at the center. He looked the part of head Elder in his vestment. Clara stood at the bottom of the stairs on the other side, waiting for her cue. She wore a ceremonial robe with her coven's insignia on it. Her hair swept into a partial updo like mine. Her face was tight with worry that I recognized. Duty forced us into strange positions. I'd have to tell her about Ivy afterward, and I dreaded it.

"Are you ready, My Queen?" He asked.

I inclined my head.

"Long live Queen Brielle," Fergus said. The Coven repeated after him in unison. Darkness gobbled up any nerves I had from that many eyes on me.

Fergus used my given name instead of my preferred name to drive home a point. He didn't need to say it for me to understand. It was one way for him to draw a line between us. He held his hand up for Clara.

She walked at a guarded pace to the center of the altar in front of me. She knelt on her knee and placed her fist over her heart. Her head bowed in reverence.

"Please rise," I said.

She stood, fear in her eyes.

"Whenever you are ready, Your Majesty," Fergus said.

"Air," I called to the element. It whistled through my hair. Casting a circle was like breathing for a witch, and if I didn't cast this one, gossip would run rampant among the coven and help Fergus gain control. It didn't take much magic, but my barrier between Darkness was thin. I centered myself on my pink aura and turned a quarter turn.

"Water." The rushing sound of the ocean pounded in my ears. Another quarter turn quieted the sound.

"Earth." The scent of moist mossy dirt filled my nose. One last quarter to turn to call the element I feared with Darkness in me. *Goddess, please help me find Light for this one.*

"Fire." The aroma of a campfire circulated in the air.

"Authentic revelations are what we seek today. Grant us

your wisdom." My voice boomed like Cecily's had when she'd been queen. My dead aunt would have been proud to see me in control. The elements swirled around us and bound the room in a circle of truth. The same circle Cecily had bound me in when she named me her successor.

Fergus stepped forward. "Clara Diana Carmichael, you have been elected by the European Coven to be the chosen representative. Do you accept this appointment?"

"Yes," Clara said, her voice strong and unwavering with duty. "I accept."

"Do you swear your allegiance to your queen, Brielle Katerina Danforth?" He asked.

I cringed at my last name. He wouldn't use a vampire's name for the ceremony, especially the powerful Domenico name, but we hadn't formalized our styling yet. He'd followed the rules whether I liked it or not.

Clara looked me in the eyes. "I swear my allegiance to you and you alone, My Queen." She went off script, and I liked the fire I saw in her. Fergus would see it as a break in tradition, but the confirmation of where she would stand if the coven fractured was clear for me.

"Would you lay down your life and all your magic for your queen and your coven?" Fergus asked her.

"I would lay down my life for my queen and my coven," she said. With Alastair's followers and likely Alastair himself close, it could come to that, not only for Clara but all of us. I wasn't ready to watch them die, and I'd use every last bit of magic, even Darkness, to make sure they didn't have to.

"Your appointment is official with the closing of the cere-mony," Fergus said, his irritation audible. He nodded to me.

His annoyance gave me some sense of satisfaction, but I held it in. There were enough issues to battle to give him another notch against my character.

I closed the circle. "Thank you, Air. Thank you, Water. Thank you, Earth. Thank you, Fire. Blessed be." *Thank you, Goddess.*

Clara stood still.

"It's done," I whispered and leaned in to hug her. *Add that to your chapped ass, Fergus.*

"Thank you," she said.

"Go enjoy your reception. Tomorrow, we get to work."

She gave me a tight smile. She wouldn't feel like celebrating with her sister still with Alastair. I'd find her at the reception where I could at least tell her Ivy was alive. And somehow, I had to find a way to break the news to my husband he was a witch before he was vampire. He wouldn't be back from the vampire castle and his meetings there. I'd wait up for him and tell him when he got home tonight.

And Michael said a powerful enough witch could reverse it with the right incantation. It had to be my father. *Dad. He and Mom are still on a sabbatical though. Would he come back to help us? Would Nick even want to be turned back from a vampire? He'd been a vampire for centuries, and he'd never even lived as a witch.*

He wouldn't be immortal any longer, and there was no way for me to know if his lifespan as a witch would start after we turned him back. He could age up to where he would have been had he never become vampire. Nothing in the visions had shown that, but the visions were flashes in time not all-encompassing.

Goddess, help me make the right decisions. Guide me down the path of Light.

Pain lanced through my chest. I looked down expecting to see a sword buried to the hilt, but there wasn't any outward damage. Darkness wasn't a fan of my prayer. It cracked through the box I'd put it in and oozed out. I sent energy to plug the hole, but some had already seeped into me. It tainted my aura with the stains of the evil it created.

I excused myself from the reception as ill. It wasn't a lie. Darkness poisoned me with every second that passed. Alan escorted me back to my suite. He cut his eyes at me several times.

"Ma'am, forgive me for asking, but are you okay?"

"Just not feeling myself tonight but thank you for asking." It meant a lot that he was comfortable enough to ask. He'd been steadfast in his allegiance since the day I healed him and probably before then. The scar had long since disappeared from my leg where his injury transferred to me, but I'd bore it proudly until it faded away. He was one of the warlocks in the coven that gave me hope for our future.

We reached the door, and I turned to face him. "Thank you, Alan." I forced a smile. "You've been unwavering in your support, and I appreciate you."

He cocked his head to the side. "It is my duty, Ma'am, but

I hope you know I'd be loyal to you even if it wasn't my sworn oath."

I hurried inside and closed the door; afraid he would see the tears in my eyes.

My phone buzzed. *Nick.* I pulled up the message willing it to say he was on his way here.

> My love. My life. My everything.
>
> Thinking of you. See you soon.

I closed my eyes. Hot tears slid down my cheeks. Even now, the Darkness lapped at my agony and offered to take it away. A trade. My pain for the power it offered. It whispered in my mind. The compartment I'd put it in crumbled, and anger and hate chipped like ice picks at me. I wanted to inflict the worst kind of pain, starting with Fergus. But it wouldn't stop there. It built like a nuclear power plant in a meltdown. There would be less and less of me. I wasn't like Sorin. I couldn't give up magic. Despair encased me, and my world collapsed in on me.

When I said I would do whatever it took at any cost to protect my loved ones, I meant it. Darkness drank up every last bit of Light and goodness in me. I wouldn't be able to control it or myself. There was one outcome I saw. I had to find Alastair and hope the eruption building inside me took him out too. Only one thing to do... like my father but so very different.

I picked up my phone and typed out a message to my husband, the love of my life. Darkness rejoiced as I tapped each letter.

Don't return to the Great House. We're over.
It's over. This is goodbye.

It was like I wasn't in control of my own actions. I swallowed against the knot in my throat. My finger hovered over the blue up arrow. I pressed down on it and my life swished away with the message. My grip on the phone loosened. The cell banged against the floor. I glanced down at it. Nick's moniker in my phone flashed across the screen. The call vibrated the cell across the floor. Darkness dried my tears and swallowed my suffering. I stomped my foot on the phone and crushed the glass. The phone buzzed over and over. I closed my eyes and let Darkness consume all my anguish. My thoughts steered to the Fire Book.

A single thought was all it took to teleport me into the shadowed room. I landed several feet away from the altar. The book flipped open for me, inviting me to take the medicine I needed to end the remaining heartache. I steadied myself at a distance, not ready to surrender again. *I might not come back. I might not want to.* Fire spiraled up from the center. It beckoned to Hell's Fire in me. I circled the altar where the book resided.

Hate grew in my heart. Hate for the book. Hate for Darkness. And most of all, hate for myself.

Darkness pounded a rhythm in my blood like it knocked on a door. Flames rose up and licked at my feet. *Hell's Fire.* If I called it, it would obey my commands. If I called Darkness, it would consume me.

I turned to face the door and held my palm out toward it.

"Lock me in and everyone else out. Soundproof the room so I don't hear them, and they don't hear me."

The words weren't needed, but they solidified it for me. If Darkness wanted me, it would only have me. The fire from the book shot into me and out my open palm. It spanned out across the room. The orange light coated the walls, floor, ceiling, and door. Darkness obeyed my wishes, and I had to make my payment. Maybe there was another way to end this. To end the prophecy with just me.

I faced the book and placed my hands on the open pages. "Take me to Hell but leave the ones I love alone."

Darkness pushed back against me like it struggled to obey my command. I gripped the book in my hands. "I've made my request and I'll make my payment. Drag me to the abyss of Hell and leave all those in my life to live in Light."

A sting sliced through my back. I doubled over and gasped for air. Another slash struck me. "What in the actual fuck?" I struggled to get the words out. If I called Darkness, it would take the pain, but the pain held me in the present. Maybe that was the point it tried to make. Another strike hit me, and I dropped to my knees.

"What do you want from me?" I cried out. My sight clouded, and I knew a vision was next. I laid the rest of the way down on the ground and let it come.

The vision took over my view. Fuzzy around the edge, but I recognized Nick. He sat on the floor with Michael's crumpled body in his lap. His eyes met mine. His lips stained red. It played like a movie, and I could barely concentrate through the constant throbbing of my back.

"Did you..." I sucked in a deep breath. "Is he..."

"He is dead at his request. Michael insisted you would have foreseen this moment."

"So, what are you some kind of assisted death expert now?" I knelt next to Michael. "You drained his blood."

"Also, his request. He said it was necessary to prevent the secret from being found before we are ready."

"What secret?"

"My understanding is he already told you."

"He told you?"

"What I am?" He narrowed his eyes at me. "Yes, he did. Why didn't you tell me?"

"He just told me, Nick."

"We agreed to be honest with each other."

"Then trust me when I say I did plan to tell you."

"We'll never know now."

"No, but we do need to prepare for what is going to happen when we tell our people."

"I'm not sure we should. The vampires will reject me as their king. The witches are already split and questioning our leadership." Blood dripped from his chin.

"We can't keep it a secret forever. Michael told me time was against us."

"It will create anarchy."

"We're headed that way anyway."

"If it gets out on its own, it will be even worse."

"What will the vampires do?"

"Some will remain loyal. Others will seek to assassinate me."

"Without an heir?"

My vision cleared. I gagged at the memory of what

Michael's body looked like in Nick's arms. I curled up in a ball on the cold floor. Darkness would warm me, but the coolness soothed me.

Michael hadn't mentioned this. *Had coming here, to the Fire Book, changed the path and caused his death? Would Nick actually do that to Michael? How am I going to stop it?*

Visions hadn't made me weak in some time, but my eyelids weighed a ton tonight. I closed them and gave in to the weariness. I drifted between sleep and wake, and the images of the vision flashed in front of me over and over.

The Fire Book rejected me. I'd tried seven times, and it refused to answer me every time. Light didn't answer my call. It was like I'd short-circuited with the vision.

My magic worked. I could create energy balls and recite incantations. Darkness wouldn't take me over, but it took my pain away. It took all my feelings except anger or nothingness. *What was the point of leaving me in limbo like this?*

Alastair had to be behind this. Something he did to me prevented me from communing with Darkness completely. It had to be him, and this had to be about control. The question was why he would want me like this unless it was just to make me vulnerable. I was half a witch in my current state and a bundle of explosive anger. Answers were what I needed. *If I found him, would I be playing into his hand? Would he use me against my family and my coven? Was the answer worth the risk?*

I glanced around the room. Not sure what I was looking

for. I teleported to the old church. I landed right inside and faced his guards. They waited in a fight formation like they were expecting me. Darkness smiled with me at the opportunity for a fight. It tingled up my spine. *Don't leave me hanging here Darkness. Now would be a great time to show up.*

It spidered out in readiness but recoiled in the same fashion. *Fuck me.*

Ivy emerged between them. It was unmistakably her. She looked almost identical to Clara except for the birthmark at the corner of her mouth. "Queen Brie, welcome to our little project." She held her hands up like she welcomed me into her home.

"Hello, Ivy. Your sister has been looking for you. She's very worried," I said, my tone disdainful.

Sadness passed across her face. "As you can see, I'm fine. I'm better than fine."

Darkness enjoyed the moment of sorrow from her and begged me to goad more out of her. I studied her. She appeared to be fine and where she wanted to be. No dark circles under her eyes. Her posture was strong. She was conflicted despite what she portrayed and wouldn't know I'd be able to read her internal emotions. That didn't mean she wasn't where she wanted to be though.

"You will not be able to pick my brain with magic if that is what you are trying to do," she said. "I'm protected."

"Hmm," I said. "By Darkness?"

"By myself," she said in a disgusted tone.

She believed what she said. I couldn't dig into her brain, but I could see the Darkness splattered on her aura. It might not have claimed her, but it had a hold whether she understood it or not. I considered how it dotted hers like a veil. It was almost symbiotic and mutual unlike any of the others I'd seen.

"Darkness clings to you," I said.

"And to you," she said.

"But you enjoy it," I said.

She narrowed her eyes at me. "So do you."

I couldn't deny the truth. Darkness gave me a bittersweet peace I didn't have when all my senses were on.

"And what if I do?" She continued. "I like being strong,"

The trick Darkness played on us all made us believe it gave us strength, but it controlled us and made us weaker. Darkness operated on our choices led by anger and bitterness.

I hated myself, and I didn't want Ivy to feel that same self-loathing. The memories of the torture I endured at Gaius's hands before Nick saved me flooded back. Darkness devoured them like a fine dessert and asked for more. I denied the request and shoved them away. The vampires could do to her what was done to me at her age. I didn't wish that on my worst enemy. I'd help her to make a break... whether she wanted it or not.

"Let me show you what we are working on," she said, her tone casual as if we were talking about an innocuous spell.

"Does Alastair know you are showing me your secrets?"

"Alastair is my equal, not my leader," she said.

No fucking way. Has anyone told Alastair that? Pretty sure he thinks otherwise. "If that's true, why weren't you here during the other battles?"

"I wasn't ready to be seen, but I've been here plenty of

times." She smiled, not the strong but kind smile like Clara. No, Ivy's smile was a bit wicked, and her emotions were no longer readable like she'd locked them away the way I had once done with Darkness.

"I don't understand what you are saying. You and Alastair came up with this plan together?"

"Darkness chose us and guided us," she said.

Darkness doesn't guide though. It only has one mission, and that is to control and dominate in a way that maximizes the turmoil it can consume. Yet, it chose not to consume me this time. I didn't know whether to be grateful or regretful.

Ivy led the way into a room similar to the Elders' council chambers with a wall of clear whiteboards. Fragments of spells dominated the space. I read several of them, and it clicked what these were designed to do. No one would do this. It was insanity, and it scared me to think about what would happen if they succeeded.

"You will never complete these, not even with Darkness's help," I said.

"We don't need Darkness for these. We need the one that walks on both sides."

My fingers twitched with magic out of irritation. She either meant me or my father, and I knew both of us would dive into the pits of Hell before we helped them raise an army of vampires in Darkness. They wanted to eradicate all traces of the vampire's human life, so the body would be a vessel of Darkness. *Was that why Darkness refused me? Was it saving itself for this new army?*

"I understand your hesitation, but we can finally achieve what our ancestors meant to do when they created vampires.

We can erase all their mistakes. You were the best vampire hunter until you met your husband. You were a legend. Wouldn't you like to be again?" She said, her tone verged on nostalgic.

The vampire hunter in me died when I fell in love with Nick, and it was time to acknowledge that part was gone. I wanted to lash out and tell her not to mention my husband, but my mind turned to those I'd ended. My kills as a huntress were done under a falsehood we had been told our entire lives. We'd been indoctrinated to believe that we were protecting the humans when what we were doing was protecting a lie that had been perpetuated over centuries.

No, I didn't want to erase humanity from vampires. Michael had given me an option to turn my husband back to a warlock, and I hadn't even had a chance to tell him. I regretted not telling him before I left. *What if I could do it? And if he wanted it? What if I could find a way to turn vampires back into humans too? Wouldn't some of them want to be human again?* If I could, it would give vampires a choice. I wouldn't force Nick or any of them, but they might at least have an option my people had taken away.

Darkness shoved me. It didn't want me to have hope. I was sure it pushed me from the inside, but it made me stumble.

Ivy righted me. The dark ink blots in her aura migrated toward where she touched me. She dropped her hands. Darkness returned to the netted pattern over her white aura. I reached out for her, and the splatters followed like a magnet. *Interesting.* She stepped away from me.

"You're free to roam or leave or stay," she said with indifference. "I suspect you've already decided to stay though, or you would have teleported by now."

She was right, and I was disgusted with myself that I had made the decision to stay. My gut, and it could be Darkness, told me the answers I needed were here.

I walked down the corridor we came through. The guards that were so eager to fight earlier seemed oblivious to my existence. I exited to the outside and stood in the overgrown field. The moon reached Waxing Gibbous and would be full in the next couple of days. *A Blood Moon.* My power would peak during that phase. *Would it be enough to stop them? Would I even want to stop them? I didn't feel shit right now except for wanting to destroy Alastair and send him to Hell in the worst death possible.* Except when I thought of Nick. Then and only in those thoughts of my husband and his love was my only hope that Darkness couldn't take.

I turned my face up to the moon and soaked in the power of Light. If Darkness punished me for it, so be it. Nausea rumbled in my stomach. I bent over and emptied the contents on the ground. "Fuck you, Darkness," I said between bouts of vomit.

My body ached as a battle raged inside it. *Maybe Darkness will rip me apart from the inside out, and then none of this will be my problem.* I didn't mean it, but Darkness stabbed me like it warned me to watch my thoughts.

"Dad, I know you can't hear me right now, but I wish you were here. I don't know what to do or where to go. I am lost and stuck in between. Light doesn't answer my commands. Darkness toys with me but doesn't answer me when I need it. I am alone."

It was my own doing. My decisions and my choices led me here to this place in time. The consequences were mine to own. *How did I get here?* Darkness enjoyed my pity party. It filled the cracks in my confidence with dark mortar. Maybe it did want to swallow me up but in a slow fashion like a snake digesting a large meal. It became clear to me that I wasn't the top of the food chain in this situation. I was at the bottom. I was the one being hunted and consumed bit by bit. *But why? Why not just take control and force me to do the bidding?* Perhaps the slow consumption makes the control more resolute. I need to wake up from this nightmare, but the only way to do that was to purge Darkness from me.

Darkness responded with a bolt of pain up my spine and into my head. I winced and pressed my palm against my temple. I pushed back. "I'm not your servant."

Did I know how to rid myself of it? Did I have the strength to do it? I could just return to the Coven. Unless Nick showed up, no one would know I was gone yet. I imagined Nick finding my phone on the floor. The realization of how deliberate my actions were would hit him hard. I left no way to contact me and no way for him to know where I was. I abandoned my husband. Bile rose in my throat, and I doubled over again. There wasn't anything left to come out, and my throat and nose burned.

"Your still here?" Ivy came into view. Her lips pressed together in a grimace. "You look quite unwell. Awful really."

"Thanks," I said. "That really made me feel better."

"If you want someone to get up in your feelings with, your vampire is the one for that."

"No, not this time. I don't think so," I said. *Does she know something about him? Is this some kind of test to see how far I've fallen from my own beliefs? Do they have him? I'll burn this fucking place to the ground.* Hell's Fire danced over my fingertips. *Of course, it responds.*

"You don't know unless you try. Don't you want to call him?" She asked.

She wanted me to lure him here. At least she didn't know I had ended it with him before I came here.

"No matter," she said. "He's smart enough he'll figure it out in a day or so."

I lunged at her and wrapped my hands around her neck. She didn't gag or even try that hard to get away. Instead, she laughed a kind of half cough and half chuckle. I could send a surge through her to snap her neck like a twig. She didn't flinch as my grip tightened. Clara's concern flashed in my mind, and I shoved Ivy backward. She laughed harder, and it made me want to tackle her and squeeze the life out of her.

But I won't hurt her. I inhaled the night air. *I will not give in to this impulse.* Darkness will not win.

THIRTEEN

Ivy left me alone with the moon. The Moon Goddess's Light cast over me like liquid silver, and I stood there with my arms out. My eyes fluttered closed. *Goddess guide me on how to stop this madness. If the price is my life, I'll pay it.* Sadness squeezed my heart in grief for those I would leave behind, especially Nick. Darkness chased my despair away and left me empty, gutted like a fish.

Fingers gripped my upper arm. I didn't fight. I didn't scream. I didn't feel fear. Darkness armored me against it.

I opened my eyes and gazed over to my side. Nick stood there. Brandon on one side and Cal on the other like they had been for me at Clara's ceremony. *This is a weird dream.*

Nick checked me over for injuries. His eyes were bright green, brighter than I remembered. He met my gaze. His stare was pained, and our connection didn't take hold. "We're getting you out of here."

Brandon came closer. A deep frown was frozen on his

face. Cal surveyed the area, muttering something about no guards.

"Do you see any magical marks like he used on me?" Nick asked Brandon.

"No, but let me do a test." Brandon created a ball of energy in his hand.

Nick let go of my arm.

Brandon cast the ball in my direction. It blanketed me. His energy was warm and connected with mine. Our twin bond filled me with his worry and fear. Darkness slammed the door closed on it.

Not a dream. Real. I tried to feel the pain of the energy blast, but I felt nothing.

Darkness crackled inside me. It stung like barbed wire. I jerked at each painful pinch. Darkness absorbed Brandon's light with a hiss.

"Just go," I said, my voice weak from the battle inside me. Alastair needed me for his plan. Everyone else would be expendable in his eyes. He'd make Nick a test subject, and I didn't want to think about him without his humanity. "I'm where I'm supposed to be."

"We're not leaving without you," Nick said, his voice full of determination.

"It's not your choice. I told you not to come back."

"Why do you sound so defeated? Don't give into it, Brie." Nick's tone grew desperate.

His words cut through and his love landed in my heart, but Darkness relished closing it off and folding the feeling in on itself until it was no more.

I looked from him to Brandon to Cal and back to Nick.

The desperation on their faces should mean something to me, but Darkness was in control and had a barrier up. "You don't belong here. None of you. But I do."

Nick took a step toward me, but I stepped away. His hand fell to his side.

"Don't do this, Brie, my love," he pleaded.

"We've got you, Sis," Brandon said. "Come home with us."

Darkness ate up the despair and regret like I was blowing bubbles and it ruptured them. "No, this is the only way. You need to leave now. Cal, take the throne. Brandon, stand by his side. Don't come back here."

"And what about me?" Nick asked, his voice cracked. "Your husband?"

"Move on from me. Find someone else to love." The devastation manifested in me only a moment before Darkness ate at the buffet.

"You know I can't do that." Nick held my phone in his hand.

I didn't look at him. Stared at the broken phone in his grasp. It represented my heart and my soul. "You know I can make you, but I'd rather not." I backed further away. "Goodbye."

None of them moved.

A hot tear burned down my cheek. "Hell's Fire," I whispered.

The fire answered in an eruption around me. They stepped back into the shadows, and their presence faded away as the distance increased. When I was sure they were gone, I let my cage drop. I walked a few steps away and fell to my knees. The damp grass soaked through the legs of my pants. I twisted until I lay on my back and stared up at the Moon.

If Darkness didn't devour the despair in me, I'd break down. Nothingness filled me. I had no desire to move. Not sure if it was Darkness or the moon holding me in place, but I felt incapable of moving from the spot. I closed my eyes convinced I would die, but I drifted off to sleep.

))●((

"BRIE, GET UP."

Did I say that myself? I blinked against the sun.

"It's mid-morning. You need to come inside." Ivy leaned forward and blocked the blaring sunlight.

My head pounded. *Why do I feel like I have a hangover?* "Why?"

I didn't know what to do with myself, so I followed her. She'd shown me the room with the half-baked spells before and I'd take any new bits of knowledge I could get.

"Have some breakfast." She gestured to the table at the front of the room that was once the chapel. It had been set up with all kinds of food and the aroma of applewood smoked bacon drifted around me.

I stayed near the door, but my stomach growled. *Traitor.*

"You need your strength," she said. "Especially after your visitors last night."

I snapped my gaze to her. "If you did — "

"Don't worry. They are not a threat here. We didn't touch

them." She smiled the same wicked smile she had before. "Now, eat."

I dropped into one of the pews that had been pushed aside. I preferred starvation over taking anything from them, and they could have mixed a control potion in the food. "I'll pass. Why did you want me to come inside?"

"To work, but you need food to do that."

Instead of complying with her, I stretched out on the pew and let Darkness eat on the unhappiness until I was to the point of exhaustion. I welcomed sleep when it came.

CHAPTER

FOURTEEN

I let Darkness have what it would take of me. There was enough distress and sorrow in me for it to enjoy and render me useless. I did get up for one activity the next two days. The setting of the sun and the rising of the moon.

The sunset cast beautiful shades of pinks and oranges across the sky. The moon would start to rise soon. *The third Blood Moon in the tetrad.* I refused to eat any of the food offered here afraid they would use it to control me. There were plenty of spells that could be used by a strong enough witch like Alastair. My body ached with hunger and exhaustion, but Darkness gave me strength to move forward.

"Why do you come out here every day?" Ivy asked over my shoulder.

Her demeanor softened toward me, but mine hardened for everyone and almost everything. *Except the sunset and the moon.*

"I still feel like me when I watch the sun set and the moon rise," I said. Darkness didn't fight me on this, and I assumed it was because my strength grew with the moon. Strength Darkness could use.

"Don't you want to be more, Brie?" She turned to face me. Her guarded expression studied mine. "Maybe you don't. You've always been the best at everything. The best in training. The best vampire hunter. And then the best queen."

"Hhmph." I sighed. I didn't feel like the best at anything anymore, even when Ivy reminded me of the celebrated accomplishments attributed to me. "I'm a complete failure at the last one, and as far as a vampire hunter, I fell in love with a vampire. Not sure I get to keep the title." I didn't want to be praised for it anymore if I was honest with myself.

"Do you believe that?" She asked. "Like really? You will be remembered for centuries. They will tell stories of the Queen of Moons." She placed one hand over my mark and gestured with the other to the moon rising over the trees in the distance.

"Stories of a disgraced queen who fell in love with the enemy and thought she could do good in this world. Instead, she ended up in the summit of evil's nest. I'll be the reminder to children on what not to do." Like the queen in the stories Brandon had found. The history books will use me as the worst kind of cautionary tale. I met her gaze.

She looked around and took me by the arms. "Don't lose faith," she said, her voice low. "You are doing good in this world. Hold on a little longer." Her gaze drifted over my shoulder. "Don't be too long."

Huh? What in Hell's Fire just happened? Was she possessed?

I turned around to follow her gaze. Ella stood at the edge of the field. She must be here to make good on the promise she gave me. *So why am I so happy to see her?* Tears threatened my eyes. Darkness lapped them up before they could fall. I glanced back for Ivy, but she was gone.

Ella nodded at me. She wore her usual stern gaze, and it was fixed on me. I stepped in cautious movement toward her.

"Close your mouth, Brie," she said. "And take a walk with me."

"What are you doing here?" I whispered. "Are you here because of our deal?"

She frowned at me and ducked back into the woods. I followed her ready for death if my fate deemed today the day.

"Your husband is a shit show right now. Your brother and Callum Kingston are trying to hold your coven together, and Malachi and I are doing the same for the vampires. You need to come back." Some spit landed on my cheek, and I took a step back. I'd never seen her angry, and she was pissed.

"I can't, Ella," I said. "I thought you came to kill me."

"Why are you always so ready to die? As someone who has done it, I don't recommend it."

"I'm ready to do whatever I can for my family, my coven, and the world." I wanted to be with them. I knew it deep down inside, but I couldn't be around them. I couldn't trust myself with Darkness and was unable to know when and if it could take control. Not that this was the right place either, but it didn't slap me with the same constant reminders of a life I wouldn't have. Darkness devoured my feelings and left me numb.

"Well, you're killing Nick, and he's already dead, so that's not an easy task," she said, her tone flat.

My insides twisted with grief, but Darkness was there to soak it up before I explored it. "He needs to move on."

"I thought you knew him better. That will never happen," she said. "That creepy fucker, Fergus, is having Nick followed. Is there anything I need to know to protect him?"

Nick still didn't know he'd once been a witch, but I couldn't tell Ella to tell him. He needed to hear it... I lost my thought and shook my head. "He always has an agenda."

She studied me. "Hmmm."

She didn't believe me, and I didn't blame her. "Why are you working with Ivy?" I asked, curious what their connection was.

"We have mutual interests," she said.

"World domination?" I asked.

"We both hate Alastair." She rolled her eyes. "Wait. You haven't figured it out. Cal thought maybe you had got the notification before you left. She's a double agent for the Coven and Alastair. He thinks Alastair recruited her."

The sadness in her when I mentioned Clara. What she said just before Ella arrived. Seriously. How did I miss it? "Cal told you this?"

"Cal said he received a top-secret communication from Clara about the same time you sent Nick that shitty message. Cal thought you received the same info too, I guess." She shrugged.

My phone. I'd left it on the floor of my suite. "No, I didn't. Clara told me Ivy had been kidnapped, and that was the last I heard from her other than her confirmation ceremony."

Crew and Dahlia's observations slid into place. They said it didn't look like Ivy was held against her will. *Did they know? They had to have known. Why hadn't anyone told me? Did Nick know?*

"I guess that was a cover story. Maybe you took off before they could tell you," she said, her annoyance with me grew. "I have to get back."

"Take care of Nick," I said. My heart broke each time I said his name, and Darkness couldn't gobble up the anguish before it gripped my heart. I blinked back tears, and by the time I finished the single motion, Darkness took the driver's seat.

"Not my job," she said. "That's yours, and you need to get your ass back there to take care of your business yourself." She didn't wait for a response. Her legs carried her away at vampire speed.

I wandered back into the clearing and over to the patch of scorched earth from where I called Hell's fire two nights ago. I knelt and ran my fingers over it. Power lived in me. Gifts from my ancestors answered my call. I am strong. *But am I strong enough to beat Alastair? I think I am. I just have to drive enough of the Darkness away to be me. I'll be stronger tonight.*

A scuffle from inside the old grand church building drew my attention. The instinct trained in me kicked in to run toward a fight. I hurried up the steps. Ivy met me at the door and exchanged a brief look with me. She took my arm and led me forward down the aisle.

"You're just in time, Brie." She squeezed my elbow. Her jaw was set in a tight frown.

I followed her gaze to the front. Strung up in one of the medieval torture devices was my dad. *No! This will not happen again.* I jerked to go to him. Ivy pinned my arm against her side. I pushed her away, but I couldn't break her hold. *Fuck.*

"Dad?" My voice came out weak.

He lifted his head, but the device prevented much movement. I couldn't see his face. Mother wasn't in the room. *Did he have her here too? No, Alastair would have her on display to taunt me. That was his style. She was safe. I'd know if she wasn't.*

"Let's see what Alastair has planned," she said. The wicked smile I'd come to recognize from her crossed her face, but it wasn't for me. She flashed it to Alastair.

My thoughts melded with Darkness's. Death for Alastair would be slow for every ounce of pain he inflicted on those I loved, and the thought swallowed all else.

"Yes, my protégé. You know there is always a plan."

Ivy escorted me down to stand at the end of the aisle. Close enough to get a good look at Sorin, but not close enough to reach him. He looked unharmed other than being bound. Alastair him here for a specific purpose. *To bait me.* And it would work because I wouldn't let him hurt my father.

I stayed silent, waiting for Alastair to divulge his plan. *Goddess knows he likes to talk about his plans.* Alastair looked healthier than the last time I saw him. His hair had returned to the pure black it was, and his appearance was like it had been before the ceremony we did outside the vampire castle.

"I only need one of you." He glanced back and forth

between Sorin and me. The hate I carried for him festered up. I wanted to attack. To end him too. To have the satisfaction of ending his part in driving the prophecy to fruition. Darkness wanted it too. It swam around my emotions and simmered them. Yet, it didn't push me this time.

"Let Brie go," Dad said. "I'll be the sacrifice." *Not happening, Dad.* Sorin got the words out first. The prophecy was my destiny, and if anyone was to be the sacrifice it was me.

"I need your power. Not your death," Alastair said. "But it could be fun. Did you not know Brie is here of her own freewill? She comes and goes as she chooses?"

Ivy squeezed tighter on my arm. I stiffened.

"Which makes me wonder why you brought my father here at all, Alastair?"

"Insurance," he said like I was an idiot. "In case you had ideas of your own."

I did. "And my mother?"

"She should be back at the Great House by now. Why would I harm such a beautiful witch?"

"You want to keep her alive for extra insurance," I said.

"But I don't need her here for that." He smiled.

My stomach seized. I fought back against Darkness when it tried to soothe my anguish. I needed the alertness pain and anger brought, but Darkness pushed back.

"I'll do the ceremony," I said. "I'll be the conduit."

"Excellent," Alastair said. "Bring her here."

Ivy escorted me to a position inside a circle. *Dark Magic.* She backed away. She distanced herself but her hand was still around my arm. Her actions were way too careful. The circle was more than Dark Magic. Power thrummed from it.

Ivy forced my hand out in front. I jerked it back, but she yanked it forward with both hands. *It's me or Dad. I have to do this.*

Alastair grabbed hold of my finger and pricked it with a long conifer needle. "That's all I needed."

Blood spells were the strongest and most costly, like the spells used to create vampires and control dark witches. There wasn't much on the needle. Not enough for any spell I'd read anyway.

"What about him?" Ivy tilted her head toward Sorin.

A smirk plastered on Alastair's face. "Kill him."

I met Sorin's eyes. Hell's Fire flared across his pupils. Mine burned to match. No way in Hell's Fire would I let him die again. Not while I still had magic in me. Ivy's grip loosened on me. I spun and looped her arm with mine, flipping her on her back. I positioned my hand over her.

"You will not harm him. If you do, I'll kill your precious protégé. And death is nothing to me. You know my kill number."

Darkness prickled in my chest. It wanted some chaos even if it wasn't with Alastair. Ivy's life mattered to me, but Darkness shielded my true feelings from Alastair. It verged on swallowing my determination to bring Ivy back to Clara, but I pushed back with my pink aura, creating the thinnest of barriers. My pink aura held but wavered against the weight.

"Go ahead. She's not important. There will be others."

I could save them or fight Alastair, but I couldn't do both. Alastair had said he didn't need two, and I was the one with the connection he needed. He'd kill my father if we stayed. I turned to Ivy and extended my hand. She took it, and I pulled us both toward my father.

"Hell's Fire," I called the familiar heat to surround us. "Free my father," I said to Ivy.

She undid the contraption. My control wavered. The fire blinked, and I threw everything I had into reinforcing it.

"I can teleport us, but I don't know where to go," I said.

"Home," Ivy said. "You take your dad and go home."

"I'm taking you too," I said.

I couldn't take us to the Great House. *The lake house.* I grabbed a hand from each and teleported. The familiar whish formed around me, and we moved through the fold in time. The living room came into view still veiled by a bluish-purple tint.

Something snagged on me. Ivy and Dad propelled forward, but I was stuck. I tried to move forward, but whatever it was, yanked me back. I lost sight of my travel companions and fell backward. There was no line to follow. I couldn't control the end-over-end tumbling. Everything blurred around me. I smacked the ground hard at the end and opened my eyes.

The old church. How?

I sat up and found myself in the circle Alastair had Ivy put me in earlier. *Fuck me.*

FIFTEEN

Alastair sat in the front pew, a smug smile on his face. "Did you think it would be that easy?"

Did I? No. Nothing in my cursed life had ever been easy. "I like a fight, Alastair. If that's what you're after, I'm ready." Darkness stoked my urge to kick his ass.

"There will be no need for that." He leaned closer to me.

I held out my hand to summon an energy ball. There was no zing. I looked at my hand and nothing was there.

"Hell's Fire," I whispered. It spit and sputtered flickers of flame at my feet.

Alastair laughed. His head tilted back, and he cackled.

"What have you done?" I asked, mustering as much venom as I could.

"Nothing you didn't wish a thousand times," he said.

Flames shot up around me hot and herculean. I tried to pull them back, but the fire didn't listen to me. *What the actual fu...* Sweat beaded on my forehead. *That's new.*

Through the flames, I glimpsed Alastair with his hand open. He closed it, and the flames retreated.

Goddess, what did I let him do? And the Blood Moon is tonight. Alastair couldn't control my mind, but he had me as a vessel to control my powers. *How am I going to fix this fucking mess? At least Dad and Ivy are safe. For now.*

I thought of ways to buy some time to figure it out. *Keep him talking, Brie. He likes to talk about himself.* "Aren't you worried about Ivy telling everyone your plans?"

"So, what if she does? I control your gifts. How would anyone stand against them?"

"I'm not the most powerful though," I said. "That is your mistake, and I'm sure you don't know who is." *Distract and deflect. Make him angry, so he gets distracted.*

"Is that what the Elders told you to keep you in line?" Alastair laughed. "Stupid naive girl. You were marked with an ancient symbol for only those huntresses that could wield ultimate power. The ancestors chose you because you and only you can withstand the toll those powers would take on the average witch."

Dad is stronger. We confirmed it. Or did we? No one agreed, but they didn't disagree. The Elders misled me many times, except for Michael. *Was that what he has been trying to tell me? I didn't think I was deserving of the honor, and I'd just assumed it had to be my father and not me. I really do have that kind of power. Goddess. How could I have been such a dumbass?*

"Are you working through it in your head?" He asked. "They don't like or trust anything or anyone more powerful than them."

He spoke the truth of one Elder from my experiences. "Fergus for sure."

He nodded. "So, there is a brain in there."

"That doesn't mean what you are doing is right or that I will help you," I said.

"You don't have a choice, Brie," he said. "I don't need your help. I just need you alive and present."

He wouldn't have me or my power. *Fuck him.* I stepped forward and slammed into an invisible wall around the circle.

"Oh, I used your blood to bind you there. I couldn't have you running off before the Blood Moon hits its peak."

My desire to rip him apart mixed with the Darkness bubbling under the surface. *Had this been his master plan all along? Even when he had Stefan kidnap me?* "How much of your plan did Stefan know before you killed him?"

"More than you know now. He took convincing to join forces with a warlock. There were a few experiments along the way to show him what was possible. I had to make sure you kept slipping through his fingers."

Does that mean he knows about Nick's heritage?

"Why?" I tiptoed around it not willing to divulge it if he didn't.

"Because I had to make sure his death wouldn't be blamed on me, and I had no plans of sharing this moment with him."

The vampire by the door glanced our way, but they returned to their posts.

"I must prepare for the ceremony. You can wait here." He

cackled and left me alone with the vampires. The guards remained in their place.

My powers were to be used to bring peace not destroy the world. I needed a plan. *Step one: get out of the circle. Step two: break the bond. Step 3: kill Alastair.*

It sounded easier than executing it would be. *Focus Brie. Get out of the circle. You can't do anything while you are in here.*

I propelled myself forward like a leap into a mosh pit. My teeth jammed together from the impact to the invisible wall.

"What the fuck?" One of the guards said. They both stared at me.

I waved and smirked at them.

They turned their backs on me.

I held out my hand for energy. Blue sparks sputtered but never caught hold to form a ball.

"Hell's Fire," I barely uttered the words, knowing it would respond to our connection if it could. Tiny flames flickered at the edge, but they did nothing.

Even if I get out, he can just pull me back to this tethered spot. My disappointment was replaced with determination. I'd have to wait for Alastair to return in order to break the blood bond.

The scent of scorched wood filled my nostrils. I knelt and studied the little fires. They burned along the pattern of the circle. First, they darkened the outer circle and worked their way inward. Once the pattern was complete, they extinguished themselves. *Interesting.*

I walked my fingers close to the edge and tapped a finger outside the circle. A little hope spread in my chest. I reached out with my hand. There wasn't a barrier. *Could that little bit of Hell's Fire burn through a containment spell?* Both were born of dark magic, so theoretically one could cancel out the other.

I stood up to see what the guards were doing. They faced the door and had little interest in me. I scooted close to the edge of the circle and tapped my foot outside the ring. *Hot damn.* There wasn't any resistance. I had to be patient for Alastair to return, so I could complete the next two steps in the plan. With any luck, I could combine them into one task.

The blood bond incantation would be hard to break. As if I needed another reason to kill Alastair, I had it. In many ways, I wanted him to surrender and face trial, but it was clear he would never do that. He'd drifted too far in his dance with Darkness. The good part of him that must have been there at some point to produce an incredible human like Cal. Maybe all the good in him passed to my friend. Death was the only way this would end. Either his or mine.

CHAPTER
SIXTEEN

The wait for Alastair to return drove me near insanity. Patience had never been a gift of mine, and I had far less of it in this situation. I had no idea how much time had passed. One of the guards left. The other turned sideways, so he had a view of the door and me.

I went over spells in my head that I could use against Alastair's but none of the ones I knew were strong enough against blood magic. My hand slipped up to my necklace. The family heirloom gave me comfort. They hadn't taken it, and the hidden vile remained secure in its place. Alastair would have built up immunity like me. It was part of our training, but these guards were vampires. I could at least even the battlefield a little. I'd take the guards out first and let the Vampire Death do its job. It's not like the guards were innocent, and it's not like I hadn't killed many vampires before. It felt different being married to one and killing any of his former subjects without his knowledge. This is what I trained for though.

I poked at the space around me, and the containment spell was almost nonexistent. What little was left wouldn't cause much resistance and Darkness would eat up the sting of pain from any I incurred. *When Alastair enters, I'll toss the Vampire Death vile to the floor as close to the vampires as I can. Then, I'll grab whatever weapons I can and end Alastair's miserable life.*

Alastair appeared at the door and leaned in next to the remaining guard. He whispered with him, too low for me to hear. The guard disappeared. *Shit. I can still make this work though.*

Alastair approached me but stopped just out of reach. *Patience. I have to have patience.* "We're almost ready. Brie. We will change the world tonight."

Not a chance. If I have to sacrifice myself to stop him, I'll give that willingly. Goddess, I'm yours to use however we need to stop him.

"We aren't doing anything. I want no part of this," I said, portraying as much confidence as I could muster. I believed the ancestors and the Goddess wouldn't let this happen. Not with me here as a conduit.

"Too bad you don't have a choice," he laughed. "Hell's Fire." He held out his hand. The flames raged around me.

I sucked in a breath. He didn't understand how to control it. His actions were forced, and Hell's Fire fought against him. It drained my energy quicker than Darkness could replace it. They both gravitated to me. They screamed for me to take control, but I couldn't. I grabbed either side of my head with my hands. Alastair owned me. Sweat formed at my temples. If I let him go, he might kill me, and that could be the solution if I couldn't break free. I dropped to my knees.

Fire receded. Darkness replenished me. The exhaustion faded away. I worked my way back to my feet.

"I thought you were stronger than that, Brie."

"It's Queen Brielle to you," I said, forcing defiance into my voice even though he could make me do whatever he wanted.

"Not after tonight," he said. "After tonight, you will be one of my subjects, and we welcome in a new age of witchcraft as our ancestors meant it to be."

"They never meant it to be like what you want. Our ancestors gifted me to prevent this, not aid it. You are in defiance of them. I hope they punish you in a way I can't," I said, not giving up on my plan.

"The originals weren't like the passives that gifted you. They wanted a world ruled by witches," he said, disgusted when he mentioned my ancestors.

I fought the urge to drop kick him. Old Brie would have given in to the impulse, but defeating him was more important than a sucker punch.

"The Goddess might strike you down for that," I said. *Goddess, I know I've fucked up and made bad choices, but I'm here to use however you need me. I'm your vessel. I'll gladly sacrifice my soul to Hell if we can defeat him.*

"Do you even believe the Goddess exists? A single power? Where is the proof?"

"I see it every time we do good and every time we make mistakes and grow from them. I see the Goddess in the Earth and in the Moon. She is the moon personified."

A little ball of white light bounced into my view. Tears brimmed my eyes. *Grandmother*. The choice was made. My destiny led me here, and Grandmother confirmed it for me. The time to fight was now. *Goddess. My ancestors give me the strength to break these bonds and defeat him.*

Nausea rolled in my stomach, and my body glowed. The ancestors answered my request and supercharged me.

"What are you doing?" Alastair asked. I could see his hand open and close, but he no longer controlled me.

My vision blurred and white light erupted from me. The ground shook, and the light consumed every inch of Darkness. Darkness cowered before the light and retreated to the mental box I'd placed it in before. The ache of exhaustion beckoned me to sleep, but I forced my eyes open and thought of home. The welcome swish of being teleported away was enough for me to give into the rest.

☽ ☽ ● ☾ ☾

Soft sheets wrapped around me. Nick's vanilla scent wafted up from them. I woke up in my bed at the Great House. *Was it all a dream? A vision?* My body ached with exhaustion. Voices carried through the bedroom door from the sitting area. I could make out Cal, Brandon, Ella, and ... Nick.

Tears burned my eyes, but I struggled to open them. *Nick.*

"He told me it was the only way." The desperation in Nick's voice broke my heart. "She's too weak to fight. I must do it."

"She will not forgive you," Brandon said.

"The Coven will hunt you," Cal said.

"You know I hate to agree with witches, but he is right, Nicholas. The witches will hunt you for eternity," Ella said, her voice waffling between disgust and concern.

What are they talking about? Running away? Is he going to try to run away?

"Keep her safe. Make sure they know she didn't have anything to do with it," Nick said, and the door slammed.

The vision. No. He can't kill Michael. "No," I said, my voice a weak shell of itself. I stepped toward the door on wobbly legs. I inhaled a breath and grasped the doorknob. My legs couldn't hold me, and I tumbled through the doorway.

Cal and Brandon helped me to my feet and the sofa. I used the arm of it to prop myself up. Ella stood beside me like she was ready to catch me.

Her eyes met mine. "I told you to come back. Not die getting here," she said.

I snorted. My voice came out scratchy and rough. "Thanks, but I need to get to Nick before he..." I couldn't finish the sentence. "Get me to him now."

"You know?" Brandon asked. "About Michael?"

"Yes, and we don't have time to discuss it. Just help me get there."

"Jesus Christ quit staring at her. Here, Brie." Ella slid her arm under mine and helped me to my feet. "Can someone point me in that direction?"

"He's in the East wing," Cal said.

"Left out of my room," I said. "Then you should pick up Nick's scent."

"I'm not a dog," Ella said. She helped me out the door. The others followed behind us.

"But you do have heightened smell," I said.

"Among other things," she said. "Hop on my back."

"Goddess," I said. "Someone's going to have to help me."

Cal lifted me, and Ella wrapped her arms around my legs.

"Hold on tight." She sped off in the direction I pointed. "I smell blood."

Nick wouldn't do it? Would he? I closed my eyes. *Please get us there in time.*

"The fresh blood is coming from here." She stopped in front of Michael's door.

My heart dropped into my stomach. "Set me down."

I tried the door, but it was locked. "I don't have enough energy to unlock it."

"I've got it," Ella said. She stepped back and landed her heel against the door. The hinges gave, and it bent back into the room.

My eyes scanned the room and found Nick with Michael in his lap. Blood covered Nick's mouth and dripped down his chin. *No, Nick. Not Michael.* I turned away like that would erase it, but the image of my husband and the only Elder I trusted was a haunting site.

I made my way to them and slid down to my knees. I cradled Michael into my lap. *My vision came true. I didn't stop it. Michael's blood was on my hands.* "Why?" I patted Michael's face. His skin dulled, the life gone. I met Nick's eyes. He looked devastated, and I was too. "Why?"

"He said it had to be done. It was the only way."

"I had a vision of this," I said. "I thought I'd be able to stop it."

"Michael said you'd understand what this meant," Nick said, his tone defeated. Tears pooled in his eyes.

"I don't though." Tears streaked down my face. I choked on my words. "I don't know why he believed it had to be done. The vision didn't make it that far."

The door creaked. Cal and Brandon peered inside.

"Close the door, Cal," Brandon said.

"What do we do now?" Ella said. "Go to the vampire lair?"

"No, we have to conceal Michael's death until we know why it was required," Cal said.

There wouldn't be leniency for any of us if we were discovered here. I wiped the tears from my face and focused on what we needed to do next. "We aren't going to be able to hide it," I said. "Fergus has placed himself so far up Michael's ass that he probably already knows we're here."

"So, we run?" Brandon asked.

"No, you all get to safety with Nick. I'll stay behind and steer the focus to Alastair." It would be a diversion at best, but it was what I had.

Nick's gaze turned distant. "This is it, isn't it? This is where the witches turn on you and the vampire on me."

A cold chill skated over my skin as unease settled over me. I'd known the moment I'd woken to the conversation in my chamber the vision I'd been dreading was here. "Yes."

"You can't stay then," he said.

"I can teleport. I'll be fine, and I'll come to you if I feel I'm in danger." Danger was relative. I'd stay until everyone that could get to safety was gone.

"Promise me, my love," he said.

I'd sent him away. Rejected him. But he still showed me compassion and love. My heart tightened in my chest. If it compared to the pain he must have felt, I'd never be able to apologize enough. Darkness tried to claim the hurt, but I pushed back with my aura. I deserved to endure this. "I promise. Now go to the lake house. You all should be safe there for now," I paused. "Have you heard from Sorin or Ivy?"

"Dad called earlier, and said they were on the way here." He looked at the clock on the wall. "They should probably be here in about fifteen minutes."

My throat closed, and I had to swallow hard to open it back up. I sent them to the lake house to protect them. They didn't need to be here. No one close to me would be safe at the Great House. "Call him and tell him to turn around and take Mother with you. I don't think any of you will be safe here much longer."

"Help me put Michael on his bed. Then, I'll teleport you to my room and you can leave from there." I hated leaving Michael there without a vigil, but I needed to buy as much time for all of us as I could. Even if it was just minutes, we needed them all to figure out what Michael's plan was. *What did he know that he thought I did? Why would he willingly die like this? Be completely drained? There* must have been something in his blood he didn't want Fergus to have. *But what?*

We settled Michael in a peaceful position. Tears pooled in my eyes. The room was cold and empty without his presence. I blinked away the image and teleported back to the room.

Still so much to say between Nick and me. The awkwardness between us made the air heavy. I loved him. That hadn't changed. I rested my hand against his face. "Don't do anything stupid. In other words, don't do what I would do."

He pressed his forehead against mine. "I love you, Brie. I hope you know I'd never intentionally hurt you. You are my soul."

"I know you wouldn't," I said. "I love you too. Be safe and keep them safe."

He brushed his lips across mine. I opened my eyes to meet his and our connection was loud. *We'll be okay. In time.* I pulled away and ushered them toward the exit.

"I'll see you soon," I said and waved them out the door. Two vampires and two witches. That didn't look suspicious at all.

They weren't gone more than ten minutes before a knock rapped on my door.

Alan stood there, a solemn expression on his face. *Here we go. Goddess, I hope you are guiding me now.*

CHAPTER
SEVENTEEN

"Ma'am." Alan cleared his throat. "There's been..." He paused. "Michael—"

"It's ok, Alan. I know." I patted his shoulder. Tears formed in my eyes for Michael. *Goddess, let those I love be safe.* "Let's do what needs to be done."

"You're alone?" He asked, concern in his voice.

"Yes." I exchanged a look with him. "And I hope you will take your vacation after you escort me."

He gave one nod. "I'm at your side until the end, Ma'am."

I didn't deserve this loyalty. I'd been stupid. Made ignorant decisions. But Michael seemed to know we would get to this point, so maybe it was always meant to go this way. There'd be time to consider my stupidity versus destiny later. *Hopefully.*

Fergus met us in the hall. His smugness was like a cloud of poisonous gas. "My Queen." He bowed low in front of the other Elders. All for show. He didn't bow like that without an audience. The others followed his lead.

"Fergus," I said, unable to keep the disgust from my voice. Darkness begged for me to plant a knee in his chin. I resisted, but I wanted it too.

He waited. I'd leave him in that position forever, but the other Elders didn't deserve to be punished.

"Please rise," I said, my voice flat.

"We have sad and alarming news," Fergus said. He glanced at Alan.

"Yes, I am aware." I blinked back tears. "We will want to give Michael the highest state honors for his service to the Coven. I'll be grieving in private today. All meetings will be canceled." I turned to walk away.

"But, My Queen," Fergus said.

I half-turned to look at him. "Yes?"

"Don't you want the details of his death?"

I have them. The image of his lifeless body hit like a boulder had slammed into my chest. I inhaled and let it out in a slow practiced manner. The other Elders were aware of the vision, at least if Fergus had done his job as the lead.

"I know, Fergus. Michael had a vision, and I had the same vision." *Here we go. Fergus is going to get what he's wanted since I became queen.*

"Then you know it was a vampire," he said, shock in his voice. *Fake shock.*

"Yes," I said.

"And you have a vampire in your bed..." He looked around at the other elders. Their faces were masked in solemn expressions. I expected them to turn on me, but they at least had the decency not to do it in this shared moment of grief. Unlike Fergus.

I moved closer to him. Alan stayed at my side. "It is none of your business who the queen has in her bed." I knew it would provoke him, but I didn't care. We were already too far down this path to back down now, and I hoped he'd react in a way the other Elders would see him for what he was. A manipulative bastard. "Maybe you should look more at your own motives than to those in my circle."

In that moment, my reign was over. The revolt Michael and I had foreseen began. I didn't need to wait to see it come to fruition. The energy shift in the air answered my silent question. I continued on my way back to my wing. Alan stayed close to me.

"They'll order you confined to your quarters by the end of the day, Ma'am. If you want out, now is the time to go." Alan stepped inside the apartments with me and scanned the space. "I can escort you out safely." To stay with me was an end to his role in the coven and maybe even his life if Fergus made the decisions on punishments. I wouldn't ask Alan to remain.

"I can teleport," I said. "They'd have a hard time confining me anywhere." I remembered Alastair's spell. "Unless they are performing dark rituals."

His voice lowered. "I don't think he has stooped that far, Ma'am."

"Alan, something happened when I was with Alastair. He used the darkest magic I've ever felt to control me. I prayed for assistance, and the ancestors responded. What I don't know is if Alastair survived. I don't know if we're going to be fighting this war on both fronts." *And do we even have enough witches and vampires with us to handle a conflict on two sides?*

Split forces only worked if it was a surprise in my experience, and I hadn't managed to surprise Alastair yet.

"You will figure it out," Alan said. "I have faith in you."

I smiled at him. "Thank you. It gives me strength to hear it."

"Are you sure you don't want to leave?"

"I'm not going anywhere. That will just make us all look guilty," I said. *But Nick is guilty. The Elders might not believe me when I tell them about the vision and what Michael told Nick.* "Did you ever consider Fergus might be right? About me? About what we are trying to do with the conservatorship?"

"Not once," Alan said. "The moment I saw the mark on your arm, I knew you were the one that would always be right."

"If only that were true," I said. "I've been wrong so much lately I'm not sure I remember what it is like to be right."

"But your always on the side of right. It doesn't mean you say or do the right thing every time, but you course correct when you are wrong. You right the ship." Alan smiled at me. It was so genuine and real. He did believe in me, and that gave me the strength to do what my people needed.

"Thank you, Alan. Thank you for being so loyal knowing this isn't going to be an easy road and for your positivity. I could learn that from you."

"It's my pleasure, Ma'am."

Three rapid knocks tapped on my door. My fate was on the other side. This was what I was here to do. What the ancestors gifted me to do. *Goddess, I ask for your guidance and wisdom to navigate this to right the wrongs of our people.*

I nodded and Alan opened it.

"My Queen," one of Fergus's messengers bowed before me. His whole body shook.

"Yes?"

"The Elders Council requests you and your companions do not leave the grounds or mansion until the investigation into Elder Michael's death is complete."

"My companions are not here, but I will remain. I have no reason to leave my home." Strange how this circumstance was one of the few times I thought of the Great House as home.

"I've been asked to relieve guardsman Alan of his duties." *He was already on Fergus's hit list.*

"That is one request I, the queen, must deny," I said. "Please tell the Council that Alan is staying at my behest and for no other reason."

"Bu— "Alan tried to protest. I held up my hand in his direction.

"That will be all," I said to the messenger.

He turned and headed back down the hall.

"Ma'am," Alan said, his voice concerned.

"Don't worry," I said. "I'd rather the blame fall on me. If anything happens, they will think you are good at taking orders. That's not the worst thing for them to think."

I pulled out my phone and stared at the contacts for a moment. Nick's number waited at the top of the frequently used numbers, but Brandon was my Protector and sworn under the coven. I debated which one to text. I looked at the next number. *Brandon.* I typed out my message fast.

> F. is already making his move. I'm not able to leave the Great House.

> Any word on if Alastair survived?

I WAITED SECONDS, but it seemed like a lifetime.

> He survived. We need a plan.

> Teleport here so we can work out the details.

He'd hate my response, but I sent it anyway.

> Can't. Have to make sure our innocence is known first.

He'd read that and wanted to come back, but Cal was there. Cal would make him think straight, and hopefully, the two of them could manage Nick.

"I'm going to visit with some of those we know are loyal to us. I don't expect you to come."

Alan dropped to a knee and fisted his hand over his heart. "I'm an extension of my queen."

His loyalty gave me the strength I needed to push forward. It reminded me what my destiny meant to our coven, the vampires, and the world. Everything I lead us through from here on out defined all of our futures.

"Rise, my friend. You never need to kneel in front of me." I said, using a word I didn't throw around often. To be my friend, meant I let someone in and Alan had more than earned the space. "Let's go spread the truth, and hopefully, we'll make an impact before Fergus can make lies sound better than the truth."

I had to believe it was possible. If I didn't believe it, no one else would.

"Lead the way, Ma'am."

I went to the training area first. Nick and I both spent a lot of time there, and those training in combat were likely where most of our support would be. They did not disappoint. The other areas wouldn't be as accepting as this group. They'd been resistant to my breaks with tradition and a good portion didn't approve of having vampires in the Great House. I recapped what happened, being as honest and transparent as I could. The vampires training with the witches here looked nervous. The witches wore hardened faces, but behind the mask was terror. The anxiety in the room suffocated me.

"So, I don't know yet why Michael thought this was necessary, but he and I both saw it in a vision. Although Alastair survived the blast from our ancestors, I do know from that moment I still have their support. I hope I have yours too."

"What is Fergus's plan?" A woman in the front asked. I welcomed the questions. They were hearing me.

"I'm not exactly sure other than he wants me off the throne. I know he wants to maintain traditions, and I'm not here to dismantle all of them. But I'm not going to let archaic practices stand either and a threat to our coven."

"What should we do?" A warlock I'd trained with in the early days asked.

"Each of you will have to decide which side aligns with your values. I suspect the coven will divide in their beliefs over this, and you will need to figure out which side you identify with most. There will be no judgment from me. You are free to choose as you always have been." Each of their decisions mattered more than they realized, but I would not strip their right to do so. *Goddess knows I'm not the most well-liked queen to ever sit the throne.* My destiny... my legacy will be ending a prophecy that could wipe out humanity in vampires and be the end of the Coven. If that meant not being liked, I could handle that. I'd never required anyone's approval for my choices, but I needed them to understand which side was right.

A small roar from discussions filled the space. Friends and family would be separated, possibly permanently, over the inability of Fergus and me to align on the future. Having just got my family whole, it devastated me to think some of these people would suffer that same pain.

A vampire stepped forward. I recognized her as one of Ella's friends who often trained here.

"And what about us and our King?" She asked in a wary tone. "Where do we fit into this division?"

"If I'm speaking from our joint leadership, I'd say the choice is yours, but Fergus will dismantle the conservatorship. My husband is still my husband. He's still your king." Nick's support was in place, but there was a bond between a Vampire King and their subjects. They would want to hear it from their king. We took an oath as witches. It wasn't engrained in us like the bond between the vampire subjects and their leader.

"Why are we being forced to remain on this compound?"
She asked.

"That is not my doing. I can arrange safe passage if you
wish to leave," I said, confident we would be able to get
everyone out if we acted

"You'd risk your life for us?" She gestured to the small
group of vampires around her.

"I've risked my life for vampires many times in the past
few months, and today is not an exception."

"You've risked your life for one vampire, our king," she
said. "But I respect your choices. We will accept your offer of
safe passage."

"Then it is yours," I said. "And anyone wishing to go with
us is welcome. These walls will not be safe for my followers
much longer."

The crowd grew louder. Everything a witch was taught in
our generation changed today with Michael's death. It had
been building before I became queen, but the events of today
were the catalyst. There would be no going back.

A few people peeled away, and two girls that looked like
they must have lied about their age approached. They
dropped to a knee and fisted their hands over their heart. I
almost burst into tears but kept my composure. They were
too young to be here. Too young to pledge loyalty to a cause
that was the sins of their ancestors and not theirs. They were
the biggest risk and the biggest heartbreak from this. If we
didn't succeed, they would pay the price and their futures
would look very different. My strength was reinforced by the
reminder.

"That's not necessary. Please rise."

"My Queen," the one that appeared to be older answered. She scanned the room like we were taught in training. The action was new to her. She hadn't mastered how to conceal the movements yet.

"How may I help you, young ladies?" I asked. The coven children were introduced to early defensive tactics as soon as they started school, but there was no way I'd let them anywhere near the fight.

"Our parents will not side against the Elders. They've made it known since everything got sussy. We've been low-key freaking out for a while," the taller girl said.

"To be honest, we think you're fire, and this b.s. is just trash," the short girl said.

"You are sisters?" I asked.

"Yes, Ma'am," they said in unison.

I smiled. "What are your names?"

"I'm Elizabeth," the taller one said. "And this is Jane Ann."

"You should stay with your parents. As someone who spent her life up until recently without her father, I know how important those relationships are." I held out my arms and offered a hug. They accepted. I patted their shoulders. "You should go be with your parents. They will be worried about you." Survival wasn't guaranteed for any of us on either side, and they were too young to have to choose. They signified the importance of why we needed to win. Their blood would not be shed in my name.

"We'd stay for you if it wasn't for them," Elizabeth said. I doubted they would tell their parents they visited here, but even if they did let it slip, we would have everyone funneled out soon.

"I totally understand," I said.

They left and a few others peeled off. For the most part, the group stayed intact.

"We should get them out of here, Ma'am. Fergus will lock down the Great House if he knows you made this move," Alan whispered.

"You're right," I said. "And maybe it's time to call me Brie. I don't think I'll be queen after we leave."

"You will always be queen, Ma'am."

"There are too many for me to teleport. We'll have to use the passages." Anyone with advanced training, intelligence, or security was aware of the escape passages, but they were never guarded. The spells cast over them were regularly checked, but several on my team, including me, knew how to disable them.

"I'll send a few ahead to make them ready."

"Thank you," I said. This was the easy part. It would get exponentially harder from here.

The damp odor of the earth permeated everything in the tunnels. They had been no more than crawl spaces in their original form, but in Cecily's reign, she'd had them built out. Equipment could be moved through them, and they were well lit. Although they narrowed on the end to allow only one person in or out at a time.

Alan helped me organize the witches and vampires who chose to remain with me in the underground passages. I'd opted to split them into groups. Alan chose four of my guardsmen he trusted to lead the groups out. He and I remained, committed to stay as long as we could, to guide any stragglers and protect their exit if needed.

Goddess. This is actually working. We're getting them out of here.

Elizabeth and Jane Ann ran down the hall towards me. Elizabeth was a good three feet or more in front of Jane Ann. *Had they changed their mind? Could I even let them go? Should I?*

"Queen Brie," Elizabeth gasped and skidded to a stop in front of me. "They know."

"Your parents?" I asked. "They know you're here?"

She shook her head and gulped in several breaths.

"Calm down," I said, trying to keep myself calm. "Tell me who they are."

She started pushing me down the tunnel. "No, you need to go."

Did she mean her parents? The Elders? My throat went dry like I'd been in the desert for days without supplies.

Jane Ann caught up to us and shoved her hands against me. "They are coming."

I met Alan's worried gaze and inclined my head toward the passages. His eyes widened, and he moved quickly to check progress. I took the girls' hands and looked each in the eye. "Who is coming?"

"The Elders, our parents," Elizabeth said. "Everyone."

"You have to get out of here," Jane Ann said. Her eyes filled with tears.

I wanted to comfort them, but we didn't have time if there was a crowd on their way. The girls shouldn't be found here.

"Thank you for coming to tell me, but the ancestors will protect me. You two need to go before the crowd gets here. I don't want your parents to punish you for warning me."

"We'll fight with you," Elizabeth said, her voice strong. I admired her bravery.

"No, this is my fight. Yours will come one day, but this is not it." I smiled at them, even though inside I was worried about the time ahead. "I'll remember you and how you did the right thing. When the time comes, I hope to see you join us. Promise me you two will take care of each other."

Jane Ann nodded, her lip pressed in a firm line.

Elizabeth straightened her back to make herself taller. "Yes," she said.

"Go out to the right and keep right. It will eventually come out by the kitchen. You should go unseen," I said. "Until we meet again."

"Blessed be," Elizabeth fisted her hand over her heart.

Jane Ann mimicked her sister's actions. "Blessed be."

They were gone down the hall as quickly as they came. *Goddess, protect those fearless young ladies. They were conscientious despite the risk and are the innocents in need of our protection today.*

Alan returned, positioning his body between me and the entrance. "Should we bring down the way in?"

"No, it's too dangerous if anyone has to backtrack or evacuate," I said. The ancestors freed me from Alastair's trap, so I believed they would see me through this. "You go and get them to Nick and Brandon. Tell Nick and Cal I said it's their job to hold everyone together."

"What about you? I can't leave you behind."

"You can and you will because it is an order from your queen. I have an army on the other side to help me tonight," I said. *At least I think I do. Hope I do.*

Alan hesitated.

"Go. I'll only be able to hold the others off so long, and the people we sent in that cave need guidance. You can do it, Alan. I believe in you just as you believe in me."

"Blessed be." He fisted his hand over his heart and bowed his head in the same fashion as Elizabeth and Jane Ann.

"Blessed be, my friend." I clasped a hand on his shoulder and squeezed. "Thank you."

He disappeared down through the cave.

I centered myself, breathing in and out as I did in meditation. I closed my eyes and imagined my ancestors beside me. *What can I do here that will prevent them from following without hurting anyone?* A bright light flashed in front of me. I opened my eyes and realized it was in my mind's eye. *Was that the answer? Create a blinding light. Could I do that? How long could I hold it?* I ticked off the different incantations I knew about producing light, but they were all flashlight level. This situation called for something that was giant halogen spotlight level. Energy coursed through me as if answering my unspoken question. *Godzilla size halogen lamp it is.*

Footsteps, a lot of them, pounded down the corridor toward me. My heart sped up into the same rhythm. My palms started to sweat. I reached for my necklace and the hidden vial there. *Goddess, please let my instincts be right. Ancestors, please stand with me here tonight.*

A breeze blew around me and stirred the wet earth smell. Voices carried down the hall. They were close.

"Light be at my command. Bring forth your brightness from my hand. Make it bold and grand, so that none who enter can withstand. Do not harm, only turn away. Those who are against me shall not stay." I positioned both palms out toward the opening. Energy stirred in me and attempted to rupture. I held it back like a weak dam. Little bursts struck out like streak lightning.

The first of the group rounded the corner and stopped when they saw me.

"My Queen," Fergus said. "We are here to escort you back to your apartment."

"That will not be necessary," I said. The light expanded. I cut the invisible seal holding it back, and it streamed out from my hands until the entire hall illuminated with it. The brilliance was more than I could look at head on. I turned my head to the side and squinted through one eye. The glow was like a thousand halogen lights bundled together. It held back the mob, but they could still exit the way they came in time to intercept the people escaping the tunnels.

I imagined the light traveling down the hall and into the Great House. With the image strong in my mind, I pushed. The drain on me was immense, but I worked it further until I sensed the confusion from everyone inside the walls of the Coven mansion.

My body ached, and I continued to send my energy to the radiant cell I'd created. *Was this different than what Alastair did to me? Yes, I'll let the people here go. I don't plan to control them. I'm not like him.* Every time I used my power, I did some kind of check to see if I was still me. Darkness liked the power, but it didn't try to consume it. *Concentrate, Brie.*

Pain pricked at my hands and radiated up my arms. My legs trembled. The intensity of it begged me to call Darkness. *Would it answer? Did I need it?* I didn't trust myself not to give in to it and the dark thoughts that would come with it. *I can hold on like this a little longer.* The more time I gave the group escaping the better. They chose to follow me, and I'd protect them with everything. I closed my eyes and reinforced the light.

I lost track of time. My body weakened like it'd been hours, and I hoped it had been enough time for everyone to get far enough away to have a chance. My knees buckled. It was time to go. *Could I teleport after using this much energy? As soon as I let the light go, I'll be vulnerable.*

The light flickered. "Thank you," I said, my voice rough like gravel. "Thank you, Goddess. Thank you, ancestors." The light contracted in on itself and disappeared. The bulbs in the sconces were dim in comparison. My eyelids were heavy, but I held them open as I thought of the lake house. I fell into the blue swirl of energy.

My vision closed in around me, but I fought to stay lucid as time creased and the two points met. It deposited me on the floor. The fur of the sheepskin rug brushed my cheek. Voices circled around me, but my body gave into the sweet lullaby of sleep.

CHAPTER
NINETEEN

)) ● ((

The sweet and savory aroma of chocolate chip cookies and bacon roused my eyes open. A familiar figure sat on the end of the bed. A white smoke-like substance muted my vision. I rubbed my eyes. My heart pounded with excitement.

"Grandmother?"

She turned to face me. "It's me." She patted my leg. "Come walk with me." Her touch felt real. The sight of her healthy brought me joy. *But this has to be a dream, right?*

I crawled out of bed. My leather fighting suit hugged my body. *Did I have it on before?* I couldn't remember. I couldn't remember what I was doing before I got here. "Where are we?"

She took my hand and led me out the door into a field. A meadow of sweetly scented grasslands grew into a lush forest like I'd never seen. A brook babbled nearby, and the rush of a river came from the distance. Grandmother stepped onto the grass and transformed into a younger version of herself I only knew from pictures.

Summerland. I died. The realization crashed down on me, but the sadness I braced for didn't come. I hadn't gone to Hell after all. The soft smell of a fresh rain encapsulated me. *Peace.* I'd known moments of it, but never had I been so enveloped by the calmness of true peace.

Even in the tranquility, I remembered I had a mission. The details were sketchy in my head, but I recalled there were people to save. "Did I do it, Grandmother? Is everyone safe?"

"You did, Granddaughter, and I'm so proud of what you were able to do," she said. "They are safe for now."

They... everyone... Familiar faces flashed through my mind.

"Just for now? The ..." *Why can't I remember what they were safe from?*

"Just for now," she said, her voice gentle like when she would wake me from sleep as a child. "This isn't the time for rest."

"How did I die?" I asked.

"You gave all of you," she said. "All of your life force was drained."

"Oh," I said. "I don't remember."

"That's ok," she said. "We just need to talk for a minute." She stopped at the edge of a lake similar to one I'd seen in Estes Park, Colorado when she'd taken Brandon and me there as kids.

Brandon. One of the faces I saw. *My brother. Was he ok?* I rubbed my head even though it didn't hurt. My thoughts were jumbled and pieces missing like a jigsaw puzzle.

"Brie, I know you're tired, sweetheart, but you are not done. The prophecy can only be defeated by you and Nick," Grandmother said, her voice sterner.

Nick. My husband. Where was he? I looked around for him. *Vampire. Undead. Not in Summerland.* Pain overrode the peace of the afterlife. I tainted the air with my regret for not being able to say goodbye... for leaving him in a permanent way.

"Doesn't the prophecy end with me?" I asked. "So, if I'm here and I'm dead, isn't it done?"

She squeezed my hand. "No, unfortunately, it's still in motion despite your sacrifices. Your journey is unfinished."

"Do I need to gift my powers to someone else?" I asked, trying to remember who was next. *Cal.* "Do I need to pass them on to Cal?" *Why is everything so damn foggy?*

"No, that's not the answer today." She smiled a sad smile.

Trepidation tightened my stomach. "What is the answer?"

"You must return to your body." She sighed. "You must finish what you started, but I promise you that your ancestors will stand with you even when others fail you."

"Oh," I said. I didn't want to leave her. Not again. But I wanted a second chance to finish the prophecy. A second chance to make up for the regrets I'd taken to Summerland. "I love you and miss you, Grandmother. I'm ready. How do I go back?"

"I'm always with you in here." She placed a hand on my chest. "And I'm afraid it is going to hurt, and for that I'm sorry," she said. "My love."

The last two words hung in the air around me.

A heaviness sat on my chest. Agony spidered out from it. A gasp slid from my lips. I gulped in air like it was water in a Texas drought.

"She's breathing," Dad said.

She? Me? I blinked a few times to clear my fuzzy view. *I'm not in Summerland anymore. Thank you, Grandmother. Thank you, Goddess.*

"Brie, my love." Nick squeezed my hand. His love radiated into me. I felt safe and whole.

My body, on the other hand, was stiff like a hinge in need of oil. I tried to sit up, but my husband pulled me into his lap on the bed. My side pinched and stung like a dagger poked out of it.

"I think my rib is broken," I wheezed.

"That would be my fault," Brandon sat on the edge of the bed. *He's okay.* Relief replaced everything else in me. I inhaled as deep as I could with a broken rib and exhaled.

Mom knelt beside him, her chin on her hand. "We're so glad you're ok, Brie. We thought …" Her voice trailed off.

I held my hand out to her. She took it, and I squeezed hers with what little strength I had.

"You scared us," Sorin said.

I choked back a sob. *They're all okay.*

"I'm sorry," I said. "I promise it wasn't intentional. I can't say I hated the peaceful feeling of Summerland though."

"You saw Summerland?" Sorin asked, confused.

"Yes, and Grandmother. She sent me back." The emptiness I'd had since she passed was filled with the sight of seeing her in the afterlife.

"I've never heard of anyone returning from Summer-land," Mother said.

"We never heard of anyone returning from Hell before Dad either," Brandon said.

"Grandmother sent me back because the prophecy didn't die with me. It's still going," I said. Death might take me again, but the prophecy would be finished.

"We know, Brie," Nick said. "Alastair has been trying to find you since the night you lit the Great House up like an oversized lighthouse.

Night? Wasn't that this night? A few minutes ago? "Wait. How long have I been out?" It seemed like I had only been with Grandmother for a few minutes.

"Almost a month," Nick said. "Today, when your heart stopped, I thought..." he paused. "We thought it was the end. Your body had been shutting down."

I looked around at the unfamiliar space. This room was beautiful, but it was far bigger than my room at the lake house. "Where are we?"

"A safe house Cecily and I had built for you years ago. The location only known by a handful of people," Sorin said.

"Dad." I reached for his hand. He'd long since healed from the night Alastair held us captive, but the dark circles under his eyes hadn't disappeared. "How did you know?"

"I didn't, but we wanted you to have it if you need it."

"And Alan and the others?"

"Alan is here, and the others are here and at other safe houses," Sorin said.

I looked at Nick. My husband was handsome as ever, but

he worried. His forehead creased, and I braced myself for the news I needed to confirm. "And the vampires?"

"Malachi and Ella are here along with a few others," he said. "Some are in hiding but many did not follow us. They are with Alastair."

"Even knowing his plans? They still follow him?" It was unbelievable to me, and I'd had a vision. *A vision I thought I stopped but only made worse it seems.*

"Yes." Nick grimaced. "He's made promises."

"You saw your grandmother?" Dad asked. His brows furrowed.

An ache in my chest recalled the loss, but the memory of her younger self in the field reminded me she was at peace. "She said I wasn't done that I had to come back and stop the prophecy. The ancestors will support me." *Well, Nick and I apparently.*

"Fergus has convinced those remaining with him that you are unnatural," Cal said. "He's told them the power corrupted you."

"Well, he's not wrong," I said. "But I think I have it figured out now. I just had to ask for help. The ancestors came through twice for me. It was the ancestors that helped me escape Alastair and the ancestors who gave me the power to hold off Fergus and the mob."

"He's manipulating the truth to feed the fear," Brandon said. "If the others knew this— "

"It wouldn't change anything. Their minds were made up the minute Cecily named me her successor," I said, my voice rough like sleep couldn't come quick enough. The last thing I wanted to do was sleep, but my body was much weaker than my mind.

"We should let you rest," Mother said. "I'm sure you and Nick need a moment. We'll be back to check on you later." She patted my knee like Grandmother had in Summerland. "Come on gentleman." She ushered Cal and Brandon out, but Sorin hung back.

"There is much to discuss when you are up to it but gather your strength. You'll need it." He grabbed my hand. "I love you, Brie, and I'm so thankful Mother was there to help you back." His eyes glistened, heavy with emotion I hadn't seen since I brought him back from Hell.

I sucked in a breath to hold back my tears. "Don't cry, Dad, or you'll make me cry," I waved a hand in front of my face like a fan. "I'll find you in a little bit and tell you everything, but Grandmother is fine. She was strong."

He gave one nod. "Rest up." He closed the door behind him.

I scooted around so I could look up at my husband. His emerald eyes glowed like they did the night we reconnected in Club Red. Love looped around my heart and spread warmth through my chest. He'd stayed by my side like he promised in spite of the fact I hurt him. "Nick, I owe you an apology. I honestly can't believe you are even here after what I said."

He placed a finger over my lips. "You do owe me an apology, and we will settle that later, my love. I'm just glad you're okay now. How's the rib?"

His dismissal of my apology wasn't the end of the

conversation. There was a ton of worry on his face that would have to be put to rest.

"Seems fine now." I pressed my fingers into my side where the pain had been earlier. "Must have healed."

"Good." He inclined his head and brushed his lips across mine.

I leaned back, certain I had a month's worth of morning breath. "Shower with me first?"

He pulled me to my feet. "If that is your way of apologizing, I accept."

I laughed. "I plan on doing a whole lot of apologizing to you." I rubbed my thumb over his wrinkled forehead to relax him and cradled his cheek in my hand. "And telling you everything even when it's hard."

"So, you're not surprised when you look in the mirror, the red is gone from your hair. It's completely blonde again."

"Really?" I padded across the floor to the mirror. It wasn't just blonde. It was a platinum blonde. It reminded me of the way Sorin's hair lost its color. *But I'm not him. My power is still here.* Pull sparks ran along my fingers as I worked through a tangle, and the knot unwound. "That's a bit of a shock, but I bet it holds the pink better. I need a hairstylist." My hair stood up in a mess. "Did no one brush my hair while I was out?"

I glanced around the room.

Nick scooped me up in his arms and rested his temple against mine. A soft chuck rumbled through his chest. "You don't know where the bathroom is do you?"

"Nope." I pressed a quick kiss on his cheek.

TWENTY

"Want to go again?" I gazed up into Nick's eyes. My rib twinged a little, but it was healing even in my weakened state. My mind cleared enough that I didn't miss the concern on Nick's face.

"There will be plenty of time for that later." He broke the connection. "After you get your strength back." Nick rolled onto his side and studied me.

I stretched. "I don't know how you kissed me earlier before I showered and brushed my teeth."

Nick leaned over and pressed his lips against mine. "I held my breath." He chuckled.

I laughed and pushed him off of me. "Go away." My legs shook as I stood up.

Nick sped around to steady me. "Easy. It's been almost a month."

"Or maybe it's because someone had their way with me," I said. "I honestly feel pretty good except for the sea legs. I need food." I slipped out of bed and over to the mirror. I'd been pink and red for so long, the blonde didn't look like me anymore. *Who are you? I stared at the mess on top of my head.* "After I do something with my hair."

Nick slid his hands around my waist and pulled me close. "I like the way it looks after I tumbled you in bed."

"So, you think I should go down like this?" I met his gaze in the mirror and our connection swallowed me whole.

He winked at me.

"I didn't mean..." I sobered. We needed to air things. It'd been a month for him. A month of uncertainty for us and the future. "Nick, do you really forgive me? I know I said terrible things."

"I understand you were trying to protect me, and I forgave you the moment the words left your mouth." He kissed my temple. "Just don't do it again. My heart might not beat but it can still break."

My heart shattered into a million pieces. I looked up at him over my shoulder. "I love you, Nick, and I don't want to hurt you."

"Then hold my heart in yours and let them beat together as one. A single existence that can't be separated without destroying the other half. Don't send me away when you get scared."

His words melted me and formed a vice grip around my heart for the pain I caused him. "Then that's what we'll do," I said.

His mouth covered mine with urgency, and I matched his need. *It would be so easy to let the rest go and fall back into bed with him.* His touch strengthened me more than Darkness ever could, and I had to tell him all of the truth. He deserved it.

"I need to tell you something I found out from Michael before he died."

Nick's brow furrowed. Remorse lined his face at the mention of Michael. I hated taking him back to that moment, but his ancestry shouldn't be concealed from him.

"If you didn't have to be a vampire anymore, would you want that? Would you want to give up your immortality?"

"Nothing lives forever, Brie, but if it meant fewer days with you, no," he said, his tone serious and firm.

My insides melted. He wanted all the time he could get with me. "What if it meant a witch's lifetime? Would you?"

He cocked his head to the side and spun me around to face him. "What are you talking about, my love?"

The room was smaller than the apartments at the Great House, but it still had a sitting area. I led Nick to the couch and sat down next to him.

He wrapped an arm around my shoulders. "Just tell me, Brie."

"Michael said he learned about your heritage. A heritage that was hidden during that time."

"It's common knowledge I am from a royal house, but even human royals can't return from the vampire change." He tilted his body toward me.

"But what if you weren't human when it started." *Goddess, how do I convince him?* He'd known he was different from the others. I even told him when we first met how dissimilar he was. His normal wasn't vampire normal.

"I can assure you I was human, Brie. No one in my family had magical powers."

It was hard to comprehend. I understood. I'd been through something similar after all. Michael thought it was important enough to give his life, and Grandmother had sent me back with the knowledge it would take both of us to end the prophecy. It wasn't a coincidence. "That you know of. Michael said, during the time of your human life, witches were already in hiding. They'd been persecuted and spread out. Many didn't practice out of fear of it."

"I remember," he said, his voice trailing off like he went to a different place. He gave a light shake of his head. "But that doesn't make me a witch."

"No, you are vampire. But didn't you wonder why you were chosen to live out of your family?"

His face darkened into an expression I didn't recognize. "Stefan chose Gaius and me for strength. Just as Marku had chosen him. It was so long ago."

I thought he would trust me enough to accept it, but he was deep in disbelief. I thought he would come around given everything we knew and experienced from the prophecy. "Do you think it could be true?"

"I don't know," he said. "I remember my mother always checking on us, but was that different than any other mother during that time?"

The unknowns outweighed the knowns, but if it were me, I'd want to know the options in front of me. The ritual required a lot, and I'd have to get my strength up to perform it. "Michael told me of an incantation and ceremony that could return you to a warlock."

Nick's forehead wrinkled. "And you would perform this spell?"

"Yes, Michael said I was the only one with the power to do it." I didn't want to take his life in my hands like this, but it should be his choice. Stefan stole a decision from him, and I wouldn't do the same. I'd love him until the end either way.

"Would I be under your control?"

"No, you'd have your freewill if it is done right," I said. "But I want you to think about it. Really think about it."

"Could I die?"

"During the ceremony? Yes." I'd become so accustomed to it being a risk every day that I hadn't even thought to mention it. It would mean both our deaths though, and I didn't believe the ancestors would let that happen.

"No, after. Would I die a normal death?" He asked, curiosity in his voice.

Oh. His thoughts were on the future, and I was focused on surviving the prophecy. "Well, normal for a witch."

"And is there risk to you?"

"Just my power and casting," I said, assuming death hadn't changed my abilities. *I'd have to do some spells to test it out. Call Hell's Fire.* My fingers warmed with a tiny crackle. *Not now. Good to know it's still there though.*

"I'd like to review this incantation with you," he said.

My pulse quickened with excitement. *What would life be like if we were both witches? Goddess, don't let me fuck this up.*

TWENTY-ONE

‍☽ · ☽ · ● · ☾ · ☾

E veryone gathered in what had been designated my office in the time I was in a coma-like state. It was a shared space with Nick. Brandon, Cal, and Alan had set up my space. They each had their own desks in the hall. Malachi had one as well, but Ella sat at it today. She was on the phone but gave a wave and an actual smile. I smiled back.

I liked this space better than the one at the Great House. It was inviting with big windows in the hall leading to it and in the office itself. Light illuminated the space. I could see and sense the guards along the perimeter, and Brandon briefed me on the high-tech security of the place. A spell was cast over the area to prevent detection, but it meant people got lost from time to time.

A sheepskin rug like the one I loved at the lake house covered the floor in the sitting area, and oversized leather chairs that could almost hold two people. There was a matching couch with a coffee table in front of it. The aroma of Earl Grey tea drifted around me. My strength returned along with an insane appetite. Apparently, my body thought it needed to make up for a month without solid food.

Sorin and Mother sat close to each other on the couch. It warmed my heart. Brandon leaned against the desk, and Cal sat in one of the overstuffed chairs.

I beelined to the table and poured a cup adding a small amount of raw sugar and a dash of milk. "Mmm." The warm liquid slid down to my stomach. "That's good."

"You should eat something too," Nick said like I hadn't been eating since I woke up.

I glanced at the assorted pastries. "I'd rather have spaghetti."

Nick laughed.

"I was so surprised that night after our Club Red run-in to find you in your kitchen making my favorite comfort meal."

He kissed my temple. "If spaghetti made by a vampire is what you want, then I shall make it for you after the meeting."

I smiled. "I'll be sure to thank you later."

"Huh hmm," Brandon cleared his throat.

"Where are Clara and Ivy?" I looked around and down the hall. I hadn't seen them since before my Summerland visit, and I was anxious to see them.

"Training some of the inexperienced witches," Brandon said. His voice held no animosity. It made me optimistic that while I was out, they'd settled their shared history

I dropped into the other leather chair. "Ivy has firsthand knowledge of Alastair's plans. She should be here."

"They've been informed to join us after the training session," Cal said.

"Good. Now, fill me in on everything you know."

"Fergus has control of the Great House, and we are scattered," Cal said. "There are a few defectors from him as the days pass, but not enough to balance our forces." Grandmother told me the ancestors would see me through this. I had to trust in that single truth.

Malachi and Ella joined us in the office.

Nick embraced them both. "Thank you for coming, my brother."

I hugged Malachi's neck. "It's good to see you."

"Still trying to save the humans?" He quipped.

"Still trying to eat them?" I asked and raised an exaggerated eyebrow at him.

He laughed. "Let's just save the world and sort the rest of it out after we stop Alastair."

"And Fergus," I said. My stomach lurched the more I said his name, the more disgusted I was.

"Ella." I embraced her. It was a bit awkward, but at this point, we might as well get past that. I'd given her permission to kill me, and she didn't. She chose to help me find my way back. "Thank you. I don't know what else to say except that."

"You're welcome." She patted my back. "It's good to see you awake and alive."

"Everyone had just started filling me in. I'm glad you made it in time."

Nick leaned against my desk on the opposite end from Brandon. I stepped between my husband's legs and rested my back against his chest. His arms went loosely around my waist. There was a time when I wouldn't have been for PDA in front of anyone. My death changed my perspective, and this was my safe group.

Cal offered Ella his chair, but she declined. Both vampires stood. It's not like they got tired.

"So, we are short on supporters. I can't say I'm surprised from the visions I had," I said. "What about vampires?"

"They are following Alastair. I'm not sure what he has done to secure their support, but I can't sway them," Malachi said, his voice rough with frustration.

"I have some ideas. He bound me to a circle that I could only break from with my ancestors' help. I'm sure he is doing something similar to the vampires. If it was strong enough to bind me, I'm sure it is strong enough to overpower Nick's king connection too." It didn't evade me that I might have to call on Darkness to defeat him.

"The question remains as to how we will stop him," Cal said.

It was easy to forget Cal was Alastair's son. They were nothing alike. Cal was kind and thoughtful of others, and Alastair was the exact opposite.

"Fergus is a zealot, and I believe I can find a way to expose him. I just have to prove his connection to all this," I said. "Alastair has become too powerful and too dangerous. There is only one option left that we can entertain." I winced at my own words.

Ella and Malachi both stared at Cal. He stared at the desk.

I positioned myself between Cal and the view of the

others and placed my hands on his upper arms. "I stand by what I told you before. You do not have to be a part of any plan where we eliminate your father."

"And I stand by my queen and my word to her. I no longer consider him my father, and my loyalty is to you and ending the prophecy."

I'd framed it up for everyone in the room. Cal had my trust, and I knew I had his loyalty.

"You are free to tap out if you ever feel like it is more than you can handle. You are my successor and that has not changed nor would a decision to sit out Alastair's demise."

"Thank you, My Queen, but I am vested in seeing his end as well." His tone was warm, and he fisted a hand over his heart.

I nodded and turned to face the room. "Let's get to business then."

"How do we get to Alastair with so many vampires under his control and protecting him?" Sorin asked.

"Why do I have to keep reminding you all I can teleport?"

Nick shook his head. "But, my love, you are the center of his plan. The key. Handing you to him is a gift."

"No one is handing me over. I have the ancestor's power at my command now. He can't match that. Darkness shrinks away from it," I said. Darkness hadn't even nibbled at me since I died and came back, but it was still there. It lay in wait, but I didn't know why.

"We can't underestimate him again," Sorin said. "It needs to be swift and unexpected."

"Which is why teleporting makes sense," I said.

"He'll have wards up. He will know." Ivy's voice carried

from behind me. I turned to see her leaning against the door. Clara stood behind her, looking a little disheveled, and gave an apologetic shrug. Ivy walked into the room with her shoulders back. Her confidence exuded out.

"But," Cal offered. "Someone could go in and take the wards down."

Clara's face went blank.

"The only one who can get in without him knowing is me," Ivy said, working through the logistics. "And he might have warded against me by now too."

"I don't think he would. He didn't think you were formidable enough," I said, a smile forming on my lips. "I think he underestimated you the same way we underestimated him."

"My sister is not going back in there," Clara said, her voice strong but a full octave higher than normal. "Her identity is burned now. She has a target on her the size of the Great House."

Ivy frowned at Clara. "We all have targets on us Clara. I'm the only one who has half a chance to succeed. Then, once I disable the wards, Brie can teleport in and finish this."

"That's Queen Brie," Clara said in full older sibling mode. "And I absolutely forbid it."

"Sister, I love you, but this is not your decision. I am an adult, and I have already decided."

Ivy reminded me of myself. Many times, I had this discussion over the years, especially after the kidnapping when I was Ivy's age. She was strong. Stronger than Clara could see, but I understood Clara's fear well. I'd had that same fear when Brandon was captured and beaten by

Stefan's men. I would have torn down the entire vampire castle and thrown a middle finger at peace for him.

Clara was fierce too, and as a big sister, she wouldn't let this go without a fight. Her eyes were wild. "We'll discuss it privately and let everyone else know what decision we come to."

Ivy's eyes narrowed. "This is the best plan. You know it. I know it. They know it. There is nothing else to discuss." Ivy looked over her shoulder at me. "Brie, I'm in. I'll take down the wards and signal you. You can teleport in with whoever you can carry. Then we will end this."

Damn. Ivy was impressively decisive.

"Do you believe you can break his incantations? Brie said his spells had grown in strength," Brandon asked.

"I helped figure the spell out to hold her, but I made him think he did. He's not as all-knowing as he thinks he is," Ivy said. It wasn't smug the way she said it. More of a humble brag.

I smiled. "I knew I liked you."

She returned my smile. "Likewise." She looked at Nick. "Do you have a current map of the vampire castle? I can show you where we discussed putting the talisman for the wards. We can figure out the best place for Brie to teleport, and I'll work my way closest to it. Then, I can signal from there."

Ivy was the next generation of our witch leadership. She might not know it, but I could see it in her. I'd ask her to join us after this.

Everyone was looking at me. It was as awkward to me as it used to be. "Well, show her the map. I know you have one in that stack of stuff on my desk. If you don't, I'll be disappointed."

Brandon flipped the maps and pulled out the right one. He spread it out across the top of everything on the desk.

"If my sister is going in first, I'm going with her," Clara said.

I nodded to her. I couldn't argue, because I'd gone to the heart of the beast to rescue Brandon from Stefan. "Can you get both of you through, Ivy?"

"We share DNA, so it shouldn't be a problem." She studied the map.

Ivy pointed out all the places the talismans were planned to be placed. We needed them all disabled to be sure Alastair wouldn't see us coming, but there was a risk he would be alerted when they were taken down. If the alert was active for disabled wards, Ivy and Clara would be caught.

"I hadn't finished the incantation for him on how to set up the second line, but it was far enough along..."

"He could have figured out the rest." I finished. "There's always risk when we go to battle, and this is war. A war he started when he betrayed his people." I looked at Nick. He was stoic. "And the vampires."

"I accepted the risks when I accepted this role," Ivy said.

I faced Ivy and Clara. "If you feel unsafe or think for a second the wards have been triggered, you get out immediately."

Brandon's stomach growled, and I cut my eyes at him. "Everyone go power up, change clothes, whatever you need to do to get ready, and we'll start practice runs in an hour."

I was usually the one ready to go in despite the risks, but

my nerves jittered in my stomach. Everyone I cared about would be playing a part in this attack, and I was the one who had to give the order. I wouldn't be able to protect them all with this plan, and it scared the Hell's Fire out of me.

Nick waited for everyone to leave and closed the door. He linked his hands together and swung them over my head, resting them at my waist. Even though being caged in his arms was a safe space, his silence made me nervous.

"I want to do it," he said.

My belly clenched. I cleared my throat.

His eyes scrunched up at the corners as he smiled. "The vampire to witch spell. I want to do it.

Oh! My stomach tightened for a different reason. His life would be in my hands, and he trusted me. "And you're sure this is what you want? Because I love you either way. I will love you either way, Nick."

"Ssh," he said, brushing his lips across mine. "I'm as sure as I am of my love for you."

"I can't do it alone. We're going to need help from the others." They wouldn't refuse me. I knew I could count on them for help, but I expected a moment of shock.

"I read the spell. I understand."

His hands slid down below my ass and lifted me up. He sat me on the desk.

I ran my fingers through his dark hair. This man was everything to me, and I'd make sure the ceremony was perfect. He would have what he wanted. "I love you, Nicholas Domenico. No matter what I want you to know that."

CHAPTER

TWENTY-TWO

︾ ·︾ · ● · ︽ ·︽

I vy and I led drills on the plan. We'd shaved several seconds off our time. The longest and most dangerous part was the time Ivy and Clara were on their own with the wards. They were vulnerable and any exposure would mean our plan failed. The element of surprise would be lost.

"One more time," I said. "And this time we'll have Malachi and Ella simulate vampire attacks at random." My strength and energy levels had returned to normal, and the run-throughs didn't tire me at all.

"We can't cover all the possible scenarios, Sis," Brandon said.

"No, we can't." I reached for my necklace and rubbed the vial of Vampire Death. "But we can reduce complacency and always be ready for the unexpected."

"They were well trained like we were," he said.

"We only have one more day, Brandon."

"And if they are exhausted, they will make mistakes. They don't have your healing powers."

I took in the group. They were red-faced. I wasn't tired, but they were. I sighed. "You're right."

"Oh my Goddess. Did you just say I was right?"

I pushed his shoulder. "Go kiss Cal or something."

He winked at me.

I laughed. "Ok, everyone. Let's call it. We've got this. Go get some rest." I looked at Brandon with his arm around Cal's shoulders. "Or whatever you need to do." They both turned a deep crimson.

They filed out in pairs. Malachi and Ella. Ivy and Clara. Mom and Dad walked over with Brandon and Cal behind them. They were a mix of concern and weariness.

"You should get some rest too," Sorin said. He glanced at Nick. "You don't need any distractions going in tomorrow."

"None of us do, but I don't think we have that luxury this time around." I faced my parents. "Mom? Dad?" Mother took my hand. My death made me not want to leave things left unsaid. "I want you to know I love you both. I know I haven't been a perfect person or a perfect queen, but I am proud to be your daughter."

Mother kissed my cheek. "I am so very proud of you, Brie, and I love you too." She glanced between me and Sorin.

Dad wrapped his arms around me and squeezed me so tight I almost couldn't get a breath.

I'd thought this kind of family would never exist for me. "Dad?"

"I couldn't be prouder of you, Brie. You are the best queen the coven has ever had, and you will go down in history. But if you had never been queen, I'd be equally as proud of you."

"Thank you," I said, choking on the lump in my throat.

"Go rest," he said. He let go of me and took Mom's hand.

I watched them walk out together. Their love had survived the impossible mountain of Darkness. And if they made it, reason suggested Nick and I could too.

"Now that it's just the four of us," I said, turning to the group. "Brandon you heard a version of it, but death and a month in a coma have jumbled some things in my brain, so forgive me if this is new news to either of you. Michael told me before..." I trailed off unable to say the words. An uncomfortable silence filled the space, but I pushed forward. "Michael told me Nick was a witch before he was turned."

Brandon exchanged a look with Cal. *They knew.*

Nick crossed his arms over his chest but didn't speak.

"Michael gave me a blueprint on how to turn Nick back from a vampire to a witch, and Nick would like to proceed with the ceremony after we defeat Alastair. Would you two be willing to help us?"

"It would be nice to say my sister is married to a witch instead of a bloodsucker," Brandon said and smiled at Nick. Nick's jaw tightened, and he frowned at Brandon. "Sorry man. I'm just teasing. You're my brother now. I'm here however you need me."

Nick visibly relaxed.

"I'm always at your disposal, My Queen," Cal said.

"Thank you both," I said. "We'll defeat Alastair tomorrow and change Nick the next. Since the moon will still be full as the last moon in the tetrad, I should be able to draw enough power. I'll need you two to anchor me though." It sounded good, but my nerves were in overdrive. I had to get them under control before the ceremony. If they went haywire during the ceremony, so would my power, and that would make the whole ritual unpredictable. *Breath in. Breath out.*

"Whatever you need, Sis." Brandon's voice brought me out of my head.

"You sure are agreeable," I said. "Is it because you have plans right now?"

"If you'll excuse us," Brandon said. "See you tomorrow." He took Cal's hand and led him out of the room.

"Alone at last," Nick whispered in my ear. His breath tickled and sent shivers down my arms.

"Did you have something in mind, my husband?"

"As a matter of fact, I did." He scooped me up in his arms.

"I can walk to our bedroom." I laughed.

"But your father said you needed rest." He nuzzled my neck.

"So, he did," I giggled. "What about my spaghetti?"

"Ah yes," he said. "Spaghetti first and then I want you alone." He sped through the hall to the kitchen at vampire speed. I wondered if he realized it could be one of the last times he did that as a vampire.

)) ● ((

Ivy and Clara left about an hour ago for the vampire castle, and I verged on madness at the wait for the signal. I paced back and forth across the floor of my office ready to teleport. We all dressed in black for the mission. We looked like were a human funeral party. The thought hung in my head. *Please Goddess don't let this day end in plans for a funeral for any of my charges. Please be with us and bring the people, vampires, and witches, home safely.* A gentle current zipped across my skin. The soft sounds of wings fluttered around me, and sweet wet grass scented the air. *Grandmother? Goddess?* There was no answer, but I took it as a sign from the Goddess I'd followed the right path.

"You're going to wear a hole in that rug," Mother said.

I reached for the hidden vial on my necklace. "I should have given them my vial of Vampire Death."

"Stop fretting and focus on your tasks," Sorin said.

I centered and replayed the plan.

Teleport to the entrance from the kitchen off of the throne room.

Mom, Dad, and Brandon will create a distraction.

Clara, Ivy, and Nick will be my backup.

Cal stays to open a transport tunnel if I don't teleport us back by the deadline.

I'll throw everything I have at Alastair.

Nick will take control of the vampires again.

Malachi and Ella will be his backup.

"There's the signal," Brandon said.

My eyes snapped to the antique desk bell. It chimed in the correct rhythm. My gut twisted into knots. *This is it.*

"Everyone join hands." I held mine out. Nick took my left and Brandon my right. Once we were all touching. I thought of the place we intended to be. My focus was clear and precise.

I landed on my feet in the smoothest teleport. I looked around and everyone was on their feet. No one gagged. If we weren't in a hurry, I'd have patted myself on the back.

Ivy and Clara leaned against the wall. Ivy held a finger up to her mouth for us to be quiet. I listened for sounds or voices.

"We still need her," Alastair said. "I can only do so much without harvesting her power."

"How do you plan to lure her here?" I recognized the second voice, but I couldn't place what vampire it belonged to.

"I should have let Darkness consume her," Alastair said.

"Then you wouldn't have the power of Light to complete the spell," the voice said.

That fucker. I met Brandon's gaze. His eyes widened, and mine had to match his. *Fergus. The traitorous zealot bastard. He wasn't just conspiring for power. He was pulling the strings. I will blow him sky high for the Goddess to deal with.* I took a step forward and Nick's arms wrapped around me, pulling me tight against him.

"If we had one of her loved ones, we could ensnare her here," Alastair said. "They are her weakness."

"She's impetuous, yes," Fergus agreed. "But she's smart."

"Too smart to realize this is the only way to rid the world of the horrible creatures our ancestors created."

"Some of them have uses," Fergus said. "We'll need them to establish control."

"Yes, but once that is done, we'll destroy them all."

Nick growled behind me. He moved aside and advanced. I followed on his heels.

Ivy threw an arm out in front of us. Nick sidestepped it, and I ducked under it. I burst into the room. There were a dozen vampires there to guard the meeting. *Impetuous.* Fergus's word choice hung over me like a sign. I'd allowed my anger to take the lead instead of using my control. I could have stopped Nick, but I jumped in with both feet.

"Get him," Alastair said.

The vampires descended on Nick. Their eyes glowed a weird amber color like animal eyes in the dark. I fought to control the panic taking over me. *Nick can handle himself. Battle instincts, Brie. Focus.* The rest of the team took their positions like we practiced.

Alastair whispered, "come." And more vampires filed in. My palms were slick with sweat as panic sat in. I breathed in and out, but there was nothing to calm me. I assessed the situation. We'd given up our element of surprise.

I scanned the room for Fergus. He scooted back toward the door. I nodded my head at Mom and Dad. They went after him, disappearing down the hall. Malachi and Ella were at Nick's side fighting their former subjects. Brandon, Ivy, and Clara were with me. This was not the plan we had, but like all fights, I improvised.

"Well, little Ivy, you finally chose a side," Alastair said.

"My side was always Brie's," she said.

"Then I will happily watch you die." He pointed a finger at her, and a large vampire that reminded me of Gaius bared his teeth and barreled at her. I ran toward Ivy, but Clara stepped in front of her sister. The vampire swiped his arm and backhanded her. Clara's head hit the wall in a deafening crack. She slid down. Her eyes open and vacant.

I bit down on my lip to stifle my scream and hurried to position myself closer to Alastair.

Ivy cried out and advanced into a training maneuver of flips that resembled martial arts. She tossed a stake midair. It landed in the vampire's chest. She continued her flips and planted her feet against the stake. It plunged into his heart, and he turned to ash.

Another large vamp came from behind her.

"Ivy," I screamed.

The vampire wrapped his arms around her and squeezed. She gasped for air and kicked wildly.

I held out my hand and formed an energy ball to throw at the vamp.

"Save it for Alastair," Brandon said over my shoulder. "I'll help her."

I looked around for Fergus, but he had disappeared. Anger heated my body, and Hell's Fire flashed at my fingertips. If I sent it out over the room, I chanced hitting one of us. Alastair was my target. *Where is he damn it?*

Cal, Malachi, and Ella entered. *Had that much time passed? Did they abort the plan for some reason?*

Malachi and Ella flanked Nick. Their trio downed vampires as soon as they entered the room.

The fight herded Alastair until he stood a few feet away from me this was my chance. I maneuvered through the skirmish like a wild animal tracking its prey.

"I've got your back," Cal said. "Get him. End it." He told

me to kill his father, but he didn't consider Alastair his father anymore.

A scream caught my attention. I turned to see Ella's head roll across the room. *Goddess. Help me hold it together.*

"You should save the rest of them," Alastair said.

I jerked my head toward the sound of his voice. "They don't need my help."

"You can either have me or them. Which will you choose?"

"You," I stalked in his direction.

"Now," he said. He looked away from me. I followed his gaze. The vamp slammed Brandon and Ivy's heads together and dropped their lifeless bodies against the ground.

"No!" The twin bond shattered in my chest. I stumbled forward. Tried to focus through the pain. Cal dropped to his knees in front of me. A long sword through his chest. My lungs collapsed in, and I couldn't get a breath.

I found Nick across the room and took a labored step in his direction. He scanned the room and met my eyes. We'd lost this attack. Defeat buried into the broken twin bond. A vampire appeared over his shoulder.

"Nick!" I called out, but it was too late. The vampire made a clean swipe with a sword across his neck and onto Malachi's. I tried to move but couldn't. I followed Nick's head to the ground, and my heart died in my chest. It turned black and shriveled up like a raisin. I didn't want to feel the sadness. The loss. *Darkness. Come to me. Claim me as your Queen.* Nothingness filled me.

I reached for the vial of Vampire Death and launched it at the murderous vamp and watched his agony as he writhed from the poison. Alastair was next. I turned to him and raised my hand in a deliberate motion. All of the power of Darkness would be on him until he was crushed into oblivion.

The room rocked. My ears rang. A force knocked me back a few steps. I looked down. Shrapnel was embedded in my chest, but I didn't know from what or where. Nor did I care. I welcomed death. Beckoned it to me. Blood pooled on the front of my black shirt, dark and sticky. I pressed my hand to it and expected pain, but none came. *Numb. Darkness.* Darkness wanted to heal me, but blood still poured from the wound through my fingers. I didn't want to live without Nick or with the death of so many good people on my hands. My heart was dead like the people I loved. *Hell's Fire.* It answered with a walled circle around me. Alastair wouldn't be able to get to me until it was too late, and Darkness understood. It drew on my life force to reinforce the fiery wall. I lay down in the circle and closed my eyes. My wait for death wouldn't be long with this much blood. *I'm sorry.*

Endless darkness enveloped me, and I expected to see Hell. All I saw was deep dark nothingness.

My brain was foggy, but Ivy and I led drills on the plan. We'd shaved several seconds off our time. The longest and most dangerous part was the time Ivy and Clara were on their own with the wards. They were vulnerable and any exposure would mean our plan failed. The element of surprise would be lost.

"One more time," I said. "And this time we'll have Malachi and Ella simulate vampire attacks at random." My strength and energy levels had returned to normal, and the run-throughs didn't tire me at all.

"We can't cover all the possible scenarios, Sis," Brandon said. His words noodled around in my brain like I'd missed something important in them.

"No, we can't." I reached for my necklace and rubbed the vial of Vampire Death. "But we can reduce complacency and always be ready for the unexpected."

"They were well trained like we were," he said.

"We only have one more day, Brandon."

"And if they are exhausted, they will make mistakes. They don't have your healing powers."

I took in the group. They were red-faced. I wasn't tired, but they were. I sighed. "You're right."

"Oh my Goddess. Did you just say I was right?"

I pushed his shoulder. "Go kiss Cal or something."

He winked at me.

Deja vu slammed against me like the explosion of light that freed me from Alastair's control. *I'd been here before. I'd had this conversation. I'd lived this day.*

Am I in some kind of witch purgatory? The day had reset. *But why? Did I do that? Did our ancestors? Did the Goddess?* The spark across my skin when I asked the Goddess to protect us. *Had my request been honored with a mulligan?*

No one else seemed to notice or even realize, we'd done this all before.

Instead of laughing like I had the first time, I grabbed Nick's arm and pulled him to the side. Electricity passed between us. It jarred me in contrast with the memory of his death. I let out a slow breath.

"Nick, we've been here before," I whispered. My words came out in a rush.

"We've been here for a month, my love," he said in a consoling voice. His eyes were full of worry.

"No, we've lived this day before and tomorrow, and it didn't end well." I rubbed the knot in my throat and down to the vial of vampire death on my necklace. The vial was there even though I'd used it against the vampire who chopped my husband's head off. I swallowed the hardness in my throat.

Was it a dream? No, it wasn't. It wasn't a vision. It happened. I surveyed my loved ones in the room.

"What do you mean?" he asked, confused.

"I mean. We messed up and some of us died, and it reset back today." *All of us died. Including you, and I welcomed death in the end. Welcomed it. Wanted it. Yet, here we are to live it again.*

He rubbed my upper arms. "I think you were dreaming, my love. You were out for almost a month. It's just your subconscious making sense of the time."

"No, it's not, and I need you to believe me," I said. "I need you to listen to me."

"Maybe it was a vision while you were under." He hooked his arm around my waist and hugged me tight to his side.

I shook my head, knowing it wasn't. Panic closed my throat, and I cleared it several times.

"It's not, Nick." My voice came out shaky, hardly recognizable as my own. I pushed back from him. "It's not."

"Ssh," He tried to pull me back into his embrace, but I held my hands up between us. "We'll figure it out."

I dismissed everyone, and Nick and I were alone. Maybe that small change was enough to set things right. To give us the advantage.

"Tell me what happens next. We said our goodbyes in here until tomorrow. We prepped. Ivy and Clara succeeded in turning off the wards. When we teleported to the hallway in the castle, Fergus was in the throne room with Alastair. They had some differing opinions, but they both wanted to use me to create dark witches and destroy vampires, well most vampires." I grabbed his arm and held on.

"And what happened next?" He asked, securing his arm around my waist.

The usual safety of his arms vanished in the wake of the memories. Fear encapsulated me, and his warmth couldn't get in to calm me.

"We were overwhelmed with vampire guards when we entered the room. Everyone died. I was the last one standing. Something hit me in the chest. I couldn't see what it was, but it was a mortal wound. I called Darkness and Hell's Fire with the intention to die. Everything went dark, and then we were back here having the same conversation we just had." The devastation of the day seeped into my bones. The heaviness of the deaths weighed on my body. I'd lived it.

"It sounds like a vision." Nick rested his forehead against mine. "Why do you think it wasn't?"

I pulled back and looked up into his eyes. I needed the reassurance of our connection. Sparks tingled across my body. "Because it wasn't. I've never had a vision last that long. It's never been so complete. I don't know what to tell you, except I know it was real."

"Okay, my love. I believe you," he said, his face filled with concern. "If it was and we are repeating it, then you need to tell the others."

"If you don't believe me, how will I convince them?"

"I do believe you, and they will believe you too." He hugged me to him.

☽ ☽ ● ☾ ☾

Everyone assembled in my office, Nick, my parents, my brother, Ivy, Clara, Malachi, and Ella. I explained to them what I remembered and that the day reset. Confused faces stared back at me. No one said a word. I stunned them into silence and myself too.

"I know how unbelievable it sounds," I acknowledged. Even witches didn't have the power to bend time. If Alastair harvested Darkness the way he did my power, he might be able to, but I didn't see how. Maybe it was tied to the dark magic he used to bind me to the circle in the old church. I couldn't explain it, but I knew we were sent back for a reason. We had to succeed, and we had to figure out what to change to do it. "It did happen though, and we need to fix whatever we broke yesterday... or tomorrow."

"Let's break it down every step from what you remember or any blind spots in your memory," Clara said. She believed me, and it gave me a small amount of relief.

"The only blind spot for me will be anything that happened with you and Ivy before we met up. We can start from where my memory picks up though."

I walked them through the events, even the horrible ones that threatened to open me to Darkness. I shared my own death where I gave up and surrendered. Shame gathered around the memory.

"So, maybe we just need to wait for Fergus to leave," Brandon said. "No charging in. We wait patiently." He glanced between me and Nick. It was an option, but we wouldn't know where everyone would be positioned.

"No, I think there is more to it," Sorin said. "We'd still be outmatched by the guards, and we don't know what hit Brie in the chest."

"Yes, that's another blind spot. I don't know what exploded or where it came from, but it didn't seem to hit anyone but me."

"So, the only real blind spots for you are the beginning and the end," he said.

I nodded. "Yes."

"Maybe today is not the day," he said. "Maybe we wait."

"But the final Blood Moon in the tetrad is tonight. It must be tonight," I said. The prophecy had to end with tetrad. If we didn't end it tonight, Alastair would control Darkness and the army he sought to create.

"Are you sure?" Sorin asked.

"Yes," I said. "I'll never be stronger than I am tonight." Alastair had been planning this for a long time, and it would take every gift I had plus the power of the Blood Moon to defeat him.

"Then we need to change the approach," he said. "No jumping the gun. We stay on plan."

"A new plan," I said. Tears stung my eyes. "I can't watch you all die again."

"Three of us are already dead," Ella said. "If it makes you feel better."

I snorted. "Not really, but thanks for trying."

We are fucked.

᠎᠎᠎᠎᠎᠎᠎᠎᠎᠎᠎᠎᠎᠎᠎᠎᠎᠎᠎᠎᠎᠎᠎᠎ ☽ ☽ ● ☾ ☾

PLEASE GODDESS DON'T LET this day end in plans for a funeral for any of my charges. Please be with us and bring the people, vampires, and witches, home safely. The signal came, and I teleported us into the hallway. *Nothing had changed from yesterday.*

Alastair and Fergus had the same conversation. Nick was triggered at the same spot. I had to follow him, knowing how it would end this time.

When the time came for the metal to pierce my chest, I turned to it and welcomed death for a second time. Hell's Fire and Darkness caged me in, safe from Alastair's madness.

When the unending darkness came to collect me, I smiled. Once again, I expected to see Hell, and once again, it denied me. I drifted into weightless nothingness. Awake but not. I didn't remember this from last time. *Is this the end?* I'd failed in the second chance. I floated up and down like I was on one of those giant slides without ever getting to the end of it. *Shouldn't my life pass before my eyes? Where is everyone else? Are they ahead of me? Will I see them on the other side? Is there another side?*

A breeze rustled around me similar to what would be stirred up by wings. A presence surrounded me with hope, strength, and love. *The Goddess. A clear message. It was my job to save them.* I was deposited on the floor in the office again. Time had folded in half, but instead of teleporting me from one place to the other, it moved me back to the past like a chess piece.

TWENTY-FOUR

) ·) · ● · (· (

*T*hird time's a bitch. I cannot see Nick's head sliced from his shoulders for a third time. I cannot watch all of them die again. I'd rather eat Hell's Fire than face their deaths one more time.

"Stop." My anger vomited out in a booming voice. *Great. Now, they will all think I'm crazy. What the fuck. They probably already do.*

"This is the third time we have lived this day. I've watched you all die twice in the same way, and my insides are pretty much dead. I've taken a sharp piece of metal to the chest twice, and I'm not anxious to do any of it again."

"You mean you had a vision," Nick said. He moved close like he intended to hug me.

I held my hand up. "No, not like a vision. It happened and the Goddess returned me to this spot like a reset."

Cal cleared his throat, drawing my attention. "And you laid down in a cage of your own making before being swallowed into Darkness?"

"Yes, you've seen it?" *That's new from the first two times. Something had changed. Thank you, Goddess.*

"I had a vision, but I didn't understand it. I couldn't see who was there, but the cage kept folding in around the occupant until it looked like a black hole in space. Nothingness." He stared across the room, his eyes unfocused.

"That's it, Cal," I said. "Did you see anything else?"

"Yes." He glanced from me to focus on Nick. "You wielded magic. Red like fire." Red in his vision and not blue like Michael's vision. *Something had changed.* Hope lit like kindling in me. We might have a chance this time.

Nick met my gaze. His face was full of confusion. The answer clicked into place for me.

"We need to do the spell before we fight Alastair," I whispered. My fear of fucking it up threatened my confidence, but the solution sang in my soul. This was the change we needed.

"But Brie, what if it doesn't work or one of us dies?" Nick asked in a worried tone.

"It will work," I said, pushing my fear aside and allowing my confidence to be restored. "Remember how we were entwined with the prophecy. Our markings, the writings about the prophecy, and now this. We need to face Alastair together as witches to defeat him. That is what the prophecy is trying to tell us." The truth tolled like a bell inside me.

Nick looked around the room. His eyes settled on Malachi. "Then, I need to formally pass the leadership of the Vampire Kingdom to my best friend."

"I'm not sure there will be a kingdom to rule," Malachi

said, his voice solemn. "But it would be my honor to follow you as a leader."

"And you must promise me to name Ella your second in command," Nick said.

"There isn't anyone else I would choose," Malachi said.

"We'll need to set everything up for the ceremony," I said. Precision would be key, and we couldn't sacrifice it even in a compressed timeline. "And we don't have much time."

"We can help," Clara gestured between her and Ivy.

"The details are at the Great House. I need to get my hands on the old scroll. It's a delicate spell. We need to execute this with perfection."

"Your father and I will do whatever you need, Brie," Mother said.

"I can go with you to the Great House." Cal stepped forward.

"As will I," Brandon said.

"Then, the three of us will go within the hour. Mother, if you could find a suitable space and sage it." I faced Clara. "Can you gather a list of ingredients and prep them?"

"Of course," she said.

"I'll write it down for you." I met Sorin's gaze. "Can you prepare Nick for what this ceremony will be like? He needs to know what to expect, so he can keep his emotions under control." The irony of me saying someone else needed to control their emotions wasn't lost on me.

My father nodded. "Of course."

Nick studied every move I made. Even when I wasn't looking at him, I could feel his eyes on me. I wrote down the supplies and preparations needed for Clara and Ivy and passed the paper to them. I turned to Cal and Brandon. "Ready?"

Apprehension rolled off Brandon and matched my own. I hadn't called the Great House home long, but it had been a place of safety and sanctuary for both Brandon and me growing up. To imagine that it no longer was a place we belonged stung me to the core. Brandon sent off a similar vibe.

I touched his arm. "It's going to be okay."

He put his hand over mine. "It has to be." The worry in his eyes told me he had less confidence than I did.

I let go and leaned over to Nick. I'd have been afraid, but there was no fear visible in his demeanor. His eyes danced with pride. "I love you, my husband."

His hand cupped my chin. He leaned in and kissed me. "I love you more, my wife."

"Kind of hard to argue with considering what you are about to endure," I said. I believed in the path ahead, and that we were not just doing what the ancestors guided us to but also what the Goddess herself expected from us. *My husband will make a damn good witch.*

"Mark that on the calendar that you didn't argue with me." He chuckled.

I smiled. "You and Brandon always keeping score about when I agree with you. See you soon."

"Soon, my love."

I held out my hands for Cal and Brandon. Brandon on my right and Cal on my left. Brandon chose the right every time he could. I'd ask him why if we survived today.

Michael's room. I focused on where I suspected the scroll

would be. The swish came fast like it sensed my urgency. I landed feet first in Michael's room with Brandon and Cal beside me.

The memory of seeing Nick curled over Michael's body bubbled up, and it was almost too much to stay in the room. I inhaled a deep cleansing breath. The scent of sage filled my nostrils. The room looked just as we had left it minus one thing. *Michael's body.*

"I expected Fergus would have tossed the room," Brandon said.

"He probably wanted to, but in his fanatical ways, he knows the disrespect something like that would bring," I said.

"Yet, here we are," Cal said.

"Here we are," I repeated absentmindedly. My thoughts shifted to the scroll. "Shall we begin?"

We split up into different parts of the room. I watched as Brandon and Cal were careful in their search, putting things back to where they were, so they looked undisturbed.

I cast a spell over the lock to keep unwanted visitors out. The simple incantation could be broken, but it would give us the second I'd need to teleport us out if it came to that.

The bookcase drew me to it. I ran my hand across the shelves. Witches, especially in Coven walls, were known for hidden passages and compartments. The rooms at the Great House were no exception. Michael would have protected the scroll. The energy changed on a shelf. I swiped my hand over the space several times. The discrepancy was like a magical draft.

"Brandon? Cal?" I called. "Can you come here?"

They stood beside me. "Run your hand in front of this shelf like this." I demonstrated and the draft vibrated again.

Brandon did it and shrugged. "I don't feel anything."

Cal took his turn. "Nor do I."

"Michael left a calling card only I would find." *Blessed be. Thank you, my friend.* I smiled and waved my hand again, zeroing in on the vibration.

"He knew," Brandon whispered.

Of course, he did. Michael was wise. I settled on the spot and pulled an old book from the shelf. Its worn leather appearance glimmered and shifted until the scroll appeared in my hands.

"Holy shit," Brandon said. "Only Michael could have pulled this off."

Footsteps echoed on the other side of the door and paused.

"We should go," Cal whispered.

I waved my hand at the door to unlock the magical spell holding it closed.

I tucked the scroll into my jacket and extended my hands to my travel companions.

My feet touched the exact place they left.

"They're back," Mother called. "Did you find it?" She asked with a mixture of relief and anxiousness.

I retrieved the delicate scroll from my jacket. The fragile papyrus creased and frayed on the ends.

Mother took it from me and gently unrolled it on the desk.

TWENTY-FIVE

⠀

Clara, Ivy, and I wafted lit sage bundles through the air to cleanse the ceremony space. *I let go of what no longer serves me. I clear this space to create space for Nick's transformation.* The chant repeated through my head as I moved around the room. I returned the shell to the stand with the smudging stick still burning.

"Ready?" I took Nick's hands in mine. His fingers warmed in my grasp.

"Whatever happens, remember this is my decision," he said, his voice low.

"It's going to work."

"If you feel in danger, cut it off," he said. "No matter the consequences to me."

I looked away. He laid his palm against my cheek and turned my head toward him. I met his gaze and covered his hand with mine. I didn't see fear in his eyes. I saw love. Pure unending and unconditional love.

"It will work," I said.

Malachi and Ella couldn't participate in the ceremony, so they stood by the door with Alan to make sure we weren't disturbed. Not that anyone would.

Clara and Ivy would be my anchors. Two required for this powerful spell.

Brandon took the North position and Sorin the South. Mother represented East and Cal the west. Nick took the center, of course.

I faced Mother. "East solidify the earth under our feet."

A quarter turn to my father. "South strengthen our lives with water." Two more turns to go to establish the circle.

A quarter turn to Cal. "West bring your wind to blow evil from our lives."

Final quarter turn to Brandon. "North bring the fire to keep us warm on our journey."

Hell's Fire erupted around the outer perimeter.

I inhaled to settle my nerves. The incantation had to be perfect, framed like a picture to make the spell its strongest.

"Goddess, we ask you to bless this ceremony and guide us with your infinite wisdom," I said, my voice rang out with strength. "Ancestors, your strength is requested here to power this change."

Light radiated from me like a dim fire. The air swirled like a storm brewed. *Maybe we should have done this outside. Too late.* Thunder pounded outside and rattled the room.

"A child of night no more. This day shall restore you to all that you were before and more."

I focused on Nick and repeated the chant. "A child of night no more. This day shall restore you to all that you were before and more."

The third time my voice rumbled louder than the thunder. "A child of night no more. This day shall restore you to all that you were before and more."

Blue sparks made lines from Hell's Fire and ignited in a circle around Nick. The tiny bursts danced around him and covered him, but he didn't flinch. It didn't look like they hurt him. He absorbed them.

I could barely stand against the wind. I glanced around the circle and everyone else struggled to stay upright. I need to finish it. The blue sparks came to an end, and I took that as a cue.

"So mote it be," my voice boomed.

A clap of thunder deafened the room. The wind turned to a light breeze and dissipated. I listened for a moment. *No more thunder.* The spell was done, and we were all still alive.

I walked up to Nick and touched his arm, looking for any damage or signs he'd changed. He looked the same. His hands were warm, not because of my body heat but on their own.

"Did it work?" He asked, his voice full of hope. So much so, it broke my heart I didn't have a direct answer for him.

"I don't know," I said, still studying him. Nothing on the outside looked different, but the change would have been internal. "Something happened. Do you still want blood?"

"I don't know," he said. "I'm not hungry, but I was never that hungry for blood. It was need, an overwhelming desire to feed at times."

"How do you feel?"

"The same," he said, his voice draped in sadness. "I don't feel anything different."

The disappointment in his voice gutted me. He needed an answer, and I had an idea. Something simple we did when witches first trained. "Want to try to do something like make an energy ball?"

He pressed his lips in a trim line and nodded.

"Hold your hand out like this." I showed him, acutely aware of all the eyes on us in the room. They could wait though. My husband needed answers.

He held his palm out and up.

"Now concentrate on forming a small ball of energy."

A tiny red ball formed above his hand. *He did it!* My heart froze and then pounded. My husband was a warlock. After two hundred and fifty years, he'd returned to his former self. Red was what Cal saw in his vision, but the magical charge that came to Nick during the circle was blue. I chose to believe both Cal and Michael had seen parts of this.

"Red," I said. "That's an interesting choice."

"It chose me."

"Same for me," I said, giddy with happiness for him. "We need to get some practice in for you."

"If you're done, Brie, then you should close the circle," Sorin said.

The excitement on Nick's face mesmerized me. A new world opened for him, and it would be a new journey.

"Brie," Dad said. "Close the circle. It needs to be you."

I glanced around and everyone was still in their points. "Of course," I said.

"Thank you, North for your true direction and fire." I moved in reverse of the earlier order. Hell's Fire quieted and disappeared.

"Thank you, West for your winds of wisdom."

A quarter turn to Sorin. "Thank you South for the vast renewal opportunities water brings."

Finally, I came to Mother. "Thank you, East for grounding us for the ceremony and in life."

A collective sigh came from the group. I noticed for the first time sweat beaded on their foreheads. "Are you all okay?"

"I was rooted in place," Brandon said. "I couldn't even wipe the sweat off my forehead until you ended the spell."

Concern pitted in my stomach. "All of you were?"

Mother nodded.

"We all were," Sorin said.

"That isn't part of the incantation," I said. The spell wasn't blood magic, and there wasn't anything in it that should have bound them in place, not even the anchors. It was far from a normal ritual and called the ancestors.

"I suspect the power required tethered us to the circle," Sorin said.

"I'm so sorry," I said. "I should have seen that."

"No apologies needed." Mother patted my arm. "We all knew the risks when we agreed."

"I was so focused on my anchor meditation that I didn't notice," Clara said.

"Same," Ivy said. "I'm just glad it worked."

Brandon patted Nick on the shoulder. "Glad you didn't die."

Nick chuckled. "Thanks. I'm glad I didn't make your sister a widow so young."

Brandon laughed with him. No laughter from me. I'd

witnessed them all die twice, and I was relieved everyone was still alive.

"Enough death talk," I said.

Nick's fingers laced through mine and pulled me toward him. With his other hand, he touched my face. My breath hitched at the contact. His chest rose and fell in a quickened cadence. My breath matched his pace.

"This is so much better," he said.

"I..." All my thoughts jumbled. My love for him was the only thing that mattered. I looked up into his eyes, wondering if our connection would still exist. Our eyes met in a supercharged intermingling of power. A soft glow enveloped us. I sighed. My worries were meaningless.

Nick smiled. "We're still us, Brie."

"I know you want to spend time together on this new journey, but we still have to face our enemies tonight," Sorin said. "Unless you've seen a change."

I looked over my shoulder. "No," I said. "I haven't had a vision in a while." I glanced at Cal.

He shook his head. "Me either."

"I haven't had one since Grandmother helped me find my way back from the coma," I said. "But my intuition keeps prodding me that we are where we should be."

Sorin's forehead creased. "I have a theory."

"Don't keep us in suspense, Sorin," Mother said. "It's poor form."

He crossed his arm and rubbed his chin. "I think this has been a test," he said. "For you, Brie."

I turned in Nick's arms, but he held me close, refusing to break the contact. "A test? We are dealing with a prophecy, and I'm being tested." Anger flared in me and touched the compartment Darkness had retreated to.

"Not the kind of test you are thinking. A test to see if you can handle what is to come," he said, his tone solemn.

"I don't understand," I said.

"No matter what," Brandon said, his voice quiet. "You can't save us." He looked at Cal. Cal locked eyes with Brandon and threaded their fingers together.

"You're not seeing a future, because there isn't one," Ivy said.

They were wrong. There had to be a way to end this where we all lived. We'd been given a second and third chance. "But my visions are usually a warning," I said, my voice cracked. "Subjective and pliable."

"We've known from the beginning this prophecy is about sacrifice," Mother said. She wrapped her arms around me, pulling me from Nick's hold into hers. "Whatever happens, I wouldn't change a thing because I got you and your father back."

"I love you, Mom," I said. *This will not be it. There has to be a version of this fucked up prophecy where everyone lives.* Despair dragged me down, but I fought it with the anger in me. Anger I might not be able to control this ending, but I'd sacrifice all of me to save them.

"I love you too," she said. "I think you and Nick should spend some time alone. You got a special gift today, and you need to enjoy it."

Brandon and Cal stood to the side, locked together with their arms around each other.

I glanced up over my shoulder. "You should tell Malachi and Ella."

Nick nodded and went to break the news about Sorin's theory.

"I don't know what to say to you all," I said. Tears threatened the corners of my eyes. "I thought I could save us all. I really did, but one of my many wrong turns led us here."

"We have never been in control of our deaths," Cal said. "That's what makes our lives worth the voyage and a gift."

For them, I'd show acceptance, but I'll be fighting with all the magic and power at my disposal. *Tonight is about happiness. Tomorrow is about survival.*

"Thank you," I said. "Thank you all for believing in me. If tomorrow is our night to die, then let's do it here. Let's make them come to us. We deserve to spend every last minute with the ones we love."

Nick slid in behind me and wrapped his arms around my waist. The familiar position was new again. "Best plan ever."

"Shall we all go do our thing and meet up for dinner tonight?"

"I have a request," Brandon said.

"Whatever you want, little brother," I said.

He rolled his eyes. "Minutes, Brie, minutes." He smiled and turned to Cal. He placed his hands on either side of Cal's face. "I want to marry this man today." He drew in a breath. "If he will have me."

"I will," Cal said with the biggest smile.

The tenderness of their gazes on each other made me tear up. That was pure love, and it both filled my heart and broke it to know how short-lived their married life might be.

"So, instead of dinner, we are having a wedding reception?" A wedding and reception sounded more joyful than a funeral march feast.

"I can perform the ceremony," Sorin said.

"Weddings are lovely," Clara said in a wistful tone.

I wanted to tell her it would be her someday, but I couldn't guarantee it. If what Sorin believed was the truth, and it certainly made sense, then none of us would live past tomorrow. As full as my heart was for Nick, it broke for the future that wouldn't be. Not just for me and him, but all those in this room.

I opened the door to the office. Nick sat on the sofa with a book in his hands.

"Aren't you supposed to be preparing for your brother's wedding?" He held out his arm, and I slid into the safe space that only his arms could provide, and I did feel safe there despite the ultimate threat hanging over us.

"My only duty is to show up on time to stand up with him." I leaned my head against his chest. "What are you reading?"

"I found this old book on the shelf, and I couldn't stop thinking about it. It was like I had to read it," he said.

I smiled against his chest. "It called to you. Our ancestors often reach out through inanimate objects to us."

"Interesting," he said.

"Anything particular stand out to you?" I asked, trying to not sound hopeful. Grandmother had said it would take both of us. This could be the ancestors showing him his path.

"No, but I can't read at vampire speed anymore." He kissed the top of my head. "No complaints."

"Let me show you something," I sat up. "Give me your hand."

He held it out palm up, and I flipped it over, positioning it above the open pages.

"Ask the ancestors for their guidance," I said.

He closed his eyes. "Ancestors guide me through the pages of this book."

I mashed my lips together to keep from snickering. The ancestors didn't care how we asked, but that was awkward.

The pages turned so fast they stirred up a breeze. My cheeks hurt from smiling, and I didn't hide my amazement. "Open your eyes, Nick."

He stared down in wonder, and the pages came to rest. "Was that me?"

"It was," I said. "With the ancestors' help, of course. See what they wanted to share with you."

He studied the page, and I looked down to see where it landed.

A reddish-orange Blood Moon, the only color visible, sat at the top of the page. Below it read *The Last Moon of the Tetrad.*

My mark burned like Hell's Fire touched it, but it had no fire in it. I eyeballed Nick, and he had his hand over his shirt where his mark was. The ancestors were clearly sending us a signal. Dread came first, but I refused it entry into the space. *Hope. I'm holding tight for it.*

"That fucking hurts," Nick said.

"Welcome to being a witch," I said. "Let's see what they are steering us to."

"Can you read this?" He asked.

"Yes," I said. "You?"

He nodded. "And this day, when the last Blood Moon of the Tetrad shines high, a union will defeat the fires of Hell and return them to their origin."

I swallowed against the knot in my throat. Part of me wanted to believe the ancestors gave us the answer to survival, but it read more like my epithet.

I read the next line. "Light of the moon will drive out the Darkness with the sting of its sharpness."

"They will meet at the vertex of the night to conquer enemies in the ultimate fight." Nick's voice grew softer. "The sacrifice will not be slight and will not be without self-immolation."

"It's me," I stared at my hands, pressing them against my leg to keep them from shaking.

Nick's finger hooked under my chin and tilted my head up.

"It's not you, my love," he said. "It's us. We have an opportunity to end this tonight."

"I'm not ready to say goodbye to you, Nick," I said, my voice betraying my sadness. He believed it meant our sacrifice, but the prophecy had always been about one sacrifice. *Mine.*

"We're going together," he said. "And you saw your grandmother in Summerland. We will be there together."

There was a reason I went to Summerland last time, and

it was Grandmother. I wasn't so sure I'd end up there a second time.

"I'm so tired." I leaned against him. "I'm exhausted at constantly fighting."

"This is the last one, my love," he said. "We're going to leave it all on the battlefield."

"You don't remember living it two times before," I said.

His lips pressed against my cheek. "Let's go upstairs. I want to make love to you as a witch just one time."

He scooped me into his arms the same way he had done as a vampire and stood up. Every moment meant more.

I kissed and nipped his neck as he took the stairs two at a time.

He kicked the door closed behind us and slid me down his body to set me on the floor. I pulled my shirt over my head, and he mirrored my actions.

"Wanna race to see who can get naked first?" I asked. "I mean it is a fair fight now."

Nick chuckled, a sexy rumble in his chest. "You're on." He unbuttoned his pants.

Clothes scattered across the room until we stood bare in front of each other.

"It will be a shame if you don't get a rematch." He pulled me to him and pressed his lips to mine. I put up a barrier to sadness for myself.

"Who says you won?" I muttered against his lips.

"I always win, my love," he said, his voice husky with need. His mouth smothered mine and urged my lips apart. He picked me up and sat me on the edge of the bed. My core tightened with the skin-to-skin contact.

His hot mouth blazed down my neck and over my collarbone. He held my breasts and teased one nipple with his tongue. Sparks radiated between us like miniature lightning strikes sizzling across my flesh.

My head fell back, and a moan escaped my lips.

His hand trailed down my stomach, eliciting goosebumps along the way. I needed him, and I needed him soon.

"Just take me," I said.

"Have patience, my love," he said in a husky whisper. "This is the first time we are the same, and I want to savor you."

Fuck. I nearly exploded from the sound of his voice and sexy words.

His fingers slipped through my folds and inside me in a slow rhythm. A wave of pleasure grew in me with each motion.

"You are so wet for me, my love," he said.

"I'm close." I pushed against his finger wanting him in every way I could have him.

His arm slid under my waist and pulled me closer. The pleasure stopped when he took his fingers away.

I opened my eyes to see him positioning himself at my entrance. "You want me as much now as you did when I was a vampire?" He dipped his head in and out.

"Goddess, yes." I managed to rasp out. "More." I tried to grind against him, but he held me steady.

He thrust inside me hard. I almost unraveled from the stroke.

"Not yet," he said. "Wait for me. Let's have this moment together."

"I like this side of you, but shut up and fuck me," I said, my voice rough with need.

His hand grabbed the back of my neck and pulled me in for a brutal kiss. I welcomed every bit of it. I wanted everything he could give.

He ran his hands over my breasts and down my sides. I bucked against him. He took hold of my hips in a bruising grip and pumped into me.

"Nick," I moaned. His punishing strokes continue to build me toward my peak. "I'm about to go."

Nick froze. "I said we were doing this together. Open your eyes, Brie."

I lifted my head and met his gaze. Our connection possessed me in a way Darkness would never consume me. Light formed around us, and electricity coursed between us.

He started to move again, holding my gaze. His hand slid down over my belly until he reached my center. He flicked his thumb in one swipe back and forth across my clit. I was undone, and he met me in the release.

"Brie," he called my name as he finished. His forehead rested against mine. He inhaled several deep breaths, and I could feel his heart pounding in his chest. His cheek pressed against mine.

Tears sprung to my eyes.

Nick leaned back and wiped the tears from my face. "Why are you crying? Did I hurt you?"

"No," I said, smiling. "I can feel your heart." I pressed my hand against his chest. It was like a miracle. A gift I couldn't repay but would be grateful for even in the afterlife.

He brought our lips together. "Thanks to you, my love. All thanks to you."

Thanks to Michael and the ancestors and the Goddess. If we died tomorrow, at least I would have had the best night of my life. *Goddess, I'd like to have more of these though.*

Brandon and Cal stood at the front of the makeshift altar and faced Sorin. They looked happy, and my heart sank a little deeper. I didn't know if the sacrifice Nick and I would make together tonight would be enough to save them.

Sorin opened a circle the same way Cal had opened it when Nick and I were married. "May the East bring openness to your marriage. May the South bring warmth to your home. May the West bring trust to your union. May the North bring security to your marriage."

Brandon and Cal joined hands. My father wrapped the ribbon around their wrists.

"Do you promise you will honor and respect the other?"

"We will." Brandon and Cal said together.

Father wound the ribbon around in another pass.

"Do you promise you will forever bear each other's burdens and pains?"

"We will." They smiled at each other.

The ribbon wound another time.

"Do you promise you will both live in the Light and love of the other till the end of days?"

"We will." A blush crossed Brandon's cheeks.

Dad wrapped the ribbon again.

"Blessed be the binding that is made here today."

He wound it around one more time and tied it in a knot. "Like your hands now bound so are your lives. May you always seek each other in your times of need and remain steady with the earth under solid under your feet."

"Blessed be," the rest of us said at the same time. It was intimate and perfect, and I recognized the look on their faces. In that moment, there wasn't anyone else in the room. I glanced at Nick, and he met my gaze with a smile, his face full of love.

Dad snipped the ribbon and closed the circle.

"Can we kiss now?" Brandon asked.

I stifled and giggle.

"You may kiss your husband," Dad said.

Cal leaned in and made the kiss quick. Brandon being Brandon grabbed Cal and dipped him into a passionate kiss. Everyone cheered. Cal's face was flushed when Brandon returned him to a standing position.

"Congratulations," I squeezed and hugged them both. "I'm so happy for you."

"Let's get the champagne open," Brandon said.

The wedding and reception were in the same room just on the opposite side, so it was easy to find the booze.

I turned down the champagne. It took a lot to get a witch

drunk, but I didn't want to risk having dulled senses tonight. Nick declined it as well.

"This time tomorrow, the moon will be at its peak," I leaned into Nick. Each tick on the clock raised my level of anxiety. *Would we win this time? Who would live? Who would die? Could I save everyone?*

"We can go to the library a do some more research." He kissed the top of my head.

"If there was another option, surely the ancestors wouldn't have shown us the passage they did."

"Or maybe they wanted us to know what we are fighting for," he said, his voice deep and soft.

"I know exactly what I'm fighting for," I said. "What about you?"

"I'm fighting for you," he said, in his melodic voice.

"You still have the vampire voice, and I'm still a sucker for it," I said. "Let's go look. For the record, I'd rather go spend the night with you inside me."

"Don't make me second guess my choice here." A deep chuckle rumbled from his chest.

"Just go." I sighed.

We took our time and strolled the short distance to the library. Not many people were in this area of the house, and it was quiet. *Peaceful.*

"You want to take that side, and I'll take this one?" I asked Nick, not knowing where to start the search.

"Whatever you say, my love." He smiled.

"I think you are still on a dopamine high from that mind-blowing sex earlier." I looked away to hide my smile.

"Mind-blowing, huh? Good to know where the bar is I need to beat." He chuckled, and it landed deep in my center.

"That will be a fun goal," I said. *If we get the chance to...* "Hold your hand up to the bookcase and move it around. If there is a magical calling card, you should feel it."

I ran my hands over the shelves and spines of the books in the library. *Please show me a book with a better answer than what we saw earlier.* No books called to me much to my disappointment. There wasn't even one that looked as old as the one we had earlier, but sometimes secrets hid in plain sight.

"Anything?" I asked over my shoulder.

"No," Nick said, sounding as frustrated as I felt. "You?"

"Nothing."

I huffed and leaned back against the bookcase. It creaked and swung open to a passageway. "What the..."

"Didn't Sorin say they had this place built for you?"

"He did. An under-the-radar hideout." I peered into the passageway. It was darker than dark. Pitch black with not even a smidge of light and soundless like nothingness.

"Why would he build this?" Nick asked.

"I don't know." I took a couple of steps into it and the call hit me like a sweet song and a hint of sage. "But I need to see what's down here."

"Me too," Nick said.

He slipped his hand into mine, and we walked through the dark hallway toward whatever beckoned us. Death could be waiting for us, and I was prepared to accept it for me. I wasn't ready to accept it for Nick.

"Maybe you should stay behind," I said.

"Don't even ask me to do that," he said. "I don't like telling you no."

"I expected that," I said. "But I wish you would wait at the entrance."

He pulled me tight against his side. "I might not be a vampire anymore, but it's nice to see my powers of persuasion are still intact."

I conjured an energy ball to shed light in the dark hallway. A pile of iron bars stacked along the side of the wall gave me dungeon vibes.

"Let me try," Nick said, holding out his hand.

I closed my hand around the energy, absorbing it back into me.

A tiny little red ball formed. Pride swelled in my chest at how easily he controlled his magic.

"Good," I said. "Now, think about it growing to the size of your hand."

It expanded and contracted before reaching its form.

"It's harder than it looks," he said.

"It gets easier with practice." The word hung between us. If what we read was true, there wouldn't be practice on another day. "Hold your palm out and don't think too hard about it. I know that's hard for you. Not to think that is."

Nick chuckled. "You're going to have to make that up to me."

"Name the time and place." It hit me that it was easy between us again. I guess having your imminent death and knowing nothing you can do will change it does that to someone.

"I see something down there," Nick said.

I squinted. His red energy cast a strange glow in the darkness to me. It came into view. A blue glow. "What is that?"

We inched up closer to it. A book floated in front of us suspended in the blue light. *Another book. I don't know whether to laugh, cry, or run.* "What is it with these books hidden in dungeon-like spaces?"

"I've only been a witch a minute, so you tell me," Nick said.

"I don't fucking know," I said. "But Sorin and Cecily had this place built. Surely they had to know." If Dad had known there was a floating book down here, he would have said something.

"Maybe Cecily had it put here without Sorin's knowledge."

I shrugged. "That's a possibility. Dad was in near solitude for two decades."

"Do you know what book it is?"

"No, I don't recognize the cover..." The marking on the front stunned me into silence. I looked up at Nick.

"Is that?" He asked.

"Our marks," I said. My tattoo graced the upper left corner and Nick's was on the lower right. A Blood Moon suspended in the center between them. I couldn't believe what I was seeing. "This book was meant for us."

"The union in the book in the library."

"It led us here for a reason," I said. Hope blossomed in my belly, and I didn't want to let it grow until I knew more.

"How do we get it out of the suspension?"

"We take it." I reached in and took hold of the book. A

sharp charge zapped the palm of my hand. I pulled it back and rubbed the area. "You try."

Nick raised one eyebrow at me but reached for it. He jerked his hand back. "Fuck."

"Hurts, right?"

He shook his hand. "Is it too late to go back to being a vampire?"

"Yep," I said, turning my focus back to the book. "It has both our marks. Maybe we have to do it together."

"If I get zapped again, I'm going to kick someone's ass," Nick said with no humor in his voice.

But I laughed. "It's all part of living in a world of witchcraft. Sometimes we get shocked, sometimes we don't." My confidence was high I was right this time. "Ready?"

I positioned my hand hovering over the side of my mark. Nick positioned his on the other side.

"Not really but count us down."

"Three... two... one." We wrapped our hands around it and pulled it back between us. There was no shock. *Thank you, Goddess.*

"The union," Nick said.

The symbols on the cover were raised. "Hold it in your palm."

Nick positioned the book.

We both ran a hand over the symbols. They glowed. I'd never seen a book like this. The book opened, supported by Nick.

"This is beautiful," I said. The blue light radiated from the book, not the area it had been suspended in. I looked around for somewhere to place it, so we could both peruse it.

"There's a table over there." Nick pointed behind me. He walked over and laid it there. It radiated like a blue flashlight. "This book is meant for you."

"It's meant for us," I said. "It took both of us to retrieve it."

"But it glows blue like your energy," he said.

"That could mean a million things. My energy is blue, but my aura is pink." I studied the cover and opened it to the first page. The book was old but not fragile as I'd expected. Whatever enchantment was placed on it had preserved it quite well.

Nick slipped his hand around my waist and studied with me. "A queen like no other will come to pass, and she will have a king that will never be repeated."

"That certainly sounds like us," I said. "But someone could have created this to fool us." I walked my fingers over the pages and tried to sense the age.

"How do we know whether to trust it or not?"

The blue energy extended out and linked up with mine. A jolt of memories flooded into me. The vision moved like a Netflix show on fast forward. Glimpses of ancestors and battles and many many moons flashed by. I quieted my mind and focused on slowing it down. The first image it stopped on was a warrior. *A huntress.* She bore the marks of many vampire kills. A practice banned more than a century ago, because of our healing powers magic was used to scar the skin with an arrow mark. Her neck and arms were both covered with them... except for the mark on her shoulder. *The same mark as I have.* She knelt before someone. *A vampire.* He grasped either side of her head and twisted until her head severed from her body.

I sucked in a breath to steady myself, but the connection broke.

"Brie, what happened?" Nick's grip tightened on me.

"The book is old," I said. "At least as old as the Fire Book. Maybe older."

"What did you see?" His voice was soft. I hadn't projected it, but it damn sure drained me like I had.

"It was from over a hundred years and probably three times that. A great huntress, maybe a queen with the markings she had. A vampire ripped her head from her shoulders."

"Times were more violent then," he said.

"I don't know they are any less violent now. We're still delivering tactical and skilled blows across both fronts."

"Let's look through the book and see if we can find anything to get us through the night."

"And then what?" I asked. "What comes after that? I'm so tired of this fight. I want to win. I want to survive tonight, but it seems like there is always something else. Something worse waiting for us."

Blue light lashed out from the book and around my neck. *Never give up.* I heard the words in my head as if they had been spoken out loud. The light retreated to the book. I rubbed my throat.

"Are you ok?" Nick looked me over. "What was that?"

"I'm fine. It was a warning to keep going," I said. "Someone taking your side,"

"Well, I'm glad someone is." He kissed the top of my

head. "But if they touch you like that again, I'll burn the damn book."

I flipped a couple of pages. "This book was written as a warning when two powerful beings come together, but it's, also, a tale of how they fought against those who wished to cast the world in darkness and enslave the humans."

"This man looks like Sorin," Nick said.

The drawing of the man did bear a strong resemblance to my father. He could be our ancestor. "And his companion was a queen. She ruled for a century before she named a successor." I flipped the page. "Oh."

"He died," Nick said. "She didn't want to live without him."

"No, that's not what this passage says." I read it carefully.

"Right here." Nick pointed. "It says he died."

"But here. This was later, and he was there." I exchanged a knowing look with him. *Son of a...* "He became vampire," I said.

"Well, we went the other way," Nick said.

I mulled it over. *Could we be here to right a very old wrong?* "Why did she choose to end her life though?" I scanned the next few pages. "Here." I pointed to a verse.

"She tried to turn him back," he said. "But it didn't work."

"He lost all of his humanity," I said. "Nick, if that had happened to you." I touched his arm. I shuttered thinking of what our futures would be like.

"It didn't for a reason," he said, his tone confident. "I wanted to be who I was meant to be. He didn't want to return to his former self."

I followed the passage he was reading. "She tricked him into the ceremony. Forced him, and it backfired. It drove him deeper into Darkness." I stared at the last word. "For he became a shadow of himself. Smoke and nothingness. He did not love. He did not feel pleasure. He only knew hate. He was Darkness."

Holy fucking shit.

"Do you think he is what consumed my father?" I said. "What consumed me?"

"Do you think it means literally?" Nick asked. "Could a witch turned vampire become something so solitary and evil?"

"I don't know," I whispered. My brain hurt as it reasoned through what this meant. *Could Darkness have once been an actual person? A witch turned vampire and turned witch again? I will not let the same thing happen to Nick. I'd take all of it into myself before I'd allow that to happen.*

TWENTY-EIGHT

⟩ ⟩ ● ⟨ ⟨

I stared at the story on the page, uncertain of what it meant for Nick and me. *This is not our destiny.* "It's not us," I said, gazing up at Nick. "Right?"

"I wanted to be like you. We aren't the same as them." Nick shook his head. "This is not our story."

"Why would this story be meant for us?" *Am I going to turn into a creepy goo that infects people?*

"Maybe to show us what could have happened."

"But why wait to draw us here until after we did it?" I asked, confused by the message the book sent. "That doesn't make sense to me. Maybe there is something we are missing in it."

"Like a hidden message or subtext?" Nick asked.

"Yes, something like that," I said. "I have an idea. Put your hand over mine." I held mine over the book. He laid his palm against the back of mine.

Blue and red energy swirled together from the book to

the ceiling. They formed a funnel that devolved into a scene. The queen bowed before the vampire. She couldn't live without him, and she couldn't live with him like this. She knelt before him. He sneered and wielded the death blow.

I winced. Wanted to look away, but a figure in the background caught my eye.

A child. *Their child.* A young boy stood near the top of a rolling hill in the distance, but he was visible. He appeared to be about seven. The same age Brandon and I were when our powers manifested for the first time.

The boy screamed and ran toward them. He squared off against his father and began to glow. The sky darkened with only a Blood Moon to cast light on them. The boy divided into two. *Twins.* He launched all his power at his father. The newly minted twin joined him as if he knew the anguish the young man felt. Their father dropped to the ground but did not die. He did not turn to ash. He faded into a shadow.

The twins continued to throw everything they had at him. They faltered but were unyielding. I recognized this and had been there. Memories came of my own struggle to maintain when the weakness overtook every inch of my body. The twin's life force drained. When the last of their energy was spent, they turned into pure light and drifted away on the wind. *Presumably to the Goddess.*

Their father gave into the shadows around him until he looked like a black hole. He became Darkness. The replay froze in the final moment. Sadness rippled through me and weakened my knees. I flipped my hand to lace my fingers through Nick's and squeezed.

"That's tragic," Nick said, his voice so quiet I almost didn't hear him.

"Heartbreakingly tragic." I reached for my stomach with my free hand. "How did she leave her child? And to have your child give a sacrifice, because of the parent's choices." Bile rose in my throat.

"He couldn't live with it either," Nick said. "We couldn't be? Could we?" Nick's eyes dropped to my belly.

"We don't even know if you can," I said. "I doubt that's what this text would be telling us."

"I'd love nothing more than to have a child with you, my love," Nick said.

Kids weren't even a thought for me as a huntress. *Would a huntress make a good mother? Would a queen? Did I even want them? Elizabeth and Jane Ann must be the best of their parents. A little Nicholas would be the best parts of him too.* I met Nick's gaze and knew with absolute certainty I did if we persevered through the prophecy.

"Maybe the ancestors wanted to let us know we could have children," I said. "But I don't think that's what the message here is," I said, and he looked crushed. *We might not even survive the next twenty-four hours.* He needed hope, and after all he had given me, I owed him something to look forward to. "Maybe after we save the world though."

He pulled me close. Our hands no longer touching, the images disappeared.

"Agree. We will be working on the baby-making after this is all over."

"I'm looking forward to that," I said, not sure we'd see a

time after this. "But right now, we need to find something that will get us through the night. So far, I only see bad parenting choices and people dying unnecessarily." I flipped the page. The corner tore, and I expected to get a shock but none came.

He nodded. "It does seem that way from this portrayal."

"What are we supposed to do with this information? How is this supposed to lead us to peace?"

"If he is Darkness personified, he is the one we are really facing. Not Alastair," I said. "And he is old and powerful." *Maybe as powerful as the Goddess.*

"True. How do you fight something that isn't corporeal?"

"We've been fighting it all along, but we've been doing it all wrong."

He met my gaze. "Because it's just been you and Sorin fighting Darkness. The rest of us were fighting Alastair or my father or someone in their circle."

Oh my Goddess. What if he's onto the solution? All of us against Darkness, but we'd need to force him to take form in some way. "I think that's the answer, but if I'm wrong, we die again tonight. And what if it's our last chance?"

"It's the only thing we have to go on," Nick said. "Even with all of us focused on that goal, we don't know what to do."

"Maybe something to contain him. When we fought Alastair that night at the castle, Dad's plan was to disperse the Darkness between us. We channeled it then. I'm thinking if we focus it into something strong enough to hold it, we could contain him." It stood to reason. A containment spell like what Alastair had used on me but without blood magic could work.

"So, we just need to find a box that will restrain him and lock him up. Easy enough." Nick shrugged.

"Was that sarcasm, my husband?" I laughed.

He smiled. "Why are you surprised?"

"You're usually so serious," I said, still amused. "And this isn't actually fun and games."

"No, it feels like an impossible task, but I don't want to give that power." His forehead tensed.

"And that is one of a long list of reasons I love you."

He kissed my forehead. "I love you too, and together we can do anything."

"Unstoppable," I said and turned back to the book. "So, let's figure this shit out."

His hand hovered over the book. I slipped mine underneath. "Show us how to contain this evil once and for all."

The book floated and flipped from top to bottom. It spun around like it was possessed. Then it landed upright on the table and the pages turned in a slow methodical rhythm like someone was pondering as they looked for the answers.

"We could— "

"Patience," I said. "Just wait."

"My wife giving me lessons on patience." Nick chuckled.

"Right. Who am I?"

"A queen. A leader. A champion," he said. "And most importantly, the woman I love."

"You must want something." I waited, not so patiently in my head, for the book to stop on anything.

"There is something I always want," he said. "You." His words warmed me.

"Concentrate."

The book finally came to rest. I peered at the page. *That's a game changer. Do we have enough time to do it?* "We're going to need Sorin."

TWENTY-NINE

Sorin met us in my office. I recapped for him what we'd discovered about the creation of Darkness and a potential solution the book showed us.

"It can't be done, Brie," Dad said. He gave no indication he was aware the book existed.

"But what if it could." I glanced between him and Nick.

"Go find your brother. He'll talk some sense into you since you aren't listening to me." Dad gazed out the window. *Why was he being so obstinate about it?*

"Did someone mention me?" Brandon strutted into the room. He had a different gait.

"Is the honeymoon already over?" I pushed his shoulder.

"Not a chance in Hell," he said. "I had to make sure my sister wasn't out fighting the bad guys without me."

"She's certainly trying." Sorin rubbed his chin and kept his eyes on the view out the window.

"What crazy idea do you have now, Sis?" Brandon dropped onto the couch.

I scooted next to him and held my hand up to call the book off the desk. It floated in front of us open to the pages from earlier. "Show him," I commanded it.

"Where did this book come from?" Brandon asked as I passed it to him. The shock factor appeared to have been disabled once Nick and I had read what it wanted us to see.

"It found us," I said.

"Of course, it did." He studied the page. "A faraday cage for Darkness. Of course, you would find the most impossible task."

"But what if this is our one shot to survive tonight?"

"Some of these items are difficult to find," he said, his tone laced with skepticism. "It'd be hard to pull off in less than a day."

"But there is one place where we can get them all," I said, aware he was going to think it was as crazy an idea as Dad did. It was a chance for us all, and a risk worth taking.

"The Great House? You want to break into the Great House again?" Brandon's voice rose an octave, and he paced with the book in hand.

"I don't think it's breaking in since I'm technically still queen and I'll technically be teleporting."

"I guess if we're going to die anyway. It's worth a shot," Brandon said. It wasn't like him to give in so easily.

"That was relatively little fight from you," I said. "You didn't see another solution to our problem, did you?"

"No, but I haven't seen any solutions since you were in Summerland." He said, his voice sad. His lost feelings waved over me. I empathized with him because I felt the same way about not getting visions.

"I expected more from you than to agree to this plan, Brandon," Sorin said. Dad should know better. Brandon and I stayed in sync most of the time.

"She's right, Dad. We have to give it a chance. What if we can rid the world of the Darkness?"

"Tell him what the Darkness is, Brie," Sorin said, his tone stern. "He should know the whole truth."

I ran through what the book had shown us for Brandon.

"So, it's a person?" Brandon's brows furrowed together.

"It was," I said.

"Is this the right thing to do then? Caging it?" I sensed how nervous he was and shared it. We were out of time and out of options.

"How else do we stop the corruption?" I asked, glancing at Nick.

He shifted forward on the seat. "I've only been a witch for a brief moment, but it seems like we were shown this for a reason whether from the ancestors, the Goddess, or Darkness himself. I think we have to take that seriously."

"Maybe caging him, but then finding a way to release him," Brandon said. "Does he have a name?"

Darkness was dangerous, whoever he was, but if we could release him in a safe manner, I'd support it. "I don't have a name for him, but I can tell you he looks a lot like Dad."

"What?" Sorin's head snapped in my direction. "Me?"

"Yes, he has to be a relative," I said.

Sorin reached for the chair next to Brandon and lowered himself into it.

"What's wrong with you? Are you ok?" I asked.

His face paled. "I didn't believe the stories."

"What stories?" I took the seat next to him. *Were we related to this person?*

"When I was a child, your grandmother told stories about her family."

"Yes, I remember that both of her parents were killed by a jealous vampire," I said. "She had a hard time accepting Nick because of it."

"Yes, but even further back than that," he said. "The original line of witches had dissension."

"The creation of vampires and dark witches," I said. "Is that what you mean?"

"Yes," he said. "One of our ancestors was the first to use dark magic and tap into it."

"So that's the reason it is so drawn to us." It wasn't that we were evil. It was that we were part of it. Part of the history that brought us here. Shock ricocheted between me and Brandon. That's why we needed to stop it. Why the prophecy hinged on us.

He nodded. "I thought they were just stories, because how could someone be an entity like Darkness..."

"If the book hadn't shown us, I'm not sure I would have believed it," Nick said.

"Me either. It pushes the boundaries for what we know of magic," I said.

Brandon patted my leg. "Our family. Our responsibility."

"Agree. We need to fix this. I still think the first step is to capture him."

"In the magical faraday cage," Nick said, his tone serious.

"Yes," I said. "But we will not leave him there. We need to

help him find peace." If magic brought us here, it could release him from the pain too.

"Whatever that means to him," Brandon nodded.

"And if he can't communicate what that is, what will you do?"

"We are witches, Nick. We can commune with any living thing," Brandon said. "Brielle hasn't taught you that yet."

I swatted his arm. "I can't believe you just called me, Brielle. What's gotten into you?"

"I guess it's the married life." He stretched his arms over his head.

"Apparently, so. It will do that to you." I looked up at Nick.

He leaned over and kissed the top of my head. "It certainly will."

"When are we going on our supply run?" Brandon asked.

"Right away. I'm going to ask Ivy and Clara to go with me."

"I'm still your bound Protector, so just confirming I'm going," he said.

"I need you and Nick here to construct the iron cage. There was plenty of it in the secret passageway like it was placed there just for this." Had Cecily known and put it there?

"Iron is so harsh," Brandon said. Iron could be used against witches, and I shared Brandon's disgust. It had its use on occasion, and our ritual was one of those times.

"The folklore is true," Nick said.

"It doesn't hurt a witch," I said. "But when enchanted, it can be impossible for us to permeate."

"Won't Darkness just pass between the bars?"

"Not once we turn it into a faraday cage meant just for Darkness." I wagged my eyebrows at him. This spell had been chosen for a reason, and it was because it was the only thing that could hold him or it in place, whether he was in human form or creepy dark smoke form.

Nick checked my jacket like he was inspecting a parachute. "You get in and get out. Don't do anything stupid."

"You sound more and more like my family every day."

"I am your family, my love." He gave me a quick kiss on my lips. "Do your swish thing. Get in and get out."

"Yes, you are, and you chose to be here. I'll do my best swishing." I smiled. "Ready ladies?" I asked Clara and Ivy.

They extended their hands to me.

"Let's do this," Ivy said.

"I wish you hadn't told me what this will feel like," Clara said, in a nervous tone.

"You'll be fine." *At least for the teleporting.* "Hold on tight,"

The portal formed around us and swished us to The Great House. I landed on my feet and checked Clara and Ivy. They were both on their feet like they had teleported a dozen times. I'd positioned us outside what the perimeter was for the disturbance alarms to trigger.

"If the tunnels are compromised, I'll teleport us in, but let's try this first."

"We're following you," Ivy said.

We navigated through the tunnels. There weren't any wards up. It's like Fergus didn't care or intended for us to sneak into The Great House. Maybe he hoped we would give him another reason to attack us.

The first stop was my room where I had one of the rarer ingredients, a truffle gifted to me from Crew long before I assumed the queen position. I didn't ask how he'd obtained it, but my gut had told me to save it for an important moment. There was nothing more important than what we were doing tonight.

The next stop was the apothecary room for the rest. I couldn't teleport us directly in there, because the magic sensing alarms would detect it, so I navigated us through some of the hidden passages. There were almost no guards out and even far fewer people. Once everything was gathered, we made our way back down the hall in a slow methodical fashion toward the tunnels.

There were several paths to use, but I chose the one that took us by my office, expecting it to be vacant. Voices drifted out from behind the door. Anger rolled through me. They were in my offices. It felt like a personal invasion.

I leaned up against the wall next to Clara and Ivy. Fergus, Alastair, and their cronies were deep in plans. *About us, of course.*

"Once we have her power, we can use it to bring him back," Alastair said.

"Why can't we use her father? He's one step closer to the origin," Fergus said.

"Her power is purer than his. She commands everything her ancestors have to offer. Sorin is strong, but she is stronger."

I inhaled a short gasp and covered my mouth. Ivy grabbed my wrist.

Alastair and Fergus paused their conversation. I held my breath afraid they would discover us. It wasn't clear if anyone else was them, but I could take them both out if they were alone. I looked at Ivy, and she vehemently shook her head. Her eyes widened, and I took her warning seriously.

"And your certain she'll show up tonight?" Alastair asked.

"It's the Blood Moon and the last in the Tetrad. She'll be her most powerful then. It would be foolish of her not to make an attempt tonight," Fergus said, the smug confidence in his voice made the air putrid.

"We'll be ready," Alastair said. "And you are certain you'll be able to contain her?"

"Yes, the team has been working on a special weapon just for her. We'll stall her healing powers long enough to weaken her. Then restore them when we have her prepped and ready."

I clutched my chest, remembering exactly how the impact felt, how the blood oozed through my fingers and wouldn't stop. Fergus didn't account for my willingness to die to prevent them from using me. He didn't account for Hell's Fire and Darkness bending to my wish for death. Darkness gave me what I wanted in the end. Maybe there is some redemption for this ancient ancestor.

"What if he doesn't want to separate from them?" Alastair asked.

"He's been nothing but an entity for centuries. He'll want some revenge," Fergus said.

Alastair's tone came out less than convinced. "He was vampire, and if that queen couldn't reverse him, what makes you think we can or even control him."

"We'll have her power at our command," Fergus said. "He'll bend to her. He's sought her out. He wants to be free of his purgatory. Wouldn't you?"

They didn't understand him at all. He was tired of the fight. *Just like me.* That's why he showed me their history. My history. He didn't want us to repeat it, and he wanted his story to finally come to an end. It became so clear to me what the point was. He'd existed in a torment of his own making for centuries, and I was the one person who could free him. If I could stop Alastair and Fergus from ruining it. And if there was hope for this man, my ancestor, to find his peace and place after all this time, then maybe there was hope I could be the queen my people deserved and earn the mark my ancestors placed on my shoulder.

I shifted closer to the door. Ivy flung her arm across in front of me, cautioning me against my foolish nature. I wanted to take them out here and now, but that would jeopardize everything if I tried and failed. I didn't move any further and their voices faded away into the distance.

"We should go," Clara said.

Fuck the alarms. Let them know we were here and let them

wonder what we were doing.

I nodded and called our ride. I reached for their hands and swished away in the teleporting haze. Despite the crazy introduction, teleporting had become my favorite way to travel. I landed on my feet in the office. My landings were far less rocky than the bouncing and hurling of the first few times.

Dad met us and took my pack. "Nick's sick. Your mother is with him in your room, but you should go to him."

My heart twisted with the pit in my stomach. "Sick? But we're witches."

"Just see for yourself," Dad said, his voice strained.

I teleported to my room. Mom sat on the bed next to Nick. His eyes were closed and his breath shallow. He looked pale and almost unrecognizable from a couple of hours ago. I sat on the bed and took his hand in mine. "What happened?"

"He and your brother were working on the cage, and he collapsed. He's been unconscious ever since," she said.

"Did anyone try to heal him?" I asked.

"Yes, but it didn't work." She rubbed my upper arm.

"Was the iron enchanted?" I asked.

"Your brother isn't sick, and nothing came back when we checked."

Panic shuddered through me. "Nick? Can you hear me?"

He didn't respond.

I held my hands out over his body and sent my energy into him. The drain on my body instant, but Darkness was there to reinforce me. I let my ancestors replenish my lost strength. A metallic taste formed in my mouth. *Iron? No. Blood...*

"He needs blood, Mom, but he doesn't have fangs anymore. Can you go get a syringe and bring it back here?"

She disappeared.

"I know what you need, Nick. We're going to get it for you. You will be just fine. Hang on for me." *Goddess, please. Ancestors, please. Darkness, please. Whoever can help him, please.*

Footsteps echoed down the hall and grew closer.

"Here, Brie." Mother handed me the needle and syringe.

I jabbed it into my arm and pulled back the plunger. It filled with crimson liquid. I yanked it out of my arm and took the needle off.

"Tilt his head back a little, Mom," I said.

She lifted it just enough that his mouth opened. I put the tip in and slowly pushed the plunger back down. His lips closed around it, and I watched his throat move up and down. The color in his cheeks looked better but still pale. It was working.

He roused. "Brie?" His voice was hoarse.

Thank the Goddess. "I'm here, my husband. How do you feel?"

"Absolutely miserable. My head hurts and my body aches. What is going on?"

"I don't know. Did you hurt yourself? Any injuries while putting the faraday cage together?"

"Not that I recall," he said but raised his hand.

I took hold of it and examined it. "There's a sliver of iron in your finger." *Easy fix.*

"It's a tiny one," he said.

"That's all it takes if it's laced with poison or enchanted."
Enchanted or poison was the question and why.

"Where are your tweezers, I'll get them for you," Mom said.

"Top center drawer," I said. I'd seen them rummaging for a toothbrush.

I owed Mom some thanks for this.

"You scared me," I said, holding back tears. "When I walked in and you looked so pale, I thought that was it."

"I'm not going anywhere, my love." His voice was still weak, but he was stronger after the blood.

"You better not, because you promised me forever or at least our version of it."

"And I intend to live up to that promise every day we have," he reached a hand up to caress my check. "Did you get what you needed at the Great House?"

"We did and more," I turned my face to his palm and brushed my lips against his skin. Alastair and Fergus had known all along what Darkness was. *What else did they know?*

Mom returned with the tweezers and passed them to me. "Thanks, Mom. I appreciate you staying with him."

She squeezed my shoulder. "Of course."

"So, what else did you get while you were there?" Nick asked.

"Let me get this little bastard out of your finger, and then I'll tell you everything." I grabbed onto the iron piece and pulled it out with as much care as I could. "This little death trap is going down the toilet."

I headed into the bathroom and drop it in the commode. The rusty color drifted down to the bottom. A yellow tint drifted off of it. *Poison.* I hit the handle and watched it go down the drain. *What the hell was poisoned iron doing in that hallway anyway?* It was like someone left it there for us to find. *But why? Did they want to kill us?* Dad said he and Cecily had this place built, and there were just a few people who knew about it. I needed to ask him about it.

"How are you feeling?" I stood beside the bed and rested my hand against Nick's cheek. His skin was warm and in the normal range. I moved my hand to his heart and let my rhythm meld with his.

"Almost like new," he said. "Better if you would come snuggle with me."

"I need to go talk to Dad for a minute," I turned to Mom. "Do you mind staying with him for a few more minutes?"

"Sure, honey," she said.

"Don't be too long. I still want to hear what else you brought back." He smiled at me.

"I won't be," I said.

I found Sorin in the library with the book we recovered from the hidden passage.

He looked up. "How's Nick?"

I dropped into the chair opposite him. "My husband is a very resilient man. It's an interesting read, isn't it?" I pointed to the book.

He closed it. "It is. I can't believe so many of those legends were real."

"We are the legends of the humans, so it shouldn't be that surprising that ours are real."

"What's on your mind?" He closed the book.

"The iron in the hallway," I said. "Do you know where it

came from?"

"No, I guess it was brought in after I went into seclusion. Why?"

"It was poisoned. Nick had a tiny sliver in his finger. That's what made him sick." He could have died. My stomach tightened.

"So, you think someone was deliberate with the placement?"

"I do," I said. "It's like they wanted to help but hurt too. Help but not be obvious."

"Well, that sounds like the work of someone playing both sides of the game," Dad said. "There are always those like that, and if you know who they are, you can use them to your advantage." The only one I knew playing both sides was Ivy, but I was sure it wasn't her.

"Right now, I'm more interested in making them pay for almost killing my newly returned to a witch husband."

"Brie, everything can't be about revenge," he said. "You lose sight of the most important things, like saving you and your mother, Brandon, and Nick."

"And you."

He smiled, but it didn't reach his eyes. He had some of that residual thinking like me. I wondered if I deserve to be saved, and I knew he had those same thoughts. But our ancestor who is pure Darkness seemed to think we were worthy. He chose us for a reason, and I found hope in it.

"Did you find his name by chance? It would be nice to speak his name when we set him free."

"No, it seems to be stricken from what I can tell."

"I thought maybe I overlooked it or didn't understand it.

Names were so weird back then."

Dad laughed from deep in his belly. "They weren't weird. Names held deep meaning and spiritual significance then, much more so than they do today."

I nodded. Mom named me Brielle because she wanted Brandon and me to have names that started with the same letter and had the same number of letters and syllables. Our names were for a fashion statement and not significance.

"And as far as the iron, we don't know if it was put there yesterday or ten years ago," he said. "If they are here, then they will eventually mess up, and you will know then."

"You sure do seem relaxed about this," I said.

"I know this is the safest place you can be right now, and I think you have a much bigger focus for the evening."

"You make a hard argument," I said. "I'd love to know his name if you find it in there."

"I'll keep looking, but it looks to have been deliberately removed." He pointed to text that looked slightly out of place.

"With magic," I said. "Perhaps we can fix that."

I laid my hand on the page. "Reveal what is hidden in plain sight. Show us what once was written and removed in spite."

The words blurred and swirled on the page. They reorganized.

"Some things are hidden for our own good," Sorin said.

"And sometimes, they are hidden for no good," I said. "Let me know what you find. I need to go check on my husband." I welcomed the swish that took me back to Nick and teleported to the hallway to be less disruptive.

☽ · ☾ · ● · ☾ · ☾

Mom sat with Nick. They were engrossed in conversation, and I leaned against the door, pleased to see them getting along so well. She patted his hand.

Nick looked up and met my gaze. Our special connection found me and filled me with love like no other.

"My love." He patted the bed beside him.

I crawled onto the bed and snuggled up to him.

"I'll leave you two alone," Mom said. She studied me and patted my face. "Your cheeks are rosier than usual. Are you feeling okay? You didn't touch the iron, did you?"

"No, I'm fine," I said.

I did feel different today, but it had to be the tasks we were facing. The uncomfortable queasiness and the anxiety threatened to send me to bed. I pushed forward and ignored it, but she drew my attention back to it. Nerves weren't my thing. I'd fought vampires and multiple battles with my only worry being for my loved ones.

And there was plenty to get worked up about this evening. That had to be it. The risks and the plans and our futures hinged on this one plan. A little knot formed in my belly. I inhaled a deep breath and squeezed her hand.

"I'm good, Mom," I said. "Let's just get through tonight."

She smiled. "Let him rest. He needs his strength tonight too."

"Yes, ma'am. See you in a couple of hours."

She shut the door behind her.

Nick pulled me to him. "I don't want to rest."

I yawned.

"But it looks like you need to."

"I don't know where that came from," I said. "I swear I wasn't tired a minute ago."

I studied him. His dark hair was still shiny like the day we met. His eyes were still a color of green that would make the Caribbean jealous. His jaw still perfect right down to the stubble grazing it. Being a witch hadn't changed him, except for the small crinkle around his eyes now.

"What are you thinking?"

"How much I love you," I said.

"And how much is that?" He asked.

He rarely asked me to express my love, and I would happily indulge him. "I love you more than the moon and more than the stars. I love you with my mortality and my hereafter. Every last part of me is yours."

He kissed me. "Even your lips?"

"Yes."

"Even your neck?" He pressed a hot kiss behind my ear.

Chills ran down my body. "Yes."

"I like all these yeses from you." He nibbled on my earlobe.

"Mmm hmmm."

A knock rapped on the door. I closed my eyes against the disturbance. "Brie? Are you in there?" Brandon's voice carried through the door.

I sighed. "Yes, coming."

"Not yet," Nick whispered but rolled away.

"Unfortunately," I whispered back and climbed off the bed. I opened the door. "What's up?"

Brandon's face lit up with excitement. "Dad found something, and he said you'd want to see it."

"Oh, he must have found our ancestor's name." I looked at Nick. He appeared much stronger.

"Go on, my love. I'll be along in a minute." He caressed my cheek. He glanced at Brandon. "You too."

Brandon snickered. "Just don't call me 'my love.' My husband wouldn't like it."

Nick laughed. "Go you two." He waved us off.

I hurried down to the office with Brandon on my heels. Sorin was leaning against the desk.

Dad looked up when I walked into the office. "His name is Rowan."

"Rowan?" I echoed.

"Yes, and he was very powerful for a warlock, even more so than the queen. The queen originally sought him out for that reason, but they fell in love, and everything changed."

"As it often does," I said. "So, she married knowing he was the more powerful witch?"

Brandon took a seat in front of Dad.

"It was a love match," I whispered.

"When did it change? Why did he become vampire?" Brandon asked.

I dropped into the other chair in front of the desk.

Dad turned the book toward me. "They were working on the dark magic spell that created the vampires, and he decided to try it on himself."

Damn. I glanced at Brandon. His mouth gaped open.

"Why would he do that?" I asked.

"They had an agreement that she would turn him back, but he thought he would understand more if he experienced everything a vampire did." Sorin shook his head.

"Then he didn't want to be a witch again?" I glanced down at my fingers in my lap. The gravity of his decision on what started as a simple act reminded me of some of my own choices. The guilt from those choices ate at me.

"No, but she had promised him that no matter what she would turn him back," he said, his tone riddled with sadness.

"And that's why she tricked him into it and did it anyway," I said. "What about their son?"

"The image you saw must be what Rowan perceived to have happened. The boy lived and is a great-grandparent for us about 7 generations back."

Goddess. He mixed reality and the fiction of his own making and twisted into a purgatory he couldn't escape. "Do we know what happened to the son?"

"He did not practice magic after that day, but the coven suspected he was powerful like Rowan. A warlock tried to siphon magic from him. He went into hiding after that with a small group of supporters and caregivers."

"Sounds familiar," I said. "It's like history is repeating its mistakes." *Dad. Me. It seems like a cycle we can't break. Only we must break it this time.*

Dad sat the book down on the desk and focused his gaze on me. "But it's not. You are learning from our ancestors and your own experiences. Just have faith in yourself and what you are trying to do."

"I want to, Dad," I said, the stress evident in my voice. "But it's hard to not have anxiety about it when I have watched all of you die twice now, and you three times considering the first battle."

He sat down next to me and pulled me into a hug. "I am so proud of you for challenging and pushing limits, Brie." He extended an arm out for Brandon. "Both of you."

"Thank you." I'm sure that should have quieted my nerves, but the pressure grew. It made my stress worse. "I just feel like I'm the problem most of the time."

'No, you're not," he said. "And I'm so sorry I tried to force you to make a decision I thought would stop this prophecy. There wasn't anything that you could or couldn't have done that wouldn't have led us here."

These were the words I wanted to hear. The ones I needed to hear. *So why don't I feel better?*

"Let me tell you about Alastair and Fergus," I said. Dad let go of us and gestured for me to continue. It was very relaxed for him. I went through what I'd overheard in a methodical pattern.

"And you didn't go after them there," he said. "I'm impressed."

"I wanted to," I said. "I started to, but Ivy held me back," I confessed.

He nodded. "You took advice from a trusted source and adjusted course, Brie. That's what leaders do. You are growing every day, whether you see it or not."

Brandon looked me over. "How are you feeling? You have dark circles under your eyes."

"I am a little tired today. My nerves have my stomach upset too."

Dad picked up the book and flipped the pages. "If you're not too tired, I'd like to show you a passage. Then you can go get some rest."

"Of course," I said, curious about what else he had found.

He opened the book and handed it to me.

I scanned the words and couldn't believe the sentences in front of me. "Is this true? Do you think he really saw this coming?"

Sorin looks resigned. "He knew his descendant would eventually be the one to save him, and he knew it would be during a Blood Moon Tetrad as part of The Blood Moon Prophecy."

A twinge in my stomach echoed my concern. "What if they don't show here tonight? What if they are so sure we will come to them?"

"Then we live to fight another day, but Alastair isn't known for his patience. I don't think he will miss this opportunity."

"There are so many things that can go wrong," I said.

"But you only need one path that is right," Sorin said. "Go get some rest." He turned to Brandon. "Both of you. We all need to be alert when the sun goes down."

The sun set and the moon started to rise, and I hadn't been able to rest. I emptied the contents of my stomach twice. Nerves like this were a new experience for me.

I checked the faraday cage. It looked like the way zoos used to keep animals a long time ago. It was necessary but made me cringe. I walked the perimeter and validated the crystal placements for accuracy. This spell could start when the Blood Moon reached its peak in what the humans called the witching hour. Alastair and Fergus's plan could throw off our timing if they showed up too close before or after the start of the incantation. It would be disastrous.

"Crew and Dahlia arrived with a handful of witches," Brandon said from behind me where everyone gathered.

"They did?" I said, surveying our group and stepping into place for the incantation. "They never openly choose sides."

"Then you should feel honored," he said.

"The only way I'll feel honored is if we can spare lives and still accomplish our goal today."

Brandon patted my back. "It's war, and we have to accept that."

This wasn't a war of our choosing, but I would do everything I could to see us through. *Goddess. Ancestors. Be with us tonight and protect us on our path.*

"Time to start," Cal said. He took his place in the outer circle with Mom, Clara, and Ivy. Mom called each of the directions to the circle. They would be the second line of defense behind Malachi, Ella, and Alan further down the passage. Mom's circle held a barrier spell around us that would only invite Rowan to our private party.

It was my turn to call my circle. I inhaled the sage to cleanse my thoughts. Brandon stood at the East, and Sorin took the West. Nick took the North and I would take the South at the end. My husband's presence calmed me, but I was aware this was a risk with someone so new to casting. Nerves pushed aside, I began. *Here we go. Goddess be with us.* I stood in front of Brandon. "East, we call you to the circle breathe life into us and grant us inspiration.

I skipped the South since that would be me and faced Sorin. "West, we call you to the circle for empathy and reflection."

Another quarter turn to my husband. His first time participating as a direction, but he took it on like he'd done it a hundred times. "North, we call you to the circle to balance us and bring wisdom to our decisions tonight.

I moved into my Southern post. "South, we call you to

the circle for transformation and action as we bring to an end The Blood Moon Prophecy.

The air swirled around us with a mix of earth, ocean, and smoke scents. This powerful circle could do many things, but we had one unified goal tonight. Release Rowan from his purgatory, which should alone stop Alastair and Fergus. It eliminated the power source they needed to make their plan work. I'd end Alastair if he showed up. He wouldn't be given an opportunity to try to resurrect this poor soul again. Fergus wasn't any better, but his hands weren't as directly dirty as Alastair's. Politically, I needed to expose his deeds to justify whatever his punishment would be, and I'd let the coven decide that.

I steadied myself for the ritual. The power coursed through our circle, and I looked to Sorin to start the incantation that would bring Darkness wholly to us. He nodded.

"East, South, West, and North, our air, fire, water, and earth, we need you today. A mistake was made many moons ago, and it spiraled into Darkness. We seek to right that wrong. Bring forth to us all that is Darkness, so that we might name him and find a peaceful resolution. We want to bring forth only good, but we need your help tonight," I said with anticipation.

"Darkness will find a name and an end will come to this game," I said.

Nick, Dad, and Brandon joined me to repeat it. "Darkness will find a name and an end will come to this game."

Magic liked threes, so we repeated it a third time "Darkness will find a name and an end will come to this game."

The center of the circle shimmered and filled with a black smoke-like aura. It worked. *He's here.* The door to the faraday cage was open. "In you go if you want my help. Otherwise, I will banish you."

I didn't know if I was strong enough to follow through on that threat, but I didn't have to find out. He floated into the cage. Nick pushed the door closed with his foot. He didn't want to touch it after his earlier experience. I didn't blame him.

"Rowan, as your descendant, I greet you." Once I named him, he materialized. Not fully corporal but not mist. His face was startling. It was like Sorin's twin. His features were identical to my father's. I glanced back and forth between them.

Sorin's eyes narrowed like he was trying to see through the man.

Rowan inhaled a deep breath. "I haven't taken a breath in centuries."

"You speak English?" Brandon asked. I glanced at him, and his forehead wrinkled.

"Darkness speaks all languages," Rowan said, as he stood inside the cage. "As I, also, know you are of me, Brandon."

"I'm your descendant too, yes," Brandon shot me some side-eye. "At least that is what I am told." His skepticism rolled off and struck me. Even with the similarities, he didn't trust an apparition.

"You remind me of myself at your age," Rowan said and turned to me. "But you, Brie, are so much more than I could have ever been." The wonder in his eyes made me curious about what he meant. He was an eternal entity for centuries.

I was a very mortal witch who would have a death whenever that day may come.

"How so?"

"You are the only one I've ever seen who could co-exist with me," he paused. "Or with Darkness. Though Darkness and I are the same but not."

Somehow, I understood what he meant. It was almost symbiotic between us. The Darkness that was him was in me and my father, but it was not all that we are. I could have let bitterness lead me down the same path, but I had the love and support of some of the most amazing individuals. My chest expanded with gratitude for them.

"The choice you were asked to make, Sorin," Rowan looked at him. "And you, Brielle. It was my fault. My painfully wrong choices passed down in a spiral to you, and for that, I cannot begin to express how sorrowful I am. The prophecy was put in place to make sure I never walk this earth again."

"There are some that wish to bring you back among us," Sorin said.

"We cannot let that happen. It is time for me to move on. I've mourned my queen and my son for too long. I'm ready to be with them."

I let out a breath. He was ready to be reunited with his family.

"I've been given an incantation to allow you to pass on, but I need to know I have your permission. I won't do what your queen was forced to do. I need to hear you say it," I said.

He met my gaze with translucent blue-grey eyes. "I want

to be with her, Brielle, and there is only one way to where she is."

"And what if this doesn't work," I said, afraid I wasn't the right person for it. That the power would tempt me. "I'm not sure even my magic is strong enough for it."

"You know that's not true," he said. "You know the truth is that you are strong enough, and with three warlock anchors." He passed a gaze over Sorin, Brandon, and Cal. "And a dual conduit." His gaze turned to Nick.

I hadn't planned on anyone channeling except me. Putting Nick into a channeling position for a spell of this magnitude wasn't the plan. The risk was supposed to be all mine. This was Summerland not portaling into the Great House. "He's not our bloodline."

"No, but he is your equal, even though he doesn't know it yet. You will not bear the same burdens my wife and I did. The ancestors will warm to him and smile on this union. There has already been a good omen." He smiled between Nick and me.

"A good omen?" I asked, but it dawned on me what he meant. "That Nick survived the transformation back to a warlock."

He didn't agree, but he didn't deny it either. He moved to the center of the faraday cage. "Let's begin."

In the two times I lived this day before, this was the time we entered the throne room. The hope was that any decisions they made about invading here would be made after we'd released Rowan. My concern for this spell was opening the space for Rowan to travel to the afterlife. It had never been done that I knew of, and I didn't know if he would be allowed entrance to Summerland. *Where would he go? Back to an ethereal existence?*

"I feel your worry, and I do not know the answers either," Rowan said. "But my wife and my son are there, and I must try."

I worried he would cease to exist at all if he was rejected from Summerland, but if it were me, I'd choose my family too. "We have everything prepared, and it shouldn't take long."

"Do you need to close the first circle?" Brandon asked.

"No, it's a circle of three. Mom's circle being one, our first circle being two, and then this being three."

The four of us took our positions around the faraday cage, and I centered to open the third circle. *Goddess, please bless this journey. Ancestors, I need your strength if you are willing to help.*

I stood in front of Brandon as I had for the first one. "East, we call you to grant the air we need to travel today.

I skipped the South in the order and moved on to Sorin. "West, we call you to the circle for understanding on our journey."

I continued around the circle to my husband. "North, we call you to the circle to ground us here in this time and connect us to Summerland.

I moved around the wheel to my Southern post. "South, we call you to the circle to light the way of this powerful change."

The answer came in a clap of thunder and gusts of wind. The scent of rain dotted the air.

"I'm not sure if that is a yes or a no, but we'll proceed," I said.

"Our ancestors are not sure either," Rowan said. "But if they are reluctant, it is because of me and not you."

"Nick, for a dual conduit, you'll need to stand beside me. We must be touching." Nick walked around the cage to me. *Goddess, be with us on this journey as you have throughout.* I locked eyes with Nick. *And protect my husband.*

I glanced at Cal. "Ready?"

"Yes, My Queen." He fisted a hand over his heart.

"Brandon, what about you?" I met his gaze.

"I was born ready, Sis."

"Dad?" I looked over my shoulder.

"I'm ready."

This has to work. I cleared my mind and fixated on our task. Everything stilled around me. I was only aware of our ritual.

"Nick and I will link first. Then, I'll open to you three," I said. "Once I start the incantation, you must remain focused. The link must remain steady for me to escort Rowan to Summerland."

Nick shifted beside me. "You didn't say you had to escort him to the afterlife."

"Just to the edge. I won't enter," I said, unsure if it would be enough to get him across.

"That's a foolish chance," Nick said.

"He is right to be concerned, Brielle," Rowan said. "This is risky even to one as strong as you."

There wasn't another option. "It's risky for you to remain

here too. What if Alastair and Fergus figure out how to bring you here as Darkness and all your power?"

"You've already done that for them, Brielle," Rowan said.

Fuck. Was this playing into their hand? I glanced around for signs of an army. There were no noises. Rowan was Darkness. Manipulation was a strength of Darkness.

"Are you doing this so they can free you? I do all the hard work, but they finish it?"

"No, I wouldn't do that to my family," he said.

But he had turned on his family. Brandon didn't trust him and hadn't from the beginning. *Am I just wanting to see the good in him?*

I'd come this far and drug my family into it. The alternative was facing off at the castle to die, and I wasn't reliving that day again.

Nick had turned his back to me. I rested my hand on his low back. His body was wound tight with stress. He needed my reassurance.

"Talk to me," I said.

"This is risky, Brie," he said. "Very risky."

"But if we don't do this, we'll die again. You might not know the agony of watching me die but it was torture seeing you die twice."

"I do understand that. I watched you in a coma for almost a month. I watched your vitals whither, knowing death would take you soon.," he said, his voice cracked.

"Then you understand why we have to do it," I said. "Don't you?"

I looked up to meet his gaze, but he averted his eyes. My

heart clenched that he refused to connect with me in our way.

He gritted his teeth. "What if you can't come back?"

"I'll be back, Nick. I'm not going into Summerland." I rested my hand against his cheek.

"But what if you don't? What happens to me?" He'd suffered from my words and actions that lead us to this place, and his biggest fear was an existence without me. His love was my strength.

"You will know that you will join me one day after you live a very long and happy warlock life," I said, my throat knotted by the thought of not living that life with him. "Your second chance will be magnificent whether I'm here or not."

"When I was vampire, I'd planned to end my existence when you died," he said.

"I remember," I said. "And I told you then, I didn't support that."

"And I'd do it now too."

I shook my head. His death would destroy me even in the afterlife. He had to live and have babies even if it wasn't with me. "But I don't want you to do that," I said. "We don't know when it is our time, so we live what we can and face the other when the time comes."

He inhaled a deep breath. His breathing was still awkward. He could understand Rowan in a way the rest of us couldn't. They were the only two who had been through a transformation like this.

"All I need you to do is hold onto my hand and focus on my words. I'll guide our energy. Dad, Brandon, and Cal will anchor us to the here and now. They will make sure we don't use our life force to power the spell. It's not without risk, but there isn't anyone else I would trust to do this with."

"I trust you. I don't trust my abilities," he said.

"I got you," I said, confident in my ability to get us through this ritual. "There will be days when I need you to have me, but today, I've got you."

He reached for my hand. I squeezed it and led him back to his position in the circle.

THIRTY-THREE

Rowan's figure shimmered in and out, never quite complete. "His concern is valid."

"It certainly is," I said.

The power of the circle dominated the space. I thrust out my hand and drew it to me. Our ancestors didn't resist the request, but I could taste their concern in the current.

Nick fluctuated, his unsurety causing waves. Each one of us played a specific role and had to be on point for it. Any little mistake or deviation could result in failure of the spell and unleash the power from the incantation. A rupture from a stockpile of magic might kill us all. That was not an option in my book.

I leaned close to Nick and whispered. "The ancestors are helping us. Just relax and let me drive."

He blew out a breath and nodded.

I recited the incantation.

"Love was lost in darkness

Darkness was once a witch

But then his path led to a switch.

Although he is ready to revert

His destiny is blocked.

We need the door to Summerland manually unlocked."

The energy streamed from Nick and me between the cage. It swirled into a tunnel. The sound, like a tornado, was almost deafening. Our success hinged on our next actions.

"Anchors ready?"

"Ready," Sorin said.

"Ready," Brandon said.

"Ready," Cal said, his voice strained. He was the outside anchor, tethered to Mom's circle.

"Stay here and breathe steady," I said to Nick.

"Got it," he said. "Hurry back."

I let go of his hand and walked to the cage door. I unlatched it, careful not to get a piece under my skin, and held my hand out to Rowan. His hand was solid but lighter than a witch's.

"Finally," he said.

Our hands firmly together we moved into the portal to Summerland. White light blinded me as soon as we stepped through. I recognized the room where Grandmother had met me as her younger self. The flowy white curtains billowed in the open space. I relaxed in the knowledge we made it across the bridge to the entrance.

"We're here, Rowan." I turned to him. He was fully formed here.

"How do I find my family?" He asked, his voice full of eagerness and a smile on his face.

"Grandmother met me here, so maybe we just need to

wait here for them."

A feast had been set up on a large table. The colorful food of berries and fruit stood out against the whiteness of everything. I looked down to see my leather fighting suit in place, just like before. The faint sounds of the brook on the other side of the field meandered in the air. The peace of Summerland tempted me, but I was ready to live a long life with Nick and the rest of my loved ones.

He looked like the pictures of Dad from when he was younger. "Do you want to see yourself?"

"Am I grotesque?"

"Not at all." I looked around for the mirror I saw last time. It was on the wall adjacent to the feast. I guided him over to it.

He touched his face. "Is this real? Am I really in Summerland?"

"You are," I said. I gazed out the open doors, but I didn't see anyone in the fields. *Would his family just know he was here? Did I need to try to find Grandmother?*

I couldn't venture too far away from the entry, or I'd risk breaking the tether with my anchors. The field started with the grass just outside the open doors though. That shouldn't be too far.

"Let's step outside. Maybe we can see them coming from there."

Rowan stared down out the green grass. "You should wait here. I can go from here on my own."

"I've been this far before," I said. "It's fine." Grandmother had guided me to this point, and it was my turn to guide Rowan. Family helped family.

"I have a strange feeling about it," he said.

I patted his arm. He stepped down, and I stepped down next to him.

A tug yanked me back a step, but I pushed forward. "Grandmother?" I called.

Rowan knelt and ran his hand over the grass. "It feels like soft bedding. I want to lay down and look up at the sky." He tilted his head back and gazed up.

"It is beautiful here," I said. The peace of this place calmed in a way I'd only experienced in Summerland.

"Brie," Grandmother's voice drifted over my shoulder. I turned to see her with her arms open. I hugged her. Love spread around me as if I could almost see it.

"I missed you," I said.

"And I you, dear granddaughter," she said. "You should go back though. This is not your time."

"I'm helping a long-lost relative find his family," I said.

"I know who he is." She studied him. "Rowan, the decision is pending on whether you will be allowed to stay."

His shoulders sagged, a defeated look on his face. I'd advocate for him. It's why I was here.

"He's not the same person he was then," I said. "They know that, right? Do we need to talk to them? And who is making the decision?"

Grandmother smiled. "Always so full of questions," she said. "His family, the ones he remembers, are meeting with the Goddess. She will decide, but they will have to offer their thoughts."

"And he doesn't get to speak on his own behalf?"

"This is an unusual circumstance. I don't know that there

is a precedent for it.," she said. "You should go. I can stay with him."

"I can't leave him here," I said. "Not knowing." *If he were denied entry, would where would they send him? Hell?* I couldn't let that happen. There had to be something I could say or do to prove to them he was a changed person.

"This isn't like your visit last time. You are tethered, and the longer you stay here the weaker the tether becomes."

"Go, Brielle," he said. "I'd like to get to know your grandmother."

Grandmother looped her arm through mine and turned me back towards the way we came. "I'll take care of him until they make a decision."

"And if they decide to not let him in," I said. "What happens then?"

"I can't say, but I imagine he is either returned to earth or somewhere a little warmer."

I looked at Rowan. He placed a hand on my shoulder. "You have done more for me than I deserve. I accept whatever decisions they make, and I will not fight them on it." His touch was gentle and calm. He smiled, and his eyes creased like it was genuine.

I don't know what came over me, but I hugged him. I hugged the embodiment of Darkness.

The tether tightened and hauled me backward at the waist. "Grandmother."

The right thing, the thing I needed to do, was let the tether pull me back, but I wanted to stay and help. Grandmother had said she would stay with Rowan, and that was what he needed. Someone to stand with him while he learned his fate.

She leaned in and gave me a quick hug. "Go," she whispered.

The magical line wrenched me through the portal, and I landed hard on the ground at the base of the cage. Nick extended his hand and pulled me to my feet. Stressed creased his face in harsher lines now that he was a witch. "They're here. Fergus and Alastair."

I glanced at the smartwatch on my wrist and panicked. "It's about the time we died the first two times."

"Then let's not make it a third," Nick said.

"We need to close the circles," I said. "We can't leave the portal open." I moved clockwise around the circle.

"Goddess and guardians, our witness tonight
North, East, South, and West
I thank you for your power and showing here
This circle has ended, and my work is done
By the Goddess and ancestors in the power of the Moon
Blessed be."

I repeated it on the first circle. A moment of relief rested over me, but fear of the unknown ahead grew. These events hadn't been lived yet. No visions to guide us.

"Now, Mom."

She worked quickly to close hers, freeing us all to stand with our small force and fight.

I moved quickly down the hall and could hear the footsteps of the others behind me. The shouting from outside filtered through the walls. The world had been rid of Darkness, at least for now, but there was still evil to face.

THIRTY-FOUR

Our little but powerful force emerged and faced the open field. The safe house was no longer a mystery location. Across the space was the evil of our time. The battle came to us.

Alastair and Fergus were at the head of the group in front of us. It looked like the stories we heard from the Salem Witch Trials when the mobs would gather. There were no pitchforks or torches, but there were flashlights, a few energy manifestations, and some kind of weapon I didn't recognize. There were easily double the number we had here if not more, and his numbers included a significant force of vampires on the front row.

"We can't stand against that many," I said to no one in particular. "Not even with the power we possess."

"Lead your people, Brie. That's all you must do tonight," Sorin said.

"We're behind you, Sis," Brandon said.

"We will always follow you, My Queen," Cal said.

I turned to face Nick, terrified I would watch him, and the others die again. "You don't need to ask me, my love, but I'm with you every step of the way." He kissed my cheek.

Clara and Ivy were on the other side of him. They nodded in unison.

Directly behind us were Malachi and Ella. "We're vampires," Malachi said. "We fight."

Crew and Dahlia stood beside Alan. The three of them fisted their hands over their hearts and bowed their heads.

The respect and support brought tears to my eyes, but there was no time for crying tonight.

"Let's go take out some traitors and restore order then," I said.

We filed out in front of our enemies, and I recalled the battle where this all started. Where my father died, and I brought him back unknowingly. The size of our forces had grown and shrunk over time, but if we were able to manage to win tonight, we'd win the war. Those who wished to destroy this life would be stopped, and peace would be ours.

"Where is our friend?" Alastair called.

"We have no mutual friends," I yelled back across the field in my booming queen voice.

"Our friend, Darkness, why is he not here?" He asked, genuine confusion in his voice.

"I don't know what you mean," I said with fake innocence.

"You need to call him here, Brielle," Fergus said. "He must pay for his crimes."

"Hmm..." I gave it fake thought. "No, I don't think I will."

"So, you are embracing Darkness over your people?" Fergus asked, glancing from side to side.

"No, I didn't say that. I'm offering someone with a messed up past forgiveness," I said. "Are you not familiar with forgiveness? I would think an elder would be after all."

"Don't toy with him, Brie," Sorin said. "We don't need him angry."

"I'm angry I'm going to have to spare Fergus," I said. He'd let Alastair be the figurehead, and I didn't have enough proof to justify ending him.

"Or not," Brandon said. "You might have to spare him, but the rest of us don't have to make that decision."

"We have to play the politics, brother."

"You almost sound like a queen," Brandon said.

"Imagine that," I said, drawing an energy ball. I grew it in my palm, large and proud as a sign of strength.

Brandon followed with his and then Dad formed one. I met Nick's gaze. His eyes were unsure.

"It's an extension of you and your magic. If you're timid with it, that's the reaction you'll get. If you're overzealous, you might blow something up." I laughed. "Kidding but not."

I split my single energy ball into two large ones, one for each hand.

Nick held out his palm and a red energy spike flew into the air like a shooting star. *Impressive even if he didn't mean to do it.* To his credit, he held it about ten feet above us.

"They're going to think you did it on purpose, let them," I said. "Now pull it back down and split it between your hands like I did."

He reigned it in and split it like he'd done it dozens of times. He was a natural and didn't know it.

"Good," I said. "Make sure you are focused on where you are going with it when you throw them."

"Got it," he said.

"I hit back if you hit me, brother-in-law or not," Brandon said, chuckling.

That earned a laugh from Nick. We shouldn't be joking, but this was us. Our family and the friends who had become family. Maybe it would worry Fergus that we weren't begging for our lives.

"Everyone ready?" I walked around and looked into the face of as many of our small but strong group as possible. "They make the first move. We hold until they do. In our history, success has been found in greater odds. We can and will be victorious. This will be the beginning of a better world for all." I clapped my hands together and blue flames shot up into the night sky and burst like fireworks erupting above us.

I returned to my place at the front. If we die tonight, it is with a clear conscience and knowing we were on the righteous side.

"Now that sounded like a queen," Brandon said.

Nick cleared his throat.

"Focus. We have work to do," I said. "But we can put on a little display while we wait."

Brandon rubbed his hands together and sparks flew like small metal shavings from welding.

"Follow our lead," I said to the rest of the front row.

Brandon and I stepped out the width of our strides.

I stepped a few feet away, ran in his direction, and leaped in an aerial. I released blue light before I flipped into the air in front of him. He shot energy balls into the night sky while I was upside down. He fired into the air again and performed a back handspring. I jumped to the spot he'd been standing and threw out a rapid release of energy balls. Others displayed their gifts. The message was clear. We would not go easily or without a fight with everything we had at our disposal.

Alastair's voice shouted out, unimpressed. "Surrender or die, Brielle Danforth."

"It's Brie Domenico, Queen of the Witches, and you do not command me or my subjects." *Mother fucker.* I added in silence to the end of it.

"Brielle, surely you understand that we must clean up your mess," Fergus's voice traveled easily over the wind.

"My mess?" I said. "I believe you are referring to your mess since you conspired with the traitor next to you to release Darkness on the world." For every false statement he wanted to hurl, I'd rebut it with the truth whether anyone believed it or not at least it would be said.

"But you have Darkness hidden for yourself, and we can't let that stand," he said, his tone mocking innocence as I had earlier.

"Once again you are wrong, Fergus," I said. "Michael was right not to trust you. I'm glad I had him to confide it because you've had your own agenda that isn't about the greater good."

"I'm not sure what you mean, especially when you are the one harboring Michael's killer." Fergus feigned shock.

I couldn't argue it, but I wouldn't let it go. "That is the only truth you have spoken, and yet it is still not a complete truth. Michael's death was a request because he was afraid of what you would do with the knowledge he had."

"Are you so jaded by the vampire in your bed to see the truth?" Bodies stirred in his line at that statement, and I was sure they must be the vampires woven into his ranks. Alastair had them under his control.

"It shouldn't matter, but I don't have a vampire in my bed. Thanks to Michael that vampire has been returned to his original state of a witch. My husband is a warlock now." The gasps were audible, but those on our side had seen Nick wield his magic. The whispers passed around the crowd.

"Lies," Fergus yelled. "There is no spell that can reverse that change."

"Apparently, there is, since I did it," I said. "Anything is possible with enough power and the right spell."

"Brie, you're taunting," Sorin said.

I nodded. I was, and that was the intention. Fergus didn't possess the same power, and he wanted to control what he didn't have.

"Is it true?" Alastair's voice came through. "You were able to reverse Nick's vampirism." I appraised my husband next to me for the gifted warlock he was now.

"It is," I said. "Thanks to Michael."

"And he is a witch not human?" Alastair asked, his voice faltered in strength.

"Yes, he was a witch before he was turned, so a witch is what he is now. I don't think a human would survive it," I said. Alastair's wheels were always turning, so I knew he was looking at an alternative should things not go as he planned.

Raised but intelligible words floated across the field. I couldn't tell who spoke. The sentiment was anger, but I couldn't understand a word of it.

"You must come with us, Brielle," Fergus said. "And bring Darkness. This is the only way we will allow your family to live."

Showtime.

"I will not bend to your commands, Fergus. The fact that you want to kill my family if I don't comply is the exact reason I shouldn't." His madness became more evident with each word he spoke. It reminded me of Rowan's story.

"You will lose everything if you fight us." His tone was almost regretful like he would be sad if I were to die.

"I'll lose everything if I don't stop you."

He didn't know that this was our third time living this night, and we were all ready to die if that's what it took. I'd give every ounce of myself to keep my family from succumbing to a fate inflicted by him.

Fergus and Alastair's forces split, but I'd anticipated that. Ours split as well. Brandon along with Cal, Clara, Mom, and Malachi took half of our force to meet the other group.

Nick, Ivy, Sorin, Ella, and Alan stayed with me. Alan and Ella made their way through the ranks pumping up the supporters. They were soldiers, but so few had combat experience, I hesitated to refer to them as such.

The first shot they fired was aimed in a direct route at me. I spun and flung an energy ball at it. It blew apart as if on command. The battle began, and I was ready for whatever my destiny was meant to be. Live or die. This was it.

The number of energy balls increased in our direction. We deflected them with ease. They weren't trying to hurt us. The tactic used was meant to wear us down.

They moved closer with every round of exchanges. Stefan had used the same tactic on us when we fought him. I wondered if Alastair learned it from him or the other way around. Not that it mattered.

"Let's freak them out a little. Who's going to cover me?" I hadn't levitated in a while, but most had only heard of my many gifts and not seen them in action. A show of power might empower our forces while intimidating theirs. Levitation wasn't my most useful skill, but this seemed like the perfect opportunity for it.

"For what?" Nick asked.

"I'm going high in the sky," I said.

Nick shook his head.

"I've got you if he can't," Ivy said.

"Up I go." I leaped like I was a cape-wearing superhero in a comic book. The height control worked better than speed. For some reason, levitation only moved forward and backward at a turtle's pace. Up or down worked like a rocket. It made no sense.

I floated above the battlefield and rapid fired blue energy balls at them. As I expected, my actions drew the bulk of the fire. I dodged the bulk of the shots I could by moving up and down, and what I didn't, I could see Nick and Ivy's energies take out. Most importantly, our group was able to get off several good shots against our enemy.

Movement in front of Alastair and Fergus drew my attention. A man knelt in front of them with something that looked similar to a bazooka, and it was aimed in my direction. He fired off a round, and I could see sparks dripping off it as it came at me. I moved up and down, but it zeroed in on me. No matter where I tried to move, I couldn't shake it. It had latched on to me. Come on.

Someone hit it with an energy ball. None came. *At least this death isn't in vain, I did something good today. Goddess protect my loved ones.*

I peered through squinted slits anticipating the impact. A red flash came from the corner of my sight and collided with the projectile. It exploded, and the shock wave knocked me backward. I slammed into the stone face of the house. The air was knocked out of my lungs. I couldn't get my breath or focus to keep levitating. I dropped like a rock.

Something will break. When I looked down at the ground, Nick was there to catch me. I landed in his arms, and his steady grasp pulled me tight to his chest.

"Are you okay?" He whispered in my hair.

I gasped for air until my lungs filled. "I will be. Just got the wind knocked out of me."

"Sorry. My energy balls only go so fast."

"Same with my levitation," I said. "Let's get back in this fight."

"No one will ever call you weak, my love."

We made our way back to the front, and it struck me how far that was for him to go.

"How did you get around there so fast? You don't have vampire speed anymore. Do you?"

"I don't know if it was vampire speed, but it was fast," he said sounding amazed.

"Impressive. I wonder if that is what Rowan meant about you being my equal." I tossed an energy ball to deflect an incoming one. "When this is over, we're going to put you through the tests we use on witches who are discovering their powers. You might have some other hidden talents."

Hope we had changed enough this time around to survive dance through my mind.

Another energy ball came right at us. Nick caught it and threw it back in the other direction like a pro. "Did Ivy show you that?"

He smiled. "She did, and a couple of other tricks."

"Any word on how the other team is doing?"

"No, they haven't checked in, but neither have we."

I surveyed the soldiers along the way. We had few injuries which surprised me. I wondered how many were wounded on the other side.

I turned my attention back to the field and saw more than a dozen people step forward on the other side with those bazooka-like guns. As I tried to count, more of them showed up. This was ugly. One had nearly taken me out. It would be impossible to face down them all. *Are Brandon and Mom facing the same thing?* Those weapons had to go or we would have fatalities.

"Nick, we can't take out that many at once," I said. "Where's Dad?"

"He's right there next to Ivy and Alan."

I moved next to him and pointed to the new equipment. "Dad, those have some kind of beacon on their target. It can't be shaken, and we can't stop them all."

"Then, we'll protect you and Nick," he said.

"No, Dad," I said. "We need to take them out before they..."

One bang after another sounded off. Everything went into slow motion for me. *Everything we tried to change, and we're still arriving at this moment.*

Dad pushed me behind him, and Nick stood at my side. I flinched with each boom. And knew exactly who at least eleven of those shots were meant for on this field. I could teleport them, but I wasn't sure I could get to us all in time. "Goddess, what do we do?"

Tears burned my eyes. There wasn't anything within my power unless the ancestors wanted to supercharge me again. The feeling didn't take over though, so I knew we were on our own.

I flailed my hands out on either side of Sorin and let strings of energy balls go in hopes they would distract what was coming for us. I looked around Dad, and not one of them connected.

Nick's fingers laced through mine, and I gripped Dad's elbow. I could teleport them. At least they would survive.

A dark mass appeared on the field between our groups. The swirl of a portal appeared in the mass. It grew larger until it was big enough for someone to walk through. It was too far away for us to reach before the personal bombs hit us.

A figure stepped out. *Rowan.* He shouldn't be here. *Did they kick him out of Summerland? Wouldn't they have sent him to Hell?* He appeared fully corporeal. *What is he doing here?* I stepped around Dad, but he held me back.

"Watch him," he said.

Darkness grew around him like a tornado. It pulled all the little bombs toward it. They imploded in on themselves with little snippets of light when they reached the swirling mass.

He cleared them and stalked toward Alastair. "You have a

dark soul. Perhaps darker than mine, but you lack the power to control it."

Rowan put his hand on Alastair's chest and drew it back. He sucked all the darkness from Alastair. It flowed out of Alastair like dirty flood water. His body dropped to the ground. Rowan turned to Fergus. Fergus back peddled away from him. "I should do the same to you, but Brie has another plan for your punishment. I will warn you not to cross her though."

Fergus dropped to his knees.

Rowan marched over to me. "I can't kill anyone, Brie. That was part of my negotiations."

"Are you going to be able to go back? Did they kick you out?"

"The fact that your first question is about my afterlife is exactly why I had to come," he said. "Yes, I will be allowed back. They have granted me sanctuary in Summerland, but they cannot hold me there. My power is beyond that."

"And your family?"

"They are there and welcomed me. We have some mending that needs to be done, but it will be fine."

"I'm so happy for you, Rowan," I said, almost forgetting the battle he stunned into a pause. "There is so much hope for all of us in your story."

"I have to leave, but I wanted to thank you," Rowan said. "Though generations separate us, you are part of my family." He took a couple of steps toward the portal but stopped and turned around. A smile grew across his face. "And take care of your child. Never leave him."

"My child?" My hand covered my belly. *It can't be. Can it?*

"Yes, your child. He will be very important." He stepped through the portal, and it closed.

I looked at Nick. "A child." The news sank into my soul and sang a song I didn't ever think I'd hear. *I'm going to be a mother.* Joy consumed me as powerfully as the connection Nick and I shared.

"Did he mean you're..." Nick trailed off.

"I don't know. I think so," I said. My mind flashed to being slammed against the wall.

Fear creased Nick's face. "Earlier, when you — "

I put a finger over his lips. "If anything happened, he would have known, and our bodies are resilient."

Brandon ran past me. He was safe. Relief mixed with my joy. "I'm going to arrest Alastair and Fergus," he said. "I want to be the one to bind Alastair and Fergus's magic."

I looked up at Nick. "I don't want to miss that either."

"But what about the baby?" Nick scanned the massive crowd.

This was the moment destiny had led us to, and the tyrants had been defeated. The forces would fall.

Fear gripped around my heart. *Would this baby ever be safe with Alastair and Fergus as a threat?*

Yelling across the field caught my attention. It looked like a scuffle between several people took place. I could make out Brandon in the middle of it. Nick and I jogged over to see what was happening.

Alastair laughed.

"If basically a God had just sucked what made me special out, I don't think I'd be laughing," I said.

He pressed his hand against my belly. "I know what Rowan saw. There is another chance within you."

I shoved his hand away. Alastair's madness exceeded Fergus's. He'd never be able to let this go.

Nick stepped forward and grabbed his collar.

I touched my husband's arm. "You're not a vampire anymore. Let him go. We'll deal with him like witches do."

Nick dropped him.

Alastair began to mumble something and stretched his fingers toward my belly. I could feel my little one fighting against whatever he did. Hexes weren't magic, but they were powerful. Magic could strengthen one, but he had none.

"Stop," I commanded.

His fingers dug against the leather of my fight suit. *I will not have my child cursed. Goddess, help me. Ancestors, help me.*

I swiped his hands away with a blue electrical charge.

Nick stepped into my view. "I've got this. I've been a witch longer."

Alastair lunged at me and tackled me to the ground. I gasped. The force knocked the air out of my lungs. I struggled against his weight. Nick's fingers wrapped around Alastair's arm, but Alastair increased the pressure on my neck the harder Nick pulled.

"You don't deserve it," he screamed in my face. "This power is not for you." Spit peppered my face. His eyes were wild, and I recognized the lost soul in front of me. He didn't have magic. All that was left was a cruel individual who would seek to destroy what he could not have. I wouldn't let him break me, and I wouldn't let him break my family. He might not have magic, but he was dangerous. He didn't need magic to kill me or my family. There was only one way to end this. I reconciled there would be no pleasure in this outcome.

"Brie," Nick's voice echoed in the wind.

"I've got this," I said, my voice calmer than it should have been. "I'm sorry," I whispered to Alastair. Not sorry for ending him but sorry he would not get to make amends to Cal or anyone else. Sorry there would be no redemption for him.

I pushed out with a magical shove, but my ancestors answered my call. My energy speared Alastair's chest. He fell backward away from me. A gaping hole, cauterized by the heat, remained in his chest. I killed my dear friend's father.

Nick helped me to my feet and looked me over, his hand rested on my belly.

I smiled up at him. "I'm fine," I said. "We're fine." I laid my hand over his.

Fergus knelt on the ground near Brandon. His hand fisted over his heart. *As if he respected anything about my authority.*

Brandon's forehead wrinkled.

"What's wrong?" I asked.

"The vampires won't leave," Brandon said. "And if we try to bind them, they are resisting."

Alastair's body lay on the ground, so it didn't seem to have anything to do with him. As if the soda bottle size hole where his heart wasn't enough, I knelt and checked for a pulse and confirmed he was dead. *So why aren't the vampires released from the control?*

"There has to be something else holding them in the spell. An enchanted object," I paused. "The Fire Book. He has to have the fucking Fire Book here."

"I'll start a search," Brandon said.

"Brother, I think you should go let Cal know the news. I'm willing to tell him, but I think he'd rather hear it from you than me." He may have disowned his father, but the finality of it would hit differently.

Brandon nodded, a solemn look on his face, and jogged back toward our line.

I'd killed someone tonight, and it wasn't like a hunt. I'd killed before. There was a lot of blood on my hands, but I'd have to reconcile my confusion later.

I wrapped my fingers around Fergus's chin and tilted his head up to face me. He'd been the mastermind behind the attempt to bring Rowan back to walk among us. He'd pulled the strings for Alastair from behind the stage. I didn't need his confirmation to know it, but I wanted to hear him say it.

My nails sunk into his skin as I squeezed. "Where is the Fire Book?"

He barked out a nervous laugh. "My Queen, I'm your humble servant."

I dug my nails in until blood pebbled on his skin. He winced.

"We can cut the shit, Fergus," I said. "Everyone here saw you working with Alastair tonight."

"No, My Queen, I was under his control. This was his plan." My internal lie detector rumbled to life inside me, and his lie stung against my skin.

"You are a liar on so many levels. You would sacrifice your own people for power, and you will pay for it one day." I wanted to reign Hell's Fire on him. Today was not the day for those dramatics though. Our people needed to see justice and not vigilante style.

I waved Alan over. "Take him to the iron cage and lock him up there."

"With pleasure, My Queen," Alan said.

I let go of Fergus's chin, and Alan slipped a hand under his arm to lift him to his feet. Alan's hands moved in a circular motion to create a temporary binding spell around Fergus's wrists.

Nick's arm slipped around my waist.

"Now, we just need to find the Fire Book and release your former people."

"They are still my people, even though I am changed," he said, his tone conflicted. "Too bad I can't just use the sire bond on them anymore."

"Try it," I said. "We don't have anything to lose. Focus on the vampires specifically. Think about breaking the spell and releasing them from the control it has on them."

Nick closed his eyes. I didn't advocate practicing magic with eyes closed, but it helped with concentration, especially for someone just learning.

"Don't overthink it," I whispered.

"Rich coming from you, my love." He chuckled.

"But I do know magic, husband. Just let go of your apprehension and let the magic lead you down the path."

Quiet settled between us. The vampires were stuck in limbo, and the witches were in a kneeling position. Our motley crew had filtered around to surround them.

Red light radiated from Nick and around us like a bubble. *Beautiful.*

"Open your eyes but hold your focus," I whispered.

"This is me?" The bubble rippled.

"Focus," I whispered. "Yes, this is you. Can you grow it? Push it out over the rest of the group."

He glanced around the field and narrowed his eyes. His hands went up with palms facing outward and pushed, like how I magically shoved Alastair off of me. I inhaled against the mixed feelings building inside of me and tamped them down for later. My husband was doing magic, and I wanted to be present in the moment.

Nick's bubble slid out like a wave rolling across the ocean. Magnificent for someone who had only been a witch a short time.

"You're doing great," I said, keeping my voice soft and relaxed. "Now, concentrate on releasing them. Visualize cutting the thread of the spell."

His actions worked fast like a practiced witch. The vampires around us blinked multiple times and had confused looks on their faces. They looked around like they were lost. Some turned in circles trying to find their bearings. Many walked off the battlefield in small groups. My husband, once the King of Vampires, was now the King of the Witches and my equal.

"You did it. You can let go now. Just pull the magic back to you." I kissed his cheek. He was flushed and warm from the exertion.

The red glow snapped like a rubber band. He stumbled back.

I steadied him. "That takes a little practice." I smiled up into his face. "You are amazing, my husband."

"If I am, it is only because you made me so, my wife." His hand caressed my face and slid into my hair. He leaned to me and pressed his lips against mine. His touch electrified me, our connection as strong as ever.

He pulled back and looked me in the eyes, intensifying the connection. His hand went to his chest. My arm burned. I unzipped the fighting suit and pulled it down over my shoulder. My mark had filled in. The Prophecy was done. I dropped to my knees. *Goddess, is it true?*

Thankful I'd put a tank top on under the leather this

time, I slid the other arm out and tied the two sleeves around my waist.

"Look at yours," I said.

Nick lifted his shirt, and the mark on his chest was filled in completely too. I ran my hand over it. Unadulterated relief fell over me. *Is this real?*

Tears pooled in my eyes. "Are we really done? Is it over?"

Nick pressed my hand against his chest with his own. "What do you want to do now that we have fulfilled the prophecy?"

"Be happy," I said.

He growled. "Anything else?"

"Spend lots of time in bed," I said. "Is that the right answer?"

"That's a good one to start with," he said. "But there's also the couch and the shower."

I slipped my arms around his waist. "I'm looking forward to each and every one of those," I said. My thoughts shifted to the life I'd taken tonight. Justified but still, a life, and every life had value. "But first, I think I need to go talk to Cal..."

Nick tucked me against his chest and rested his chin on top of my head. "He'll understand, Brie."

"I know he will understand," I said. "But will he forgive me? It's not like Alastair was innocent or that Cal didn't see him for what he was, but he was human when I killed him. Rowan had already taken his magic."

"Power and magic are not synonymous, my love. He still held power. You made the right choice, and Cal will see it that way too." He kissed the top of my head. "Just give yourself and Cal time. You both need to heal from what Alastair and Fergus did."

"Not just us. They hurt so many people," I said. "It was Fergus. He was the puppet master. Alastair was just his puppet." His retribution should be death, but the Elders Council might not deal such a sentence for one of their own.

"Brie, that might be true, but I don't think anyone had to force Alastair to do what he did. He enjoyed wickedness."

I sighed and inhaled Nick's scent. He still smelled like he did when he was vampire, vanilla whiskey. I pulled back enough that I could look into his eyes and stood on my toes to bring our lips together.

"I love you," I whispered against his lips.

"I love you too, wife," he said. "We have an announcement to make."

"We do." I smiled.

Dad had Mom's hand and led her my way with a grin the size of Texas on his face. "Your mom would love to hear your news."

I wrapped my arm around Nick's waist and pulled him close to me. "We're going to be parents."

"I'm going to be a grandmother?" She asked. Looking from me to Nick to Sorin. "Is this a joke?"

"No joke, Mom," I said. "Nick and I are expecting according to Rowan.

"Congratulations! I can't believe one of my kids is finally making me a grandmother," she said. "I don't want to be called grandmother though. I want to be Mimi."

I laughed. "Mimi it is."

Brandon strode up and raised an eyebrow. "Cal is with

Ivy and Clara, but he's fine. He didn't consider Alastair his father anymore." He studied all of us. "I wanted to let you know Fergus is in the cell. Why is everyone smiling like they've been smoking the green stuff?"

"Thanks. We're just over here celebrating your nephew."

"Ok." He paused. His jaw dropped open. "My what?"

"Rowan gave us the best news," I said. "Nick and I are going to be parents."

"Congratulations, Sis." He smiled. "I'm going to be an uncle."

"You are," I said. "But I know your mind is on your husband. Go be with him."

"Can I tell him the news?"

"Of course," I said. "He's going to be an uncle too." I hoped it would bring Cal some joy among the sadness. He might have lost his father, but he gained us as family.

THIRTY-SEVEN

It'd been a week since the battle, and I found Cal alone in the library.

"Hey," I said.

"My Queen." He stood and fisted a hand over his heart, bowing his head.

"I'm still your friend, your sister-in-law," I said. "Or as I prefer it, just call me Brie."

He stood in front of me in silence, almost like he was frozen.

I'm just going to rip the bandaid off.

"Cal, if I had thought there was another way," I paused. "Another choice that wouldn't have required me to end his life, I would have taken it." I glanced out the window. "I know they are just words now— "

He wrapped his arms around me in a warm hug. "Brie, that wasn't my father that died on the battlefield. The man I knew died a long time ago. I thought you were angry with me because I was a reminder of him. Of what he made you do. I thought you were avoiding me."

I hugged him tight to me. "I wanted to give you space."

"Just talk to me next time," he said. "You're still the queen, so I have to honor it if I think you are distancing."

"I'm still your friend which means you say what you want around me," I said. "But I do understand."

"Looks like our spouses might be getting along again," Brandon said from the door.

"For the record, we were never not getting along," I said.

He walked over and draped his arm around Cal's shoulders. "I told him he just needed to talk to you."

Nick pulled me to his side. "And I told her to give it time."

"Good thing they don't listen to us." Brandon laughed.

"I'm starving," I said. "What's for lunch?"

"Nice subject change," Brandon said.

"Well, she is eating for two." Nick patted my belly. He touched my stomach constantly since we found out I was pregnant.

"And the other one of us two is apparently ravenous," I said.

I meander to the kitchen and pulled some items from the fridge. Nick took them from my hands. "Why don't I make you some spaghetti?"

I smiled. "I could use some comfort food right now."

"I thought so." He started putting the ingredients out.

"How about you two? Up for spaghetti?"

"Always," Brandon said. "I think your cravings are projecting on me."

I laughed. "Cal?"

"I'm not much of one for American spaghetti." His nose wrinkled.

"Nick's spaghetti isn't..." I said.

Brandon's hand covered his mouth and snickered.

I rolled my eyes and laughed "Are you sure we're the same age? That's something a teenager would say."

"Nope, you're older. Remember?" He pushed his shoulder into mine.

"Oh, I remember for sure," I said. "Older, wiser, smart, stronger, better looking." I laughed.

Brandon shook his head.

"I'll eat the spaghetti if you stop this conversation," Cal said.

Nick laughed but didn't look up from his meal prep activities.

Mom and Dad walked into the kitchen.

"Do I smell spaghetti?" Dad asked.

"You do," Nick said. "And there will be plenty."

"Any word from the remaining council?" I asked. The Council had been listening to evidence for days, and I prayed to the Goddess for justice.

"No, but we should hear their decision on Fergus soon," he said.

"I feel like a useless queen not being there," I said.

"You did the right thing by telling them you couldn't make an unbiased decision and wanted him executed," Mom said.

Dad nodded. "You gave your opinion and put his fate in their hands. They understand."

"I don't want to look weak in front of them or our people," I said.

"No one will ever accuse you of looking weak, Brie," he said.

Nick pressed his lips against my temple. "I agree."

"Me too, Sis," Brandon said. "You took Darkness to Summerland and came back. If anyone even thinks about calling you weak, I'll kick their ass."

I smiled. Through it all, we were still family.

"Spaghetti is ready," Nick said. "Who's hungry?"

"Me, of course," I said.

We fixed our plates and sat around the dining table. Not as grand as The Great House dining room, but it was comfortable. I looked around the table and felt blessed beyond any of the gifts the ancestors had given me. Everything that mattered was seated around this table. *Family.*

Dad's phone buzzed on the table. He studied the message. "They've reached a decision and are asking if you would like to be there when it is announced."

"Yes," I paused. "Yes, I would."

The spaghetti forgotten, Alan drove us to The Great House in one of the remaining SUVs and entered the hall usually designated for ceremonies. Today, it was the court where Fergus's fate would be decided.

Instead of taking my place on the raised platform, I sat with my family in the front row of chairs set up for us. The elders spoke among themselves before turning to me.

"Our Queen, we are glad to have you back in the Great House of the Coven," Orion, the youngest Elder, said.

It was the first time I'd been back, and my emotions were

all over the place from remembering the way we left to how it had become home before that. "Thank you, I'm happy to be welcomed back, even under such unfortunate circumstances."

Other members of the Coven trickled in and soon the room was full like it was during ceremonies.

A guard brought Fergus into the room. No bruises from chains. No blackeyes or broken bones. He looked far better than my brother or father had when they had been kidnapped to force me into this prophecy. I'd made my piece, but it didn't stop me from wishing the pain he'd caused others, my loved ones, on him. The guard forced Fergus to sit in a chair below the platform but facing the Elders Council. No doubt they did this to symbolize his fall from rank.

"Elder Fergus, is there anything you wish to say in your own defense?"

"Only to profess my innocence as I have many times," he said.

His lie stung my skin as it did on the battlefield. I shifted in my seat. Nick took my hand and put it in his lap. I took a deep breath and let it out slowly. The sage burning in the room filled my lungs and relaxed me.

Orion stood to deliver the sentence. He towered over Fergus. "The Council has found differently. We believe you conspired against humanity, vampires, and witches in a way that is a threat to life as we know it. You are stripped of your position as Elder, and your name will be stricken from all records save for this trial."

Erasing someone from history was worse than death. It was like they never existed. At least in a death sentence, a witch's name was still written in the book of our ancestors. To be wiped from all our books was an erasure of identity.

"You committed treason against the Coven and the Crown," Orion continued. I sat up straighter in the chair. "For those crimes, there is only one sentence the Council can deliver in the Queen's stead. You will be reprimanded to the Coven prison for a period of one year of atonement. Then a sentence of death will be delivered. Only the Queen can over-rule this sentence." Orion glanced at me. "But I suspect she will let it stand. So mote it be."

Fergus didn't grovel or cry or fight when the guards approached. He walked out of the room in silence with them and never looked back. At that moment, I made the same decision to never look back on it either. It was over, and he would pay a price that couldn't be undone for his crimes.

There were no cheers in the courtroom. Only relief floated in the air. The people wanted to return to the period of peace we'd had before The Blood Moon Prophecy, and I wanted that too.

Orion approached as the room emptied. "We, the Coun-cil, want to extend that it is our strongest desire you and your family would return to The Great House as your perma-nent residency."

Tears brimmed my eyes. It had become home before everything went to Hell. *Before Michael.* They felt his loss as much as I did. I placed my hand on his arm. "Thank you, Orion. Maybe in time, when we are healed, we will. We need respite first."

He nodded and returned to the other Council members.

"Do you really think we'll move back one day?" Brandon asked.

"I don't know," I said. "Right now, I want us all to focus on what we do going forward. I still want the Conservatorship to work, and we have to figure out what that looks like now that Nick is a witch and not a vampire."

"With Malachi and Ella leading the way, we still have it," Nick said. I leaned into him and slipped my arm around his waist.

"Let's just go home and be a family for a while," I said.

"I'd like that," Dad said, hugging Mom to his side.

"So would I," Mom smiled up at him and held her hand out to me. I took it and squeezed it with so much love. We'd all sacrificed for the prophecy, but it brought us together as a family.

)) ● ((

NICK and I walked into our bedroom, and he turned me to face him. "Things are going to change when this little one arrives." His hand rested over my stomach.

I smiled. "They are. But we have some time before that happens."

He reached behind me and unzipped my dress. He let go, and it pooled at my feet.

"Shall we stay busy until then?" He unhooked my bra and let it fall to the floor. My body came to alert for him, craving his touch.

I unbuttoned his shirt and yanked it down his arms. "If

by busy you mean lots of time in bed, then I'm in total agreement."

He leaned forward and trailed hot kisses down my neck to my breast. His lips wrapped around my nipple, and my breath hitched in my throat. Desire built in me to the point I thought I'd rupture if he wasn't closer.

"Now," I gasped out. "I need you now."

He worked his pants off, and I slipped my panties off and tossed them aside.

Nick picked me up and settled me on the bed. He positioned himself over me.

His lips brushed against the tender part of my neck. Electricity sparked with every touch. "Please."

He slid inside me and moved in slow methodical strokes.

I moaned and relished the feeling.

He moved faster between my legs. "Open your eyes, my love."

I opened them and met his gaze. The connection that could only be ours possessed me and filled me with his love. It mixed with the pleasure and spiraled me up towards a peak. "Faster."

He obliged my request. "Are you close?"

"Yes," I said, my voice breathless. His name came out in a moan. "Nick."

My muscles clenched, and he joined me in the apex of an orgasm. His warmth filled me. I took several ragged breaths and rested my head on the pillow. Nick laid on top of me, supporting his weight. His head buried in the pillow next to mine.

He raised his head and pressed his lips to mine. "I love you." He looked into my eyes.

"I love you too, husband."

He rolled to the side and stroked his fingers in gentle caresses over my body.

My eyes closed in blissful rest.

"Don't go to sleep," Nick said. "I want to tell you something."

I blinked through my heavy lids. "Mhmm. What, husband?"

"You are the love of my long life, Brie. I'd never hoped that this would be my existence. That I would have a family, and you have given it all to me. I promise I will spend every day we have on this Earth making you feel the love I have for you."

I pressed my hand against his cheek and felt dampness. I sat up. "Nick, we have this life because you fought for what was right and you fought for me. This is as much because of your sacrifices as it is mine. We went to Darkness and back for this life. We did this together."

"My love is all I have left to give you now, and it is yours with my whole beating heart."

Tears streamed down my cheeks, and he wiped them away with his thumb.

"You have all of my love until our last day on this Earth," I said through the knot in my throat. "And through eternity in Summerland. But we still have a lot of pages left to add to our book in the library. Happy pages about our family."

He smiled and pressed his lips to mine. "That we do, my love. And without a prophecy hanging over our heads."

We'd completed the prophecy without ending the world and now our days were our own to live. Our love gave me more than I had ever dreamed I would have, and our life together was up to us from here until the end of my reign.

The End

EPILOGUE

28 YEARS LATER

Nick's tux fit him like a glove. I admired how well he looked in it.

"You keep looking at me like that, and we're going to miss the ceremony. Then you and I would both be in trouble."

"How did I get so lucky?" I smiled up at him.

He grinned back. "Because you cast a spell on me in a bar almost thirty years ago."

"It hasn't quite been that long, and as I told you that night, I didn't cast a spell." I laughed.

"You most certainly did. It wasn't a magical spell, but it was a spell nonetheless." His love radiated off of him and warmed my insides.

"Come on or we're going to be late." I checked myself in the mirror one last time.

Nick rested his hands on my hips. "This blue dress

reminds me of our wedding day, and how beautiful you looked coming down the aisle."

"That dress is in our closet," I said. "I can pull it out later."

He stepped back and held his arm out for me. "Well, Your Majesty, I'll hold you to that."

I took his offered arm, and we headed down the hall. Alan led the security team and would have been our escort, but he was at the ceremony for a different kind of duty on this day. I welcomed the change of our quiet walk alone.

Although the lake house was what we considered our home, we spent a large part of our days here. I'd been apprehensive about moving back to the Great House, but a few years after the battle with Alastair and Fergus and several renovations to the old mansion, I agreed to return in permanent residence. It was a symbol for the witches, and I was the head of that symbol. The chapel would always be a special place for Nick and me, and we couldn't stay away from it for long. He didn't need my aura any longer to enter, and we visited it often to remember our special days here. We stopped at the doors in front, and they opened. We stepped through for our arrival announcement.

"Her Royal Highness Queen Brielle and His Royal Highness King Nicholas."

We walked down the aisle arm in arm and took our places of honor on the front row. Malachi, now the Vampire King, was seated next to us along with Ella. She served as his Consort. Their love had been slow to blossom, but once it did, they were inseparable.

Ivy sat on the aisle across from us with an open spot for

Alan. Brandon and Cal were in their seats next to them, and Clara was seated behind Ivy with her beau of a few years next to her.

Love. I felt it in everything here today. Its warmth filled every corner of the chapel.

I'd learned when to embrace the formality of tradition and when I could dial it back. Today, I was here as a mother and could relax my duties some. Cal still served as my successor in waiting, but Ro had recently stepped up to start learning the ways. Cal helped me see how wise my son had grown in his short years. Wiser than I was at his age but equally as stubborn.

The side door opened and Ro, short for Rowan, strolled in and took his place at the altar. Our son had grown into a fine warlock. He was more like Nick in many ways, and I was thankful not to have burdened him with my overthinking. The ceremony was a binding ceremony with Alan and Ivy's daughter Willa. We'd long thought they were just friends by his reaction to her presence when we were near them, but Nick and I had been wrong. We were so surprised when he came home with a ring and showed Nick. Willa was a gifted witch, but her kind heart was what won Ro over. She'd given up a corporate job offer to return to the Coven and teach the children. Even though I offered them a private ceremony, my son understood the value of a royal wedding during these trying times.

The witches needed a reason to feel positive after so much of our negative history had been exposed. After we defeated Alastair and Fergus, Orion led the Coven on a full audit that took almost a decade to complete. Nothing shocked me anymore after the findings. A burden I was determined to not leave to Ro if he decided to take on the successor role. I pushed those thoughts out of my head for the day. I was here for my son. My smart, handsome, and grown-up son.

Nick was much more patient about the engagement news than I was. I had a million questions from living arrangements on. To his credit, Ro had an answer for everything, another example of why he is more like his father than me. But he does have my blonde hair and some of my gifts.

I glanced over at Brandon and Cal. They were still going strong and decided to adopt an orphaned witch. Harper keeps them on their toes. She's a sweet girl, but she knows how to push all her dads' buttons. Harper and Faith found lots of trouble together. Mom sat next to them and entertained Harper.

Tears pooled in my eyes.

"Don't you dare cry, my wife," Nick said. "Faith told me I'd get a spanking if I cried."

Our daughter came five years ago, and she is as much like me as Rowan was like Nick. Headstrong and would do what she wanted whether you said yes or no to her requests.

"And she probably will. Fortunately, our little princess did not make me the same promise."

The doors opened again, and our daughter entered in a pale blue dress with a crown of flowers. She made for the front in a dead run and scattered flowers from her basket in wild patterns along the way.

"You could never deny her," Nick whispered, his breath tickling my ear.

"No, even if she didn't look just like me at that age."

Faith stopped to wave at us, and Rowan had to coax her up to her place on the raised platform.

I motioned for her to turn around and face forward. She spun around in a circle several times. Ro got her righted.

The music changed to a love song, and everyone in the chapel stood.

Willa glided through the doorway and she was absolutely breathtaking.

She wore a traditional wedding-type dress for witches. She'd chosen to wear blue as I had, but instead of a ball gown, she chose a simpler look. Simple but elegant. She walked down the aisle to turned heads and whispers. I'd check in on her after the ceremony. Nick and I had decades to adjust to the buzz around us as our normal, and I would help her with the transition to being a public figure in the witch community.

"It's the beginning of a new era. A new generation to lead," I whispered to Nick.

"Don't count us out yet, my love. We are witches with a witch lifespan."

"Do you miss it?" I asked.

"What?"

"Your immortality. Being a vampire."

He kissed my temple. "I think I was only ever meant to be vampire temporarily, while I waited for my soulmate It was a means to keep me here until you were ready for me."

"You always say the right things," I whispered against his ear, letting my breath brush against his earlobe.

"If you keep doing that, I'm going to have to carry you

out the door and to our bedroom."

I giggled softly. "Let's get our son bound first."

"Remember how impatient I was at our reception?"

"Absolutely, you kept asking when we could leave."

"I'm feeling antsy about this one too," he said.

"As soon as Ro and Willa exit, we will too. I'll ask Brandon and Cal if Faith can spend the night with Harper."

"I already asked them, and they said yes," Nick said.

"Then you have me all to yourself when we see our son and daughter-in-law off on their honeymoon."

"The anticipation is killing me," he said.

"Everyone, be seated." Sorin stepped up to the center of the alter and began the binding ceremony

Goddess, thank you. Ancestors, thank you. It is because of you that we can be here today. If not for you, I wouldn't have survived The Blood Moon Prophecy to have my family today. I thank you for this life and my family.

I gazed around at our family both blood and found and looked up at Nick.

He winked at me and squeezed my hand.

To think I prayed for human-like normal before I met Nick, and now, I wouldn't want anything but my messy, complicated life together whether it be then or now. Goddess, I hope you have a lifetime of these chaotic days in store for us.

A ball of light danced in front of me, and I smiled, my heart filled with love and gratitude. Grandmother brought the answer to my prayer on behalf of the Goddess.

I slid Nick's hand into my lap and held it between both of mine. We were exactly where we were meant to be for the rest of our chaotic amazing lives.

SUSAN PERSON

QUEEN OF MOONS

QUEEN OF DARKNESS

QUEEN OF SACRIFICE

Queen
of Sacrifice

The Blood Moon Prophecy Book 1

3

2

1

ACKNOWLEDGMENTS

First, I feel like I need to say sorry for the hard cliffhanger in Book 2, Queen of Darkness, but for me, it was the end of a phase in Brie and Nick's journey. Everything changed for them after their honeymoon. I hope, after reading the final installment of the trilogy, you will agree. It was incredibly hard for me to say goodbye to these characters, but I have an announcement coming soon on a new series.

To my beta and ARC readers, you are the MVPs that aren't afraid to say "how dare you" when I do end on a hard cliffhanger. Your comments and reviews make this journey magic for me.

To the fans, thank you for your messages, TikTok videos, and especially for taking the time to write a review. You are the reason I do this writing thing!

To my family, your support means more than I can say. And to my sister, who read the first two books in a weekend and wanted an ARC for Book 3 because she couldn't wait for release day, your questions and comments made me laugh and your cheers made me smile. I promised there would be a happy ending in this book though, and I hope you enjoyed being surprised along with everyone else! Thank you!

I nearly always save her for last in the acknowledgments but she is certainly not the least - thank you to my editor,

Dawn Alexander, who calls me on it when my writing gets lazy and makes me ask all the questions. She keeps me sane and helps me get all the emotion in there even when I don't want to go there at times. There are not enough words to tell you thank you, but thanks for all you do, Dawn!

About the Author

Susan Person is a multi-contest finalist in the paranormal and dark paranormal romance categories. Recently, she returned to college to pursue a degree in anthropology and graduated in 2021. Susan enjoys meeting writers and readers alike at conferences. She knew at an early age she wanted to write powerful heroines and fulfilled that dream by writing badass empowered heroines who take charge in their paranormal worlds.

Susan grew up on a thoroughbred horse farm before moving to the big city of Dallas. She considers herself a Texan but is loyal to her home state of Arkansas. A lover of travel, she has visited several countries with many more to go on her list. She particularly loved dowsing at Stonehenge. The outdoors are a place Susan finds inspiration and can often be found in a park, at the lake, or on a road trip. She especially loves the mountains. Furry animals hold a special place in her heart, and dogs tend to seek her out as a friend.

Connect with her at susanperson.com

instagram.com/susanwritespnr

tiktok.com/@susanwritespnr

facebook.com/susanwritespnr

goodreads.com/susanperson

bookbub.com/authors/susan-person

Also by Susan Person

The Blood Moon Prophecy

Queen of Sacrifice, Book 1

Queen of Darkness, Book 2

Queen of Moons, Book 3

A Vampire Ice Age Series

In Blood & Ice, A Vampire Ice Age Series - Book 1

Reclamation In Ice, A Vampire Ice Age Series - Book 2

Book 3: TBA in 2023

Enchanted Rock Immortals World

Fae Undone, The Enchanted Rock Immortals Clan Fae 1

Fae Redone, The Enchanted Rock Immortals Clan Fae 2